A LIFE
INTERCEPTED

Also by Charles Martin

Unwritten

Thunder and Rain

A LIFE INTERCEPTED

A Novel

Charles Martin

CENTER STREET

NEW YORK BOSTON NASHVILLE

Center Street
Hachette Book Group
237 Park Avenue
New York, NY 10017
www.CenterStreet.com

Printed in the United States of America

RRD-C

First edition: September 2014
10 9 8 7 6 5 4 3 2 1

Center Street is a division of Hachette Book Group, Inc.
The Center Street name and logo are trademarks of Hachette Book Group, Inc.

The Hachette Speakers Bureau provides a wide range of authors for speaking events. To find out more, go to www.HachetteSpeakersBureau.com or call (866) 376-6591.

The publisher is not responsible for websites (or their content) that are not owned by the publisher.

Library of Congress Cataloging-in-Publication Data has been applied for.
[TK]

For David Wainer

A LIFE
INTERCEPTED

PROLOGUE

He sat on the floor, towel around his neck, drenched in his own sweat, eyes trained on the screen. Football in one hand, a half-eaten banana in the other, a bottle of Gatorade in his lap. She sat next to him. Jeans. Older sweatshirt. Legs crossed. Remote in one hand, laser pointer in the other. Staring through reading glasses. Her hair had turned. Once deep mahogany, now snow gray. The turn was not unexpected; the timing was. Life had amplified genetics. In her early thirties, she was technically old enough to be his mom, but the last third of those years had not been kind. It wasn't so much the wrinkles as the shadow beneath them. He was a rising senior, a seventeen-year-old kid strapped with immeasurable talent, high hopes, and dreams he'd only whispered. At six feet three inches—nearly five inches taller than her—almost two hundred pounds and very little body fat, there wasn't much kid left. She didn't need magnifiers to see that. When she wanted his attention, she raised an eyebrow, lowered her voice, and spoke slowly, "Dalton Rogers." At other times, she just called him Dee.

He respectfully called her Sister Lynn while in the presence or earshot of others. When they were alone, he called her Mama.

Having some experience with talent like his, she was realistic about his prospects and had been careful to temper his expectations while not dashing his hopes. A delicate balance. The game on the screen moved in slow motion, a frame at a time. In the middle of the field—and the screen—number 8 stood under center. Well known during his time, he was the plumb line by which all others were measured. Which is why they were watching the film. Dee wanted to learn from the best. Few, if any, had been better than number 8.

She pressed pause and lit the screen with a green laser. The focused beam circled his feet. "Everything starts right there." She tapped him gently on the head with her remote. "Feet. Feet. Feet. They're the first link in the kinetic chain. When he throws, what comes out of his hand starts in his feet."

Dee quoted from the article *Sports Illustrated* had later written about number 8's performance in this game, " 'Million-dollar arm, two-million-dollar feet.' "

She tapped Dee on the head with the remote again. "Neither of which happened by accident. Remember..." She laughed once. "Football is chess played in 3-D with a little cardiovascular challenge thrown in for good measure. Not to—"

"Mention the marauding horde." He waved her off like a gnat buzzing his ear. "I heard you"—he took another bite—"the first five hundred times."

She smiled and lifted the green dot to his helmet. "Where's he looking? Show me his eyes." She spoke in present tense even though the game had been played fifteen years ago.

Dee followed the line of sight to the left cornerback on the opposing defense, who, at the moment, stood lined up three yards off number 8's primary receiver, a rather gifted individual name Roderick. Better known to his friends and those who worshipped him as Roddy.

Dee pointed him out with what remained of the banana. Mama made Dee eat one a day because the potassium and magnesium helped alleviate muscle cramps in his calves. He spoke through a mouthful. "Three yards off Roddy. Man coverage. He's playing inside, which means he's taken away the slant, challenging Roddy to hug the sideline and forcing the Rocket to throw outside shoulder." It had been a close game, and the opposing team had not been impressed with the undefeated Saints or their star quarterback.

She pressed play and the video continued in slow motion. The quarterback began his count, checked right, and then paused. Noticing movement by both the weak side linebacker and strong safety, he stopped his count, pointed at both of them, and began walking up and down his offensive line hollering a change of play. Given the crowd noise, the quarterback then motioned hand signals to the receivers and the lone tailback. They nodded and made adjustments, spreading out slightly wider. All of this took less than four seconds.

Dee sat mesmerized—eyes large, mind taking notes. Taking everything in. He never grew tired of this. He'd watch these all night if Mama let him. Her film library consisted of more than a hundred films. Most of the high school games were reel-to-reel. By college they'd converted to VHS. Some of the ESPN stuff and most of the championships were HD. To give Dee access to the entirety without having to constantly switch back and forth between three types of technology, she'd had it converted to electronic files now stored by game and date on a Mac laptop that projected onto an enormous TV via an HDMI cable. She didn't need to watch the screen to see the play developing—she'd been there. Could still hear the crowd's roar and echo. The pennies rattling inside the milk jug. Smell the cut grass. She saw this and lots of other videos almost every time she closed her eyes.

She advanced the film several frames and the green dot rested on his helmet. "Eyes. Show me. Where are they now?"

Dee's hand dwarfed the ball when he pointed. "The umpire."

"Why?"

"He's got the play clock."

She circled the umpire with the green light. "Watch what happens when his hand goes up." The light flashed back across the screen to rest on the quarterback. "What's he doing?"

"Back under center. Restarting his count. Right now he's racing the clock 'cause he knows he's got about three seconds left."

She smiled. She'd taught him well. The light created a green halo as she circled the number 8 on the screen. "Think about everything going on in his head right now. Yes, he's physically talented, but the thing that sets him apart is the stuff you can't see." She then circled the entire screen. "This is a chess game. He's just moving the pieces around the board."

He nodded. Eyes fixed. The Rocket was about to expose a defensive weakness and win a Class 5A State Championship. Again.

She pressed play and whispered, "Checkmate."

The play proceeded. The center—a giant, fun-loving, faithful Labrador of a man called Wood—snapped the ball and then created a seemingly impenetrable wall of protection. The quarterback faked a handoff to the lone running back as he stepped into the B gap, bolstering Wood's wall and blocking the blitzing strong side linebacker. The quarterback then took three quick yet long steps backward to gain distance from the line and give the receivers time to make their cuts and get open. When the defensive tackle broke through and threatened to sack number 8, the Rocket turned, rolled right, and began checking down his receivers. While he was dangerous inside the pocket, he could dismantle you when he broke outside. Everybody knew that. In recognition of his talent and speed, *SI* had coined the phrase "the Rocket." The name stuck, and more than a hundred scouts and coaches stood in the stands that night, salivating over possible takeoff. The crowd rose to their feet, and the entire stadium sucked in a collective gasp. When he threw the ball, he didn't throw it where his receiver, Roddy, was. He threw it where Roddy would be when the ball got there.

She turned off the video and clicked on the light. Dee began packing up his books. It used to bother him that she never watched the ending. Then he learned that some memories fester, and if you pick at them, they cause the most pain. They walked outside under the covered walkway that would lead him across the grounds, back to school and his dorm, and her to her cottage, sequestered behind the massive brick wall. Her shield against the outside world. She hung her arm inside his. "You finished calculus?"

He smiled, nodding. "Yes, ma'am."

"Physics?"

"Test tomorrow. Second period."

She raised an eyebrow, asking him if he'd studied without having to ask him.

He shrugged. "Some."

She checked her watch. It was already after ten p.m. "Not too late." She pointed her finger at him. "And no *SportsCenter*. You can't watch that stuff and study for a test."

He smiled and pointed back inside the room. "He did it."

She nodded. He was right, he had. They'd watched it together. Some of it had been about him. "And you see where it got him?"

He chuckled but didn't respond. He knew better. Some things were still tender. A pause. He wanted to comfort her but didn't know how. "It's all over the news—he's getting out tomorrow."

She nodded and stared toward the garden.

He pressed her. "You made any plans?"

She shook her head.

"He know you're here?"

A single shake.

"You think he'll come find you?"

"I don't know." She crossed her arms. "I don't know what he'll do."

He felt the heaviness but didn't know how to help her carry it. And she'd always been careful not to let him. That weight she carried alone. He bent at the knees, bringing him eye level with her. "You need anything?"

She kissed his cheek. "Get some sleep and ace your physics test."

"You know," He slung his backpack over his shoulder, "I do have an A in the class."

She held up a finger. "A minus."

He lowered his voice, whispering, "It's an AP class."

She smiled. "Night."

She meandered through the walkways, her shadow appearing before and then retreating behind as she passed beneath the overhead lights and under the arms of the towering oaks that blanketed the private cottages. She pulled the door shut and curled up in a ball on the bed. Moments passed and she found her fingertips tracing the edges of the dove hanging from the chain around her neck. She'd always wanted to work with kids. Just not like this.

Two hours later, she twisted off the cap, poured three pills into her hand, and chased them with water. She showered, the pills kicked in, and her eyelids grew heavy. She turned on the TV, clicked resume, and tucked her knees into her chest. She drifted off to the sound of the crowd chanting his name. *Rocket! Rocket! Rocket!* The last image she saw was familiar to everyone. The whole country had seen it. On the screen, a kid in the stands held up that week's *Sports Illustrated*. It was the first time a high school quarterback had graced the cover of *SI*. Even the angle of the shot was deliberate—the photographer had taken the picture lying on his back on the grass. Number 8 stood on the field, ball in hand, all promise and possibility, goalposts rising behind him, the world at his feet. The title read THE GOD OF FRIDAY NIGHT.

She blinked, the tears spilled, and she drifted off to a time when all her dreams had come true.

CHAPTER ONE

Thirteen years ago

The assistant clipped the microphone to my lapel, smoothed my shoulders with a lint brush, and admired my day-old suit. "Moldone's Off 5th?"

Busted. "Yes."

A brush of my collar, then she turned to Audrey. "Nicely done."

Audrey nodded once, accepting the compliment. The lady looked over her shoulder and then handed me a Topps football card with my picture on it. "My brother'll disown me if I don't ask."

"What's his name?"

"Ben." She blushed. "He watches all your film. Wears your number. Your picture covers the door of his bedroom."

Topps had printed a special run of all the guys they thought would go in the first round. Glossy. Thick cardboard. Picture on one side. High school and college stats on the other. I signed the card and she clicked back into assistant mode. "The audience will filter in through those doors in a minute. Feel free to mingle. Or

7

not. Your call. They have strict instructions not to cross that line, but you are free to do as you wish." She pointed. "Those guys over there in the black T-shirts, with arms like yours but not quite as tall as you, will help keep order if needed. Jim will be in"—she eyed the digital clock on the wall—"in twenty-three minutes. We're live in twenty-three and a half. Any questions?"

"No. I'm good. Thanks."

She left and I glanced over my shoulder where Audrey had raised a knowing eyebrow and waved her finger at my suit. "Told you."

I sat on the sofa, sent two texts on my phone, muted the ringer for the third time, and then sat while my left leg nervously bounced. My tie felt tight. Face flushed. Suit stiff, awkward. Along the far wall, behind the cameras, sat a table covered with danishes, bagels, and fresh-cut fruit. My eyes fell on the raspberries. I thought about sneaking a few, but then there was the issue of the mic and the cord and what if part of it stuck in my teeth and I didn't know it. Sweat trickled down my back. Eight years as a starting quarterback, but little had prepared me for the media blitz of the last several days.

Audrey stood offstage, out of view of the camera. Hands tucked behind her. Shoulders relaxed. Wood called her "the real power behind the throne." He was right. Between high school and college, she had endured more than ninety-six games. Sun. Rain. Snow. Thunderstorm. Power outage. Sacks. Concussions. Sprains. Pulls. Injuries. Little phased her. That had earned her the rather unflattering nickname—one of several—of "Prestone."

As in, antifreeze.

The producer had given her a set of headphones so she could hear the interview. I motioned to the space next to me on the couch, then pointed to Jim Kneels's empty chair. "He won't mind."

She shook her head. "Don't even think about it. You bring me out there in the middle of this thing and you're not getting any loving for a month."

Two days ago, Audrey had taken me to an appointment-only, custom men's shop called Moldone's Off 5th. For three hours, I modeled various colors and patterns and textures in a process that gave me a newfound respect for runway models and new cars. I'd walk out of the dressing room, climb the platform, and stand there in solids and pinstripes while she tilted her head from side to side and considered me. I felt naked. She'd then twirl her finger and I'd turn in place, allowing her to study the whole of me where she'd either nod in approval or be rid of me in much the same way she shooed pigeons in the park. After the fifth costume change, I protested.

"I'm quite happy with my wrinkle-free from Sears."

"Honey, one of the things I love about you is that you're small-town grounded and proud of it." She turned to Moldone, who stood attentive with a measuring tape draped around his neck and reading glasses perched on the tip of his nose. "Mr. Moldone, you'll have to forgive him, he's been playing football a long time. One too many hits to the head."

I smiled and turned to leave, confident she had begun to see things clearly. "Thank you."

Evidently I was mistaken.

"But…" She held up a finger, stuffing my end around. "We're uptown now."

I pointed discreetly at the price tag, knowing that she was a miser at heart and reason would prevail.

She stood and smoothed my lapel. "I know. Crazy isn't it? But this city is full of crazy people. Have you seen the numbers attached to your contract?"

"Yeah, but—"

"Get over it."

"Everyone I meet will know I just bought all this stuff."

She brushed my cheek. "It makes your eyes dance."

When I opened my mouth to object to one more combination, she pointed her finger at me and raised both eyebrows. So I tried on a dozen more suits and just as many pairs of shoes.

We walked out with three suits, six custom shirts, five ties, two belts, two pairs of shoes, a maxed-out Visa card, and one very happy Mr. Moldone. I'd only ever spent that much for one other thing on the planet, and she was wearing it on her left hand.

At T-minus twenty, the double doors swung wide and the audience shuffled in, jockeying for front-row seats. Most waved, sat quietly, mumbled in hushed tones, flashed pictures, or held up their phones and recorded me just sitting there. Others hollered, cheered, or shouted words of encouragement. One guy whistled. Might have been two hundred people in total. Sensing a growing chorus, the "bouncers" moved in. It seemed silly to keep sitting, so I untethered from the mic and mingled among the audience, shaking hands, signing autographs, and posing for pictures.

One lady hugged me. "Sweetheart, I drove 264 miles. Been standing in the rain since lunch." I thanked her and signed her ticket stub and T-shirt and then laughed as the bouncers stepped in to pry her off me from one final hug. I worked my way through the first few rows, climbed the stairs, then made my way down to a woman in a wheelchair who was wearing my college jersey. Said her name was Jenny. I knelt for a picture and signed her sleeve. She just sat there crying. I kissed her forehead, and she squeezed my hand. She couldn't really control her muscles and neither of her eyes would look at me, but I found her beautiful and tender. A small boy, about ten, dwarfed in my college jersey and wearing the hat of what in a few hours would become my NFL home team, tapped me on the shoulder and shoved a Topps card in my face. I signed it, stood on my knees posing for a picture, and said, "I like your hat."

He shrugged, shook his head once, and put both hands on his hips. "You've made things really difficult for me."

Still on my knees, I chuckled. "Really? How so?"

He turned the hat in his hands. "I hate these guys, and now I've got to pull for them."

Knowing I had met my match and was about to have my hands full, I extended my hand. "I'm Matthew."

"Mac. Mac Powell."

The kid had the confidence of a man in his midforties. "Well, Mac..." I leaned forward, my face just inches from his. I lowered my voice. "Since you brought it up, I didn't used to like them much either. Pretty much hated them." He smiled at my admission. "But—" I looked over each shoulder as if sharing a secret. "I didn't have much choice, and from what I can tell from the meetings I've had so far, these new owners are pretty good people. Between you and me, I'm starting to wonder if they haven't gotten a bad rap. I mean, that whole thing two years ago in the playoffs, I don't think that was their fault." He started nodding in agreement. "They totally got robbed by the refs on that third and one."

He held up a finger. "Yeah, but then there was that four-for-one trade fiasco for that injured running back Jackson, who hasn't seen the field since he signed."

A crowd had gathered. One of the ESPN guys had turned on a camera and was filming our interaction. Impressed by the kid, several of the adults had started recording on their phones. "Yes, but—" I paused, also holding up a finger. "That trade fiasco is what created the salary cap room so they could sign"—I poked myself in the chest—"me." I paused. "And...that Jackson kid? I met him, and he's healthy now. Like, really healthy." The kid smiled. "I think you're going to be pleased with what he can do," I proffered. "So, let's give him the benefit of the doubt, at least until he proves otherwise." The kid nodded like he understood completely. "Not to mention he's now my teammate, which means I'm pulling for him." The kid's eyes told me that had sealed it. He examined his hat, pulled it down tight over his head, and shoved his hands in his pockets. I asked, "You play?"

He looked at me and turned up a lip. "Really? Do I look like I play?" Kid probably didn't weigh sixty pounds soaking wet. He shook his head. "I want"—he pointed at Jim Kneels's chair—"his job."

I told you the kid was bold. I chuckled. "Well, maybe when you get it you'll have me back and we can do this again."

He stuck out his hand. "Deal."

I turned to Audrey and pointed at the stack of footballs that the producers at ESPN wanted me to give to the audience after the show. She handed me a ball, and I signed it: *Mac, Blessings on your life and dreams. Matthew #8.*

He examined it, and after it met his approval, he tucked it under his arm and said, "Well, okay."

Behind me, a door opened, several feet shuffled in, the lights flashed, further blinding me, and the assistant waved me back to my perch on the stage, where she hurriedly reconnected my tether. Once I was seated, the iconic Jim Kneels strode in and sat to my left. I'd been watching Jim on TV for a decade. Maybe longer. He had interviewed more of the greats than anybody save Howard Cosell. He shook my hand and glanced at the smiling crowd, his eyes coming to rest on the kid. "You learn quickly."

"I don't mind."

"Enjoy the moment." I felt he wanted to say more but didn't. He straightened his papers, scanned the top sheet, and said, "Any questions?"

I shrugged. Jim is a big man. Broad. Tall. Thick. Former All-Pro linebacker. First with the Raiders, then the Steelers. One of four World Champion rings on his right hand. I had his card at home in a shoe box. "I was sort of figuring that was your job."

He laughed and nodded once. "You'll do just fine."

The light flashed green, and as one of the only living inductees to both the Football Hall of Fame and the Sports Broadcasting Hall of Fame, Jim crossed one leg over the other and paused. If his relationship with the camera was a dance, he was definitely the lead partner.

He began. "Let's back up." He eyed a sheet of paper. "Four-year starter in high school. Never lost." He paused for effect. "Passed for more yards than any kid ever in high school history." Another pause. "Threw for more touchdowns than anyone. Ever." Longer pause. "On to college, where you were offered more than fifty Division I scholarships. Defying most, you chose to stay close to your hometown of Gardi and attend a state university, where you promptly broke almost every NCAA freshman record—on record." He cleared his throat. "Then you won a couple of awards." The audience laughed. "A few big games." Audience laughed again. "Two hours ago, you were picked number one in the NFL Draft." He studied me. Leaned back. "They write stories about guys like you. How're you feeling?"

"Grateful."

He let the answer filter out among the seats and settle. "I've watched you from high school. Interviewed you a half dozen times. Know you better than some who are watching this. After almost thirty years in this business, I am, at times, skeptical of a guy in your position who can do what you do, finds his face on Gatorade bottles and Nike commercials and cereal boxes, and yet uses words like 'grateful.' However, in your case, I find it genuine and difficult not to believe."

He glanced over his glasses at me, then back through them toward his sheet. "In a few hours from now, you are flying out of New York City on a red-eye to Hawaii, where you and your wife, Audrey, are to enjoy a long-awaited and much-earned two-week honeymoon." He glanced off set at Audrey and then, at the camera, said, "For those of you who don't know, Mr. Modest here made good on a high school promise and married Audrey..." He nodded to her. Another camera flashed her live picture on the screen alongside us. She waved. Confident. Comfortable in the shadows. Not seeking to share the spotlight. "...his high school sweetheart, prior to returning to college to prove his critics wrong and play his senior year. Most who follow football know her as Lady Eight or"—a chuckle and a single shake of his head—"Prestone." He glanced at her. "Sorry. Had to. And then my personal favorite, the Spider Monkey." A shrug. The audience clapped in approval. "What is it with football and nicknames?" The screen flashed several pictures of Audrey wearing my jersey. "Through snow, sleet, rain, scorching heat, and undaunted scrutiny from the press, she is and has been cool under pressure. His number one fan..." More screen shots. He looked at me. "She is as much identified with the number eight as you are." Another glance at his cheat sheet, which he didn't need but did for effect. A rehearsed sidestep in the dance. A natural segue to me. "You have an uncanny ability to win wherever you are. You've been described by your teammates as a surgeon, a commanding presence, a field general, a T. rex of defenses, and yet those same teammates are quick to follow with the word 'unselfish.' That you're quick to defer credit. Which is unusual, given what you've accomplished. To what do you attribute that?"

I thumbed over my shoulder. "If my head starts to swell, she sticks a pin in it."

The audience laughed easily. Jim waited. "And when that doesn't work?"

"She sticks her foot someplace I don't want it."

More laughter. Jim motioned to the producer, who took the headphones from Audrey and led her to a seat on the couch beside me. "Audrey?" He stood and proffered. "Please."

Audrey pinched my leg as she sat down alongside me. A whisper, "One month."

The audience applauded. Jim waited. "What does she bring to your team?"

"Despite what's been said and written, I didn't get here by myself. We did. Two years ago, when I forced a back shoulder pass to Roddy in the end zone in the final minute, losing the national championship, my critics said the success had gone to my head and I'd never win the big one. Audrey disconnected our cable, literally unplugged the radio from my truck, adjusted my workout schedule to avoid the media, and got me back on the field with Roddy because she didn't want all those doubting voices having access to my thinking. A few months ago, with seven seconds to go in the game, I threw that same pass against the same coverage—and possibly better personnel—to Roddy. I'm not taking anything away from him. He's as good as they come. He made me look good on more than one occasion, but if he were sitting here, he'd tell you that catch had everything to do with Audrey and much less to do with us." I waved my hand across Jim's sheet of paper. "That's a record of us—of Audrey and me. What *we* did. Not what *I* did. Big difference."

He turned to Audrey. "Anything to add?"

"Matty was born to do what he's doing. He reads defenses better than most. Great arm strength. Good hips. Vision. Decent enough speed in his feet." She chuckled as did Jim. "Not bad looking." She glanced at the audience, baiting a response, followed by cheers and whistles. She returned to Jim. "Calm under pressure. A student of the game. Watches film ad nauseam. Has a film library that probably rivals this place. But his intangibles are what set him apart. He cares about those around him. The eyes in the huddle. They matter. And they know it. And you can't coach that. His teammates are not numbers on jerseys or means to an end. They are the end. He is the first set of eyes they see when they wake up in recovery after surgery, the voice on the other end of the phone at five a.m. when it's time to cut weight for camp, and he has been late to more than one dinner with me because somebody was having trouble with a route or a read or an exam that would hamper their eligibility. If you check his cell phone, you'll see that the texts he's sent since being drafted, even some while sitting on this couch, were to his teammates, coaches, trainers. Just saying 'thank you' or 'it never would have happened without you.' Matty's authentic. Not pretending." She looked at me. "He is who he says he is."

Jim turned to the audience. "Pretty good commercial right there, folks. We'll be right back." When the light flashed to red, Jim looked at Audrey and then at me. "You, my friend, married above yourself."

I nodded. "That I did."

Jim fielded a few questions from the audience before the light flashed to green. I signed a few more balls, tossed them into the audience, and drove the producers crazy when I stood and stretched my mic cord across the set to hand a ball to Jenny in the wheelchair. When the light turned solid, Jim returned to me. "It's no secret that you put Gardi, Georgia, on the map. Given what you've brought your hometown, most everyone is a vocal, loyal fan. You're the honorary mayor. They gave you the keys to the city. If you have critics, they don't venture out much and they're pretty quiet about it." A chuckle. "And for good reason. Between high school and college, you've brought home seven championships. Your high school and college jerseys have both been retired. This past year, the main thoroughfare through town was renamed Matthew 'The Rocket' Boulevard. Your high school field at St. Bernard's was renamed in your honor. According to birth certificate applications, the most popular male name in Gardi the last five years running is Matthew." He raised an eyebrow. "So…what's left to accomplish?"

I pointed to my new friend in the audience. Young Mac was sitting on the edge of his seat, beaming. "I'm now a rookie in the National Football League. I wake up tomorrow lowest man on the totem pole. Everything you've described, everything you hold in your hand, served to get me here. That's it. Doesn't mean squat to the veterans. So I'm going back to school with the best in the game. A game I love. I seem to have been given some talent for it, although I can certainly improve. But it's still a game played between two sidelines where eleven guys in a huddle can do things together they could never do alone. That in and of itself is the majesty and wonder of football. It's why we play the game."

Jim paused. Then paused again. "Favorite moment in any game?"

"When we're down and the momentum is stacked against us. Those are the moments when we find out what we're made of. When we learn to trust and lean on each other. When the eyes behind the face mask matter."

Jim paused and folded the paper, slipping it into his jacket pocket. Twirling his partner. Holding her at fingertip length. "Word is that you'll leave this interview en route to a conference room where you'll sign several endorsement deals worth reportedly tens of millions, followed by the signing of a contract worth reportedly even more tens of millions, much of which is guaranteed—provided you show up to camp. And then, by all accounts, you'll fly"—he chuckles—"*coach* class to Hawaii. You're moments away from being a multi-multi-millionaire. Will this change you?"

A deep breath. "I hope so." The audience laughed. He glanced at Audrey. "She won't let me run the AC very low at night. Says we can't afford it. Not with the way I eat. I'm hoping she'll let me bump it down a few degrees."

He held up this week's *Sports Illustrated.* My picture graced the cover—the second time in four years. I was standing on the field at State, holding a ball, my back to the camera, staring downfield. The goalposts in the distance. It was a good picture. One I was fond of because it focused the viewer's eye on the field—the game—and not me. Jim held the cover for the camera, which projected it onto the screen for the audience. The title read CAN THE GOD OF FRIDAY

NIGHT REIGN ON SUNDAY? Jim tapped the title and waited. "Your response?"

I chose my words. "It makes me uncomfortable."

Jim probed, "Why?"

I shook my head once. "I didn't make me. I'm just being me." I pointed to Jenny in the wheelchair. The camera flashed her smiling, severely cross-eyed face on the screen. "Jenny, forgive me if I'm out of line, but—" I glanced back at Jim. "I'd imagine she knows a good bit about hurdles. About difficulty. I throw a few touchdown passes, and people talk about my 'greatness.' They make statues that look like me and give me the keys to a city. It might take all the energy she has just to get out of bed, get dressed, and be in this studio. Where's the applause for that? I'm playing a game. She's playing for her life." I paused and scanned the audience. "I love this game. I'm grateful I get to play it. I love seeing smiles on faces, and I understand the desire to read about the lives of guys like me, but in the grand scheme of things, what I do between the sidelines just doesn't hold a candle to what others do outside them."

Jim glanced at the screen. "Ladies and gentlemen, Audrey Rising with her husband and sometimes football player, Matthew Rising, commonly known around town as 'the Ice Man,' 'T-Rex,' 'the Mayor of Gardi,' and 'the Rocket.'" He extended his hand to Audrey, then me. "Thanks for stopping by on what promises to be an eventful and well-deserved evening."

"Thank you, sir."

CHAPTER TWO

Present day

Gray walls. Steel bars. Locked door. No handle. Least not on my side. A stainless steel toilet. Half a roll of paper. One picture. Concrete floors. One window. Eight feet by eight feet.

My life in sixty-four square feet.

Any sound echoed, dancing around like a pinball, finally finding an exit through an open window or unlocked door. Above me, daylight crept over the sill. Some mornings, the mourning doves would sit outside in the yard and call to each other. I couldn't see them, but their calls reached me.

I folded my hands behind my head and let the pictures return. During the day, I could push them aside. Busy myself. But here, in the quiet before dawn, not so much. So this morning—like every morning—they returned. Single file. An endless parade. They were once clear. Technicolor. Even IMAX. Over time, they faded, became stained, and the edges curled up. Turned sepia. Despite their condition, they are what I have. I thumbed through each one.

The first was always Audrey. Various pictures of her. Most often the picture from the last night: the way her dress draped across her shoulders. The flickering candle. The sparkle of Central Park stretched out before us. The silver dove reflecting in the base of her neck. Her forehead pressed against mine. Soon the smells returned. New clothes. Audrey's perfume. Then the faint taste of raspberries. The champagne burn going down my throat. The horns of taxis on Broadway below. The feel and weight of a pen in my hand. The sight of my own signature. The hotel. Her wearing my pajamas.

The discomfort of my ankle returned me to my bunk. I studied it. They had installed my black anklet yesterday and then attempted to warn me of people's reactions. Said that guys like me were often surprised that something so inanimate can evoke such a hate-filled response. Visceral, even. Pragmatically, it weighs a few ounces and allows them to track me and my movements within three feet. Twenty-four/seven. Emotionally, it's the second-heaviest thing I've ever carried.

In twelve years here, more than four thousand three hundred days, I'd learned a simple truth: there's a difference between a dream coming true and a dream lived out. Prison holds your body while your memories come and go as they like—sifting through the bars like water.

In here, the tortured remember. The lucky forget.

The sound of Gage's steps closed the picture book in my mind. In a few seconds, he appeared on the other side. A strange dichotomy—freedom separated by an inch plus a million miles. The ball looked small in his pawlike hands. He tossed it into the air. It spiraled, rose, reached its summit, and fell again, where he quickly grabbed it and launched it again. I climbed off my bed, prompting Frank, in the glass control room at the end of the block, to punch a button and unlock my door. He did, it swung open, and, following Gage's nod, I walked out into the common area of the ward. Cell block D. Wiregrass Correctional Penitentiary—though few here were penitent.

The common area is four stories high, open in the middle, and rectangular. A stairwell stood behind each of us. Twenty-five yards separated us. He smirked and tossed me the ball.

Before prison guard, Gage was a receiver of note. I remember watching him on TV. Rose Bowl MVP. Following college, he had been drafted and then injured during the second year of his career, re-signed by a few teams, hung around a few years, made a few appearances, but it never stuck. Five years after entering the league, having gambled away most of his money, tired of hoping and unable to surgically fix the shredded knee, he landed this job— complete with a steady paycheck and benefits. Had he snorted his guaranteed money up his nose, he'd have been disqualified from getting this job. On the other hand, while gambling broke him just as quickly, it didn't disqualify him. In fact, it ingratiated him with the other guards, who lived vicariously through his stories of Vegas, Atlantic City, and one storied week in Monaco. When we first met Gage smiled, but it did little to hide the resident sadness. Taking the kid out of the game was one thing. Taking the football out of the kid was another.

A pressure cooker without a vent is not a pressure cooker. It's a bomb.

Ball in hand, Gage stared at me across the open area. "How long we been doing this?" He knew the answer but asked anyway.

"Couple of years."

"Seven years, ten months, and fourteen days." He shrugged. "Give or take."

"Fifteen."

"You sure?"

I caught the ball, dropped to my knees, and threw. Throwing from the knees is a drill for QBs. It forces a better throwing motion—coming over the top. And, in all honesty, it makes it easier on Gage's early-onset arthritic hands 'cause I can't throw it quite as hard. I loaded and fired it across the short distance between us. "It was a Tuesday."

"Seems like a long time."

It had been. "A lifetime."

We tossed the ball back and forth, working up a sweat. After a few minutes, the ball started whistling through the air. Like any good receiver, he caught the ball, tucked and covered it, then threw it back. "Where will you go?"

"Home."

"You sure you want to put yourself through that?"

I made no response.

"I thought you said it'd been sold on the courthouse steps."

"I did."

"Where will you stay?"

"I'll find something."

He paused. "She worth it?"

A pause. I pointed at his bum knee. "If a team called you, any team, and said, 'Hey, we'd like you to come try out.' How long would it take you to get on a plane?"

He mimicked the Heisman pose again. "About that long."

I nodded. He understood.

When two boys, or men, play catch, a rhythm can develop. Something like a pulse—catch, throw, release, catch…It doesn't happen all the time, but with Gage and me, it happened most of the time. And it was my therapy. I released the ball, flinging sweat from my forehead and fingers. The ball shot from my hand and struck his palms, stinging his skin. He shook his head. "You remember throwing that hard in college?"

A shrug. "Doesn't matter."

He chuckled. Some of the others were awake, the whites of their eyes showing through the bars. "Not if you've been listening to talk radio the last couple of weeks. A few of the coaches have expressed interest in evaluating you. Several players have done it."

I lifted my pants leg, revealing the black anklet.

Silence followed as the ball arced between us. Our time was almost up. He glanced at the door, the window, and the distance to the fence. "One time?"

I shook my head.

He shrugged. "For me?"

I knew the cameras were recording.

Gage trotted over to the door that led out into the yard. He pressed a button to lower an automatic window above the door that served as a ventilation draw. The window was eighteen inches square, hung twelve feet off the ground, and funneled cooler air to the cells. No screen and no bars, it led out into the yard, which was surrounded in double rows of fifteen-feet-tall, electrically-charged fence, all of which was covered in multiple rows of concertina wire. It also allowed a man with a football an uninterrupted throw to the corner of the exercise yard, fifty-nine yards away—provided the thrower could thread the needle of the foot-and-a-half-square window, which hung at the halfway mark. Not much room for error. He tossed me the ball and then jogged through two doors that electronically unlocked and then locked and into the far corner of the yard. By this time, the other inmates were awake and staring through the bars of their cells. A couple were making odds, taking bets. The pass required precision and meant that the ball never rose above twelve feet off the ground. In football terms, that's called "throwing on a frozen rope." It also required the thrower to release the ball at about 600 rpm—roughly the same spin rate as an air wrench used by NASCAR teams when they spin the lug nuts off race cars in the pit.

Gage waved, signaling all clear. I had to look through the two windows of the two doors, so his outline was distorted. Blurred. I turned the ball in my hand, my fingers reading the laces, measured my target, dropped three steps, and fired the ball at Gage. The ball left my fingers, whistling in a tight spiral. It cleared the window, spun through the air, and crossed the outside yard, striking his hands an inch or two left of the imaginary bull's-eye I'd placed on his forehead. He caught and held it still, in place. His silent reminder to those watching that "that just happened." He trotted back, waiting for Frank to unlock, open, close, and lock each door.

He handed me the ball, shaking his head. "You know there might be one, maybe two guys in the entire league right now who can make that pass. Maybe only a couple ever."

I shrugged.

I stepped inside my cell and turned. I wasn't allowed to extend my hand, and he knew that. In return, he handed me the ball along with a Sharpie. In all this time, he'd never asked. Over the years, the sweat and oil from our hands had darkened the ball. I signed it and handed it back. He turned it in his hands. He glanced over his shoulder at the window, then the corner of the yard, then back at me. "I'll keep it—some place safe."

"You should hide it." I waved my hand across the interior cameras that filmed our morning sessions. "Along with everything else."

He stepped outside, whispered into his microphone. The door swung shut and locked. Him on one side. Me on the other. He glanced at his watch. "Don't get too comfortable in there. Couple of folks will be along shortly to finish paperwork on you."

I glanced around my cell. "I haven't been comfortable since I walked in here."

He smiled, then turned and began walking away. "Take care, Rocket."

My voice stopped him. "Gage?"

He waited but didn't turn.

"Thank you."

He glanced to his left at the inner courtyard, then at the eighteen-inch-square window above the door that led into the yard. He shook his head, mumbled to himself, and then his steps faded away as he tossed the ball into the air.

CHAPTER THREE

American football derived primarily from rugby, and until the late 1860s, it was tough to tell the two apart. Then in the late nineteenth century, Walter Camp, the father of American football, suggested a few rule changes. The effect Americanized the game, and what they played then is essentially what we play now.

In rewriting the rules, Camp suggested several fundamental changes. The first was an unheard of concept of "down and distance" rules. The team with the ball, the offense, was given four downs to gain ten yards. If successful, they were given another four downs. Next, he reduced the number of on-field players from fifteen to eleven, thinning the crowd.

But Camp's most game-altering change to this point was the snap. The snap transferred a stationary ball off the line of scrimmage, through the legs of a giant-bellied, hairy beast of a man and into the hand of another man. A different man. A man unlike any of the rest on the field. The quarterback, a.k.a. the QB. When Camp instituted the snap, he created one unintended consequence—both for the players and the fans. The snap created a pause. A regrouping behind the lines. And it became known as the huddle. In the huddle, the players got their marching orders and were reminded who they're fighting for—and who's fighting for them. In those brief few seconds, the quarterback stared at the men looking back at him and, without ever uttering a word, asked one undeniable question.

Do you believe in me?

The answer was either the tether that joined their hearts or the wedge that drove them apart.

In any game, one half of those on the field—the defense—hates the quarterback and wants to rip his head off. The other half—the offense—does whatever it can to prevent that and to help the quarterback move the pigskin across one of two goal lines separated by exactly a hundred yards.

In the early days of the snap, the quarterback handed the ball to a halfback or ran the ball himself. But doing so play after play became predictable and lacked a certain luster. In truth, the game was simply boring. So Father Camp proposed one more change.

The forward pass.

And the game was never the same.

Overnight, entire strategies evolved, developed, and changed, or were thrown out. The game's popularity skyrocketed, as did the reputations of the men who played it. Before the forward pass, men of stout stature, able to lift freight trains, were simply lined up across from each other and then cut from their tethers to shove and scrum their way around the field in a cloud of dust and snot and blood. But after the forward pass, non-Goliaths, Davids tending the sheep, were included. Even sought after.

When the rules changed, so did the responsibilities of the players, and none more so than the quarterback. No matter how complicated it's become—and it has become complicated—the quarterback's job is to get the ball into the hands of other playmakers and let them make plays, to know where to dish it out and not turn it over, to help his team cross the goal line with the ball.

In short, to score.

His role is essential, and while the game could technically be played without one of the other ten players—albeit not very successfully—it could not without him. The QB is the decision maker, the brain, the deciding factor; without him, there is no play and the ball never crosses the goal line.

Today, almost a hundred and thirty years later, American football is a multi-billion-dollar industry. Fans idolize teams and players, stadiums hold a hundred thousand wearing clothing that identifies them with their on-field heroes. They name their children or dogs after them, wager small and large sums of money, tattoo themselves in all manner of locations, and own fantasy football teams.

Because greatness is possible with each snap, fans put these mortals on pedestals. Some are still there. Men like Heisman, Unitas, and Starr. And we are shocked when each is reduced to a man whose bones break and muscles stretch and tear. They pull off their helmets and we discover that they are not the winged Pegasus, smiling Hercules, or thundering Zeus we had imagined. We love them when they win, mourn when they don't, cheer when they return from retirement. And we despise them when those of great promise fail to let us appreciate the promise we held for them.

We hate it when our idols let us down.

Truth is, quarterbacks have a shelf life. A limited shelf life. Each is a mist that wafts across the field. Every one will only throw so many touchdown passes, so many yards, win so many games, so many championships. Finite careers are composed of finite numbers, and every quarterback plays a first and last game. There is a definite difference between a Hall of Famer and an also-played. Because of this, the fans are in constant search of the next coming of whomever to fill an insatiable appetite. We toss them about like plastic chips in a smoky poker game.

Either by God's design, the exercise of their will, or both, some quarterbacks hang around longer than others. And we love them for this. Some achieve greatness. Some immortality. And while we love the greats, we worship the immortals. We hang our hopes on them, and in return, they do something no other player can.

The also-playeds, even the greats, give some. The immortals give all. They empty themselves. Carrying the hopes of others requires a selfless emptying. Strip away the colors and the conversations and all the noise, and the game of football is a war. It's a barbaric, violent war. And those who play it know this well. That's why every time they strap on that helmet they are digging into a deep place. Some tell you they play with a chip on their shoulder, out of their anger, their hate. Those players are deceived. Anger never won a football game, and in the end, when the last whistle has blown, players are judged not by how well they hate, but how deeply can they love.

That's why, when our idols disdain and spit on us, when they don't value what we do to the extent that we do, when they unshoulder our hopes, casting them off like unwanted rags, brushing them like crumbs from a table, the pain of betrayal is soul-deep and only one thing heals it.

The gates of Wiregrass Correctional Facility swung behind me, locking me out rather than in. Puddles dotted the asphalt below a hovering gray mist. Weeds sprouted up through the cracks. Concertina wire serpentined off to my left atop the eighteen-foot fence. The humidity wrapped around me like a blanket. Gage stood stoically in the guard tower—a rifle in his hand. A single wave, half a nod, and the beginnings of a smile. The quiet around my exit stood as a stark contrast to the media circus that accompanied my entrance.

Standing there didn't improve my situation, so I started putting one foot in front of the other. I pulled up my collar and turned my face into the wind—twenty pounds lighter and dragging twelve years tethered to my ankle.

Just out of town, a man in a van with a Bible on his dash stopped at dark, offering me a ride, and I was about to accept when I saw his daughter in the backseat. I thanked him and kept walking. Late afternoon, I stuck my thumb in the air. Not long after, a woman—maybe midforties—pulled over in a box-style Chevrolet van. "Where you headed?"

"Gardi."

"Where's that?"

"East of Jesup."

"I can get you halfway."

I opened the door, sat down, tried not to make eye contact, and made sure my pants leg covered my ankle.

She was chatty, seemingly nervous, and did most of the talking for the first twenty minutes. Then she turned the conversation to me. "Enough about me. Tell me about you."

I felt something tighten in my throat. "I'm headed home. To see some folks I haven't seen in a while."

"What happened to your car?"

"Don't have one at the moment, but I'm looking to get one soon as I can."

"You got a job?"

"I'm in..." My mind raced. *What's that word that everybody uses to describe being unemployed?* Finally, it came to me. "Transition." I made some awkward movements with my hands. "I'm between jobs right now. Hoping to find one when I get home."

"Got a girlfriend?"

"No. No girlfriend."

"Wife?"

"Not anymore."

If suspicion has a body language, it was starting to spread across her face. "Well, honey, you've got to do something. Got any hobbies?"

I was never very good at lying—or telling half-truths. "Ma'am, I just got out of Wiregrass." The name alone spoke to the severity of my crime.

"When?"

"Couple hours ago. I wouldn't blame you if you want to pull over."

She looked at me. Sizing me up. Our speed decreased, but her foot was still pressing the accelerator. Her left hand drove while her right hand slid across her lap and buried itself in her purse, which was wedged between her and the door. "What for?"

"I...I did twelve years."

Her right hand had yet to move. She thought out loud but took her foot off the accelerator. We coasted. "Twelve years?"

"Yes, ma'am."

She wasn't angry. Least not yet. There was no easy way out of this. "Ma'am, my name is Matthew Rising."

It took about three seconds for the words to circulate through the car and finally come to rest in that part of her brain where memories reside. We made eye contact, she recognized me, and her lips tightened and eyes narrowed. Revulsion and anger replaced kindness. Without saying a word, she pulled to the side and pressed the unlock button.

I stepped out quietly, said, "Thank you," and pressed the door closed. She never looked at me. Without a word, she pulled around me and disappeared into the distance.

CHAPTER FOUR

In the feeding frenzy leading up to the draft, several agencies offered to represent me. Many made strong cases. Said they could protect me and my interests. And while that was true, I needed someone I could trust. For seven years, Dunwoody Jackson had been my center. Literally my shield from those who wished to rip my head off. And at six feet two inches, three hundred and twenty pounds, and with the ability to bench press a house, "Wood," as I affectionately called him, was well-suited to the job. We were inseparable on and off the field. He must have had some Viking in his blood because everything about him was big and strong. Hands, feet, arms. His hair was reddish blond. His face was dotted with freckles, and his laughter was contagious. For three years in high school and four in college, he pointed his sweaty butt at me, slammed the ball into my hands, and took my sacks personally. And while he was a great football player, he was also a pretty good student. He majored in finance, graduated in three years, and then as a senior, he started his law degree. After he passed the bar, he went to night school to complete his MBA. A bit slimmer now at two hundred and forty pounds, he had taken to his new role as my agent and described himself as my "first line of defense," saying he always wanted to play both sides of the ball. During our week in New York, while I'd been getting fitted for suits and sitting in front of cameras, Wood had been talking with other players and signing up new clients. Strutting a bit under the haze of adoration, and relishing the strange juxtaposition of telling me what to do, life was good for Wood.

Following my interview with Jim Kneels, Wood mother-henned us out the back door of the studio where he had hired a limo to chauffeur us five blocks away. Exiting the door, he pressed his left hand to the secret-service-looking earpiece stuck in his left ear, and muttered something into the mic hidden in his right hand. An engine cranked to our right, and the block-long black limo slowly approached. I raised an eyebrow. "We could walk, you know."

In the agent-picking process, Audrey felt strongly I didn't need one more person kissing my butt but someone who knew me and wasn't afraid to get in my face and tell me when my issues were my issues and not somebody else's. She said I didn't need another yes-man but a your-swollen-head-is-getting-too-fat-for-your-shoulders-man.

Wood checked his watch and tugged on the cuff of his shirt just below the sleeves of his jacket. He looked down the street. "Shut up and get in the car." He was exactly what Audrey was looking for. She laughed.

I pointed to the earpiece and mic. "Nice touch."

Nine minutes later, we walked through the rear entrance of a building. Above us, two different teams of people waited in two different mahogany conference rooms. The first was a slew of endorsement companies—eight in all. The second was the owner and general manager of my new team. In the deal, I had requested, if possible, to take two of my receivers and two of my linemen with me. They were eligible, had declared for the draft, and the team agreed it was a good fit, provided the draft worked in our favor. Between second- and third-round picks and one trade, it had. Those four guys would also be there, waiting to sign alongside me. And as Wood represented each, he stood to have a very good night. It promised to be fun for all of us. Other agencies, those competing against Wood, told me to hold out, wait for more money. Wood said take the money. The team had offered me plenty, more than any rookie ever, there was no reason to hold out, nor did I want to. I wanted to get on the field. Get the ball in my hands. And, in truth, I'd have played for free. Something Wood and Audrey agreed would be our secret.

Last, but certainly not least, sat Coach Ray. Coach Ray wasn't really a coach, but we all called him that. After almost fifty years in football, he'd earned it. He'd started as a janitor, worked his way into the laundry and then into the training and equipment room. I'd met him eight years ago as a freshman at St. Bernard's. I was sitting in the film room early one morning when he walked in, looked over both shoulders, and whispered, "Mr. Matthew, would you mind reading me this letter? I can't—"

We've been pals ever since.

He was the first person to greet me before daylight every morning. And the last to turn out the lights after I'd left. He had a great eye for defenses, and as a result we'd watched a lot of film together. He'd been at St. Bernard's for the thirty-eight years prior, had always wanted a job in a college, and so State made room for him when I said I'd like to declare early and asked if they had any room in their training staff. Then, during contract negotiations the last few weeks, and with Coach Ray's permission, I asked my would-be team if they had any openings—anywhere in their organization. Ray's reputation preceded him, and they welcomed the addition. Albeit with a few concessions of my own. In anticipation of tonight, Ray had bought a new striped suit along with a top hat, a cane, and new penguin wing tips with metal heel counters. Audrey said he looked like a cross between Gregory Hines and Fred Astaire and his walk sounded like the guard at the Tomb of the Unknown Soldier.

Audrey was floating. Her feet barely touching the ground. She was wearing this skin-colored dress that wrapped around her hips like a cocoon. A slight slit up the thigh. Stunning. The antique elevator climbed and dinged at each floor while Wood joked about having just met a female track star who'd made the jump to movies. In the lobby, she'd pulled on his coat and asked for his number. "I love what you've done with Matthew," she had said. "Let me buy you a coffee and see if you'd have any interest in representing me." Wood didn't bother telling her that not only did he not drink coffee but the smell made him nauseated. Audrey laughed and rested her arm in mine.

We exited the elevator where the two conference rooms sat to our right. Loud, nervous laughter spilled from beneath the door. As did the sound of men holding their breath. To our left, a single room. Wood nodded. "Take all the time you want. They'll wait."

Audrey looked at me, confused. Then suspicious. I took her hand and led her in, closing the door behind us. Broadway shone like a runway and the lights of Central Park glistened in the distance. The city sprawled and sparkled below us. A couch and two designer chairs faced the window. Champagne on ice and fresh raspberries waited. A small box, wrapped with blue foil wrapping and tied with the same color bow, sat on the glass table. A lit candle flickered. Eyebrows raised, she said, "And you did this all on your own?"

"Yep."

"Really?"

"Yes, really."

I've been in a lot of locker rooms and I'm pretty well acquainted with what guys do and where they go to fill up their empty spaces, to find fulfillment. Most are counterfeit. Nothing but emptiness. I stood there, staring at her. Flickering candlelight. The slight upturn of her lips. The small of her back. The beauty that's her, the part she only shared with me, the part of us that was just our secret, hidden from everyone but me. Whatever it is that God hard-wired into the heart of man, into our very DNA, which is satisfied only in and by knowing the mystery and wonder that is a woman's heart wrapped in the layers of her external beauty—I'd found it in my wife.

She hung one hand on her hip. "And just when did you have the time?"

"Honey, I do have some experience at calling an audible."

She studied the room and crossed her arms. "I think you actually just succeeded in surprising me."

"Good."

One of life's simple pleasures, Audrey loved to unwrap gifts. Especially those with a bow. Her finger tapped the box, anxious at the possibility.

I said, "Much of the last couple of weeks...no, let's be honest, months, even years, has been about me. Before it gets out of hand—"

She smiled. "Before?"

"Okay....*any more* out of hand, I want to push the pause button."

She was half-listening. Her finger still tapping the box. My rehearsed speech would have to wait. "Go ahead."

My junior year of high school, two women vied for my attention. I only gave it to one.

I was walking to class. Books in one hand, football in the other, going over the film in my mind for Friday night's game. It was mid-September; we were three games into the season and winning. Decisively. In fact, we hadn't lost in two and a half years. I'd thrown five touchdown passes the previous Friday night, and my numbers were pretty good. Word about me was spreading. A dozen or so scouts at every game had become the norm. I turned a corner headed to physics and a sultry voice echoed across my shoulder.

Ginger Redman was captain of the cheerleaders, president of the drama club, an undefeated member of the debate team, and number three in her class. To make matters worse, she was six feet tall—most of which was legs—with auburn hair. As a result of her constant overachievement, she was well accustomed to getting her way. I don't think our meeting was accidental.

I didn't really know what drove Ginger, or why, but she left little to happenstance. My guess, and it is just a guess, is that she liked the attention I was getting and she wanted it. I suppose she thought we were a match made in heaven.

She thought wrong.

She said, "You always carry that football?"

"It gives my hands something to do."

A step closer. "Your hands get you in trouble?"

"Not when they're holding this ball."

"You sleep with it?"

"Most nights."

"Linus with his blanket."

"Something like that."

"Rather self-effacing, aren't you?"

"Only if you think football is a fault."

"Football is a game you use to get someplace better."

"Well, you and I agree on one thing."

"What's that?"

"Football is a game."

"And?"

A shrug. I wanted out of this conversation.

"So now you're the tall silent type."

"It's a game that requires me to give myself to something bigger than me."

"Like?"

"The idea that eleven men can do what one can't and never could."

She knew the answer. As a result, the question was insincere. "Quarterback, right?"

A nod.

"Some say you're best in the country right now."

No response.

"You don't care?"

"I care what eleven guys do. Not one."

She stepped closer, her face inches from mine. "Then that makes you a fool."

"I'm okay with that."

She turned to leave, but my question stopped her. She had tried to disguise it, but guys in my position do well to notice the subtleties. "You always bitten your fingernails?"

She paused, didn't turn, and shoved her hands in her pockets. Her body language suggested she didn't like knowing that I'd spotted her imperfection. Wanting the last word, she eyed the ball, then me. "Call me when you get tired of holding that ball. I'll give your hands something to do."

It was the longest conversation we ever had in high school.

Audrey Michaels was an athlete in her own right. She ran track—the 800 meters and the mile—worked on the yearbook, was three questions shy of acing the SAT, thought cheerleaders were silly girls, started and led the Rose Garden Club, and stole the lead in the high school drama—away from Ginger our junior and senior years. A fact not lost on Ginger.

We met in the training room Saturday morning after a game. The night prior, we had played a rival team from Valdosta. A brutal game played in the rain. I was sacked seven times, had rushed for a couple of TDs, and had taken more than my fair share of shots. By the start of the fourth quarter, I could barely stand up. Come Saturday morning, I rolled out of bed and hobbled to my car for the drive to school. My shoulder was sore, ribs and thigh were bruised, calves were still cramping up. Deep purple contusions dotted my chest and back. Some guy's fingernails had raked across my neck. Hamburger meat had suffered less than me. I limped into the training room and climbed up on a table, and our trainers pretty much packed me in ice. Audrey had just finished a workout of her own, and lay on her stomach on the table next to me thumbing through a magazine while a trainer worked on her tight hamstring.

Unimpressed, she looked up from her magazine. One eyebrow raised. A slight smirk. "What's your problem?"

I glanced at her out of the corner of my eyes. I'd seen her before, but we'd never really talked. I grunted. "Everything from the scalp down."

She lifted an ice bag off my knee and dropped it on my face. "Pansy."

I lifted the ice and tried to focus on the condescending voice that showered me.

She dropped her magazine and dug in a bag next to her. "You QBs are such prima donnas. A hangnail and you're screaming for pain killers and ice."

My head was splitting so I glanced through narrow eyelids. Medium height. Lean. Muscular thighs and calves. A runner's build. Hair cut short like a boy. Only prettier. Painted fingernails and toes. She had rolled over and was sitting up, leaning against the wall while the trainer worked the ultrasound wand in a circular motion over her left quad and hamstring. While I thought I was the focus of her attention, I was only half of it. Her voice might have been pointed at me but her eyes were focused on her hands—she had begun knitting or something with two silvery-blue needles, each about eight inches long. Spilling out of the bag was what looked like the beginnings of a sweater or a scarf. I didn't have the energy for a debate, so I lay back down. Thought maybe if I let it go, she would too. She didn't. She dug at me again. "You disagree, Mr. Street & Smith's number four?"

Rankings were posted every Saturday morning. Last week, I'd been ranked number seven. The fact that she had checked it today said more about her than she knew. Her hands were moving at the speed of hummingbird wings, suggesting that she'd crocheted a good bit. While she was digging at me, I detected a playfulness in her tone. In a sense, she was befriending me. Albeit while playing her cards close to her chest. Sort of a we're-sitting-here-so-we-might-as-well-make-the-most-of-it sort of approach. I could take it or leave it. I admit, while she may not have known what I went through last night, there was something in her voice I really liked. And it was refreshing. I said, "You forgot one thing."

"What's that?"

"The pillow."

"Pillow?"

"Yeah, so we don't bruise our huge, swollen heads during our weekly pedicure."

She considered this, then spun one of her crochet pins, point out, holding it like a spike. "Hold still and I'll help you with that."

That was the moment we became friends. And I've loved her every second since.

———

Nearly a year passed. Our senior year. November, and my birthday, rolled around. I did not know it, but Audrey had worked with a jeweler to custom design a rather hefty silver signet ring carved with my initials. She had made the down payment and was working two jobs to pay for it. Ginger got a whiff of the idea, convinced the jeweler she was Audrey's emissary sent to collect it, and bought it out from underneath Audrey.

That night, I walked into my room, clicked on the light, and there stood Ginger in her birthday suit, her waist wrapped in a red ribbon, the ring displayed on the index finger of her right hand. The room was bathed in soft music and candlelight. I told her she needed to get dressed and go home. When I stepped out into the hall and pointed toward the front door, she pulled on a trench coat, strolled across the room, and sucker-punched me—with the ring. The ring split my skin above the eye, eventually requiring seven stitches. And no, I wasn't expecting it. Admittedly, I was distracted. Something all of my teammates, and Audrey, didn't let me forget. Anyway, with my face covered in my own blood, and my left eye nearly swollen shut, she threw the ring at me. It ricocheted off the doorframe. She then stomped out of my house. To further complicate the night—and my life—somewhere between my house and school the next day, Ginger obtained a black eye and some rather deep bruises on her neck and back.

The following day, the police paraded me out of second period and into an inquisition in Principal O'Shaughnessy's office. Ginger stood crying, throwing accusations at me. I denied every one. A tense forty-eight hours followed. Fortunately, cracks surfaced in her inconsistent story, not to mention that the bruise marks on her neck were too small for my pawlike hands. Suspicion lifted and I was exonerated, but the mystery of the black eye and bruises remained.

While the issue faded, the ring remained. As did the question of what to do with it. We couldn't return it, as it was custom made and no one would want it because my initials were carved into it. Not to mention that Ginger had bent it when it impacted the doorframe. We were stuck with it. So, in a turn of good humor, Audrey secretly took it from my dresser drawer only to return it to me for

Valentine's Day. She had slipped it over the trunk of a white plush elephant.

A fun gag.

The ring soon passed between us anytime we needed a good laugh. Audrey had last given it to me just prior to the beginning of my senior college season, when she'd slipped it over one of the arms of a pair of Rock 'em Sock 'em Robots and placed them on top of the cake she'd baked for our one-month wedding anniversary. Another good laugh. But after a dozen or so passes back and forth, we'd worn out the joke and moved on. The memory of Ginger had faded, and I'd started wondering if I should craft it into something else. Something that mattered. That represented us.

Our bedroom window overlooked a park that we soon learned sat in the migratory pattern of what seemed like most every bird in North America. If it had feathers and it was heading north or south, chances were good it'd pass below our window in the married dorm. To help the throngs along their journey, Audrey hung a feeder. One grew to three, which expanded to five, and soon we were buying hundred-pound sacks of seed once a week. Word must have spread along the bird hotline because we were covered up in color, song, and flight. About once a week, we'd wake to a new melody or different patch of color. And while they were all beautiful, none of them held a candle to the mourning dove.

A couple weeks into this, just after daylight, a mourning dove lit on the sill of our window and began pacing back and forth. Audrey propped her head on my chest, and we watched the ritual. Once he'd determined the sill was safe, the male—signified by a bluish-gray crown and purple-pink patches on the neck—hopped to the wire "limb" of the feeder where he flicked the seed with his beak, cleaning the seat next to him. Having prepared a place, he then began to lament, in that low, almost sub-audible throat-rattling call to his mate. A sound commonly mistaken for an owl. Seconds later, the more slender, less colorful female descended from the treetops, landing inches away on the same limb. Once stable, she scooted sideways and rubbed her head and face along the sides of his, gently nibbling around his neck, a pair-bonding ritual called "preening." Eventually, the pair progressed to grasping beaks and bobbing their heads up and down in unison—almost comical—all while calling to the other in a song that gives them their name.

This occurred every morning—their approach and departure accompanied by the whistle of their wings. Sometimes, during the frenzy of afternoon feedings, when the crowd and competition grew, we noticed that when one called, only the mate would answer. Above the noise and chaos of the hundreds of birds surrounding them, they knew each other's singular voice and could differentiate it. We called it "bird sonar." Amazed by this, Audrey did some research and learned that doves mate for life.

One morning, when a male sat on the window ledge calling, Audrey tapped me on the shoulder and whispered, "Know what that means?"

"No."

She tucked her arm inside mine, pulled my cheek to her lips, and kissed me. "Hope is the anchor of the soul."

When larger, more aggressive birds, like crows and blue jays, migrated through, they'd bully and dive-bomb whatever or whoever happened to be feeding. This did not go well with my wife. One afternoon, I came home from practice to find Audrey lying prone across our bed with a pellet rifle pointed at the feeder. Didn't take her long to even the score.

The doves and their beautiful songs hung around, filling our mornings and evenings. Out of this, the dove became a symbol of us.

———

Standing next to that window, New York City spread below us like a blanket of lights, her finger tapping that bow-wrapped box, she was not expecting what she got. She untied the ribbon, opened the small blue box, and revealed the half-dollar-sized, intricately carved silver dove. She laid it in the palm of her hand. "Wow."

Speechless was good.

She tilted her head. "I wasn't expecting this." And the not-expecting was even better.

"I considered a spider monkey, but—" A shrug.

She laughed. "Thank you."

Months prior, I'd googled and found a picture online of a dove in flight. Wings outstretched, landing or taking off was tough to say. Could have been either. Picture in hand, I contacted a custom jeweler in Jacksonville named Hugh Harby. Hugh had been a rather talented college water skier who, following graduation, realized he was attracted to things that glitter, so he turned his attention from carving water to shaping metal and stone. Turns out he was good at both. Enticed by my idea—and the challenge of it—Hugh worked with me to craft Audrey's gift. It came out better than we'd hoped. Elegant. Detailed.

I tucked her hair behind her ear. "It's the only one like it."

Her whisper cracked. "She's beautiful."

My eyes never left her. "Yes, she is."

She turned. "Help me."

I clasped it around her neck and she leaned into me, her back pressed to my chest and my arms wrapped around her.

We stared through our reflection out across the flickering city. The moment speaking for itself. She locked her fingers inside mine. Minutes passed. Finally, I spoke. "When you heat silver, melt it down, it burns off the impurities, or dross. What's left comes out of the fire better. More pure." I waved my hand across the conference rooms down the hall. "Where we're going...some are going to like me. Some won't. Few will be indifferent. You and I been doing this long enough to know it's the nature of the game. I just want you to know that amid all this, you're what matters. Not the numbers on those contracts in there, not my face on TV, not my name on a jersey, not some naked woman waiting to catch me alone in my hotel room."

She turned and adjusted my tie. "If you walk into a hotel room and find a naked woman waiting on you, it'd better be me."

I nodded. "You know what I'm saying. I just wanted to remind you—us—before the noise and static of our life increases, that *we* are what matters to me."

I centered the dove in the small of her neck. "This represents both a landing and a taking off. Promise and possibility."

The tear rolled down her cheek. Her chin fell to her chest. "You made me cry."

"I do that sometimes."

Her smile lifted her chin. "Yes, you do."

Sometimes during the heat of a game, or maybe just after, if you watch carefully, there is a thing that we football players do. It can be after a win or a loss or a great play, but it's mostly when one or two have given their all, held nothing back, emptied themselves for another. Helmets on or off doesn't matter, but in recognition of the moment, they lean into one another, touching foreheads. Just for a second or two. It's not a head-butt, it's a quiet honoring of the other—when words can't really say what needs saying.

Audrey leaned into me, touched her forehead to mine, and cupped the back of my neck with her palm. She whispered, "Call to me . . . and I'll come to you."

We entered each conference room to smiles, handshakes, and hugs. What had taken a lifetime to achieve occurred quickly. Each of us signed above several lines, prompting bank representatives to ask each of us to type in our predetermined passwords, triggering the transfer of seven-figure amounts into various numbered accounts. The guys were delirious. Coach Ray made more bonus money in five seconds than in five years of washing laundry and showers. Staring at the papers and the numbers, he broke down and cried, staining his new tie. Said he was going to buy his wife a new car—her first ever. Wood became an instant millionaire and promptly broke out into a cold sweat, but he recovered enough to speak into his mic, which caused somebody to roll in a cart of chilled champagne. Corks popped, foam spilled, toasts followed, and grown men slapped each other on the back, hugged again, and cried some more. Their shoulders shaking. The emotive release palpable. Audrey watched me with satisfied delight—one finger tracing the lines of the dove.

Seconds before he summoned the limousine, Wood quieted the room and raised his glass. "To the night that all our dreams came true."

But I never made that flight to Hawaii.

CHAPTER FIVE

I'd been walking an hour when a run-down Suburban passed me, slowed, and stopped in the emergency lane. A skinny spare had replaced the right rear tire, which now sat lashed atop the roof racks. I didn't recognize the car or the driver until he opened the door. Wood stepped out, pushed his Costas up on top of his shiny head, and smiled.

Figures.

Wood met me at the back of the car and bear-hugged me—the first hug I'd had in a long, long time. It spoke volumes.

His clothes were old. Cracker crumbs dotted his lap. Tie wide. Collar yellowed. Shaved head. Whatever money he'd earned was gone. Tough years. Tougher miles. Tainted by association, the glamor had flown and, one by one, his clients had departed. Over the years, he'd spent most of his money, and then some, trying to get them back. Convince them he could represent them.

It had not worked.

He was two inches shorter than I am, but his shoulders were

a good bit wider and thicker. He worked out a good bit but had thickened in the middle. Looked to be about twenty-five pounds over his playing weight. He held both my shoulders in his hands and smiled. Neither of us really knowing what to say. Finally, I broke the silence. "You should get as far away from me as you can."

He laughed. "That's exactly what Laura told me 'fore I left the house."

"Smart woman."

His belly bounced as he chuckled. "Come on."

I sat and closed the door. He sized me up. "You all right? Get the flowers I sent?" The humidity inside the car matched the outside, as the AC didn't work. He pulled the Suburban onto Hwy 90 and laid his arm on the console. "Sorry I'm late. Flat tire."

"I see that."

Prior to the draft, Wood had bought the vehicle he thought should go along with his new image as agent. A Cadillac Escalade. Sleek, fast, the throaty rumble of a high-powered V-8, leather seats, wood-grain dash, twenty-inch wheels, entertainment system—the envy of would-be clients. A week before the draft, he'd told me, "People like to do business with successful people." He was so proud. Tinted windows. Cold AC. He'd never owned a car with power windows. As he talked, he kept lowering and raising all four windows. He smirked. "Image is a big part of that."

Like everything else, Wood's image had suffered, and the Suburban he drove was not the Escalade he'd bought. This vehicle had worn tires, faded and chipped paint, a couple of fender dents, and quarter-panel scratches. The carpet was stained, leather seats torn, dashboard cracked, and stale french fries covered the backseat. It was a good reflection of him. Of his life.

Within the first few months of my sentence, Wood had petitioned the court to move me to Wiregrass. They'd agreed, and he'd come to see me at least once a month. The only connection I had to the outside world. The first time he came to see me, I could barely lift my head. He spoke across the table. With the echoes of my conviction and sentence hanging over me, he spoke words that I so desperately needed to hear. "Matty, we'll get through this."

I asked, "Why're you doing this?"

He lifted his hands, his voice cracking. "Where else would I go?"

For twelve years, Wood brought me lunch. He couldn't stop my soul from cracking in half, but once a month he sutured it shut. How I love that man.

He brushed a few crumbs off the dash and threw some trash in the backseat. The car smelled of fast food. "Sorry about the mess. Laura and I are sharing one car right now. Just till I can find time to find something else. Work's been keeping me busy." I didn't believe him. I also knew him well enough to know that the admission was more painful than he let on.

He broke the silence with small talk. "Coach Ray says hello. Said he'll check in on you."

"He still at the school?"

A nod without looking. "Says they got a kid this year who's pretty good."

"He says that about everybody."

Wood smiled. "Lucky for us."

Gardi lay two hundred and twenty miles in front of us. He asked without looking. His tone of voice told me it was a rehearsed question, and while I'd never met his wife, I'd bet she put him up to it. And no, I don't blame her. "You, uh—thought about where you'll go?"

I pointed at the car. "Where's the Suburban going?"

"Gardi."

"I'd like to go to Gardi."

He shook his head, weighing his words, trying to be careful in how he said it. "That's probably a real bad idea."

Wood had married Laura Truman six years ago. She had worked

for the clerk of the court and had met, fell in love, and married him after he'd lost everything. Which told me everything I needed to know about her. "Laura tell you to say that?"

Another painful admission. "Yes, but she's right. And if you're honest with yourself, you know she is."

That's the old Wood—the one that hasn't been beat down and is not afraid to tell me the truth. He wiped the inside of the fogged-up windshield with a dirty T-shirt. "When word got out that you were, you know—good behavior and all—a group of parents got together. Mothers of girls mostly. Drafted a petition. City council passed it. Unanimous. It'll keep guys"—he gestured to my ankle—"like that . . . away from towns like us."

Still my protector. "I won't be any bother."

He pushed down on his blinker. "That's what you think." The headliner had fallen and was flapping in the wind from the open window. Wood's broad shoulders pushed his biceps out over the sides of his seat, and his hands dwarfed the steering wheel.

Despite the concern on his face, marriage agreed with him. I tried to take his mind off me so I pointed at his stomach. "Laura a good cook?"

He rubbed his belly, smiling like a kid who'd found the toy in the cereal box. "You don't know the half of it."

Gardi was three and a half hours by interstate. A good bit more by US 84. He pointed at the sign for I-10. "Highway, or—" He turned his finger toward the sign for US 84, which connected southeast coastal Georgia to west Georgia. Maybe south Georgia's version of Route 66. It meandered across the southern rim of the state, stopping in all the little towns and at every light along the way.

"You in a hurry?" I asked.

"Not especially."

I pointed right and Wood obliged, following my finger along US 84.

We rode in silence, traveling just under the speed limit and avoiding one of the other two elephants in the room. When he finally spoke, the words took a long time to exit his mouth. He stretched out his arm and put his right hand behind my headrest. "I don't know where she is." I stared at him out of the corner of my eye. He continued. "Nobody does." He shot a glance at me. "So help me. Nobody's seen her since the trial."

What he said was true. She'd disappeared. I knew that much. The memory of the courtroom flashed back as did the echo of her sobs as they walked me out of the courtroom in chains. One of the most painful pictures in my mental album is the one of her doubled over, holding her stomach like someone had just kicked her or sliced open her stomach, as if her soul spilled out between her fingers. She never raised her head to look at me.

He fidgeted in his seat, switching hands on the wheel. "You could spend the rest of your life looking."

"I know."

Not getting anywhere, he tried an end around. "There's nothing to tie you to Gardi. There might be some real advantages to starting over someplace new."

I lifted my pant leg, flashing the anklet. He made no response.

He started scratching his stomach, then squeezed my shoulders and bicep. "You're skinny. Looks like you could use a cheeseburger."

Last night for dinner I'd eaten chop suey with one slice of white bread and a glass of water. "A cheeseburger sounds good."

Within a few miles, he pulled into a Sonic. We sat a little round table while a waitress on roller skates took our order and disappeared. Above us, the speakers played a drive-time talk show that aired on satellite radio called *Fighting Back*. The theme song had been borrowed from one of the Rocky movies. The show's host was a successful victim's rights attorney who counseled and shared her wisdom, expertise, and legal advice with callers every weeknight over a three-hour primetime slot. She was empathetic, knowledgeable, articulate, and easily fired up. Listeners loved her. Her ratings were off the chart—and had been for years.

And Wood and I knew her all too well.

The show continued with Ginger picking up where she'd left off prior to commercial. Her voice came through clear, strong, and confident. I heard her, and Wood knew I could hear her.

"Sorry. She's gotten pretty popular. Seems like her show's on twenty-four/seven sometimes..." He pointed east down Hwy 84. "You want to go someplace else?"

"She doesn't bother me."

"Her voice—" He shook his head once. "Always takes me back to the courtroom. Man did she ever put on a show." When he realized that the memory was probably more painful for me than him, he recovered. "Sorry." He swallowed. "You been following her career?"

"I've been in prison. Not Mars."

"Well, just in case you missed it, let me catch you up to speed. She completed her PhD in psychology or psychiatry or some such psycho-thing. Graduated Harvard Law. Number three in her class. That's right." He held up three fingers. "Number three. She hung up her sheepskin, took some pretty high-profile cases, never lost in court, loves to work a jury, and salivates at working the media. Written a couple of best sellers. Says she's the 'unofficial spokesperson for the victim.' As in—" He pointed again at the speakers. "1-800-R-U-A-VICTIM. Goes by the name of 'Angelina Custodia' now. It means—"

"I know what it means."

The words spilled out his mouth. "Guardian angel." In both high school and college, Wood and I watched a lot of film together. It was our way of getting to know the competition so we could put together a game plan. Given that we'd played more than a hundred games together, we'd watched a lot of film. Whenever we did this, Wood would often take every opportunity to point out players on the other side with rather aggressive tendencies, those that might try and rip my head off, and make sure I kept clear of them. To make sure I knew what was at stake and that I hated them as much as they hated me. For Wood, the line of scrimmage was a line drawn in the sand, and his film-room reaction mirrored how he played the game. Passionate. Black and white. No gray.

Ever my defender, he took my protection personally, and he never could understand why I wasn't as mad and angry at those people as he was. Further evidence that we are each called to play different roles. Different positions. I'm no center. He's no quarterback. It's not a statement of our value, simply a description of our gifts. As much as I love him, I could not afford to play angry then and I could not afford to live angry now. This description of Ginger's rise up life's ladder of success while I've been buried beneath it sounded like one of those film sessions. Deep down, Wood wanted me to exit prison and go to war against Ginger. To grind her into the earth. I knew this. He'd never seen me lose, and it was tough for him to watch.

He motioned toward the speakers. "When she's not doing this, she's on TV. And if you thought she was annoying in high school, she travels with an entourage. Hair stylist, security, personal trainer, manager. She's got this huge black custom tour bus said to cost over three million—" He swiped the air in front of him with one hand. "Got 'Angelina' written in blue stardust. She's famous for road trips where she broadcasts from street corners, courthouses, Central Park…anywhere she can fan the hype." He sat back, nodding. "Small-town girl made the big time—" A nod. "Last year, she was one of *Fortune's* top ten most powerful women. The cover was a picture of her standing in front of her own G5. You can probably guess what's painted across the tail of the plane."

"She has a bit of a cult following on cell block D." I shook my head. "Every now and then a guy would get hold of a cell phone and make a call, crying for help. She'd play along."

"You think she knew you were in there?"

"Every year, postmarked on the anniversary of the night of the draft, I'd receive an unsigned postcard from an exotic destination addressed to 'Matthew Rock.' The message was pretty clear." I reached into my pocket and handed him the cards.

He counted out loud. "Twelve." He shook his head. One of the pictures had been taken over the toes of the person staring out across a blue lagoon, waterfall, and lush vegetation. A woman's bikini—both top and bottom—lay on the beach in the forefront of the picture. The suggestion was clear enough. "That's cold." He handed them back.

Our burgers arrived. Wood took a bite, then followed it with a handful of fries. He spoke with a mouthful, pointing a fry at my ankle.

"You can bet your cheeseburger she knows you're out. Given her influence, she's probably got the GPS codes of that thing."

Another shot across my bow. "I know."

He swallowed, paused, and lowered his voice. "You got a plan to set things straight? I mean, for everything that's happened—"

Occasionally during our film sessions, Wood would step out of his role as my center and try to step into the role of offensive coordinator and suggest plays or schemes. To make sure I saw the obvious. What was at stake. Most of the time he was just talking out loud because it made him feel better. I learned to let him vent. But today was a different. Today I'd been freed from prison, and Wood needed to get something off his chest. A wound that had been festering for twelve years. If he could get me to show some passion, anger, or rage against the machine that had wronged me, he'd feel better about believing in my innocence. I raised an eyebrow. "Really? That's where we are?"

Another jab. "Twelve years is a long time to sit there and watch the world spin."

"If you're trying to help, you're not." I finished my burger.

He looked at me several seconds, finally shaking his head. "I don't think you've quite grasped the idea that she sits on top of the world and you're buried beneath it."

I wiped corners of my mouth with a napkin. "You want me to pound my chest?"

"Couldn't hurt."

"Shout at the world? Tell everyone how she done me wrong?"

"Might give people a reason to believe in you."

"And what would I gain?"

Silence.

"Wood, try and see this from my side of the table. I'm not interested in defending my name or my reputation, building my long-lost career, or gaining people's adoration and belief."

Wood eyed my empty burger wrapper and his tone softened. "You want another?"

I shook my head.

He wiped the burger grease off his chin. Doing so brought me close to his hands and arms. Both were tinged with black grease. Like he'd tried to scrub it off but the shadow remained. "You moonlighting as a grease monkey?"

He brushed me off. Changed the subject. "Just keeping the world running." He pointed at me. "And speaking of running, you should eat three more and shove two in your pockets. Man, you're skinny."

Wood ordered two milkshakes and we sat waiting. Something I was better at than him. Angelina Custodia's voice showered us from the speakers above. Seductive. Raspy. Polished. Controlled. She'd never lacked confidence, but it'd grown since I'd been in.

He scratched his chin and didn't look at me. "You've been on the news a good bit lately." He spoke softly and let the statement float around us. He wanted a response, but I knew where he was going so I didn't give him one. This time he looked at me. "One of the guards at Wiregrass told Jim Kneels at ESPN that you been doing more than three thousand push-ups and sit-ups a day. Said he personally saw you do more than sixty pull-ups—at once. Said you been doing the whole Hershel workout. Press is going crazy over it. Saying you're making a go of it. That true?"

"Just keeping busy."

He retrieved last Sunday's *Atlanta Journal Constitution* and set it in front of me. "You take up most of the first couple pages." I scanned the article. The headline read, FALLEN ROCKET: MISFIRE A DUD. WILL HE ATTEMPT TAKEOFF? He continued. "Two nights ago, ESPN aired a two-hour documentary. Called it *The Best Who Never Was*. They interviewed about a dozen guys who still think you got a shot. *HBO Sports* is said to have something in the works. And one of the major cable channels is talking about a reality TV show."

"Showing what?"

"Your road back."

I shook my head and said nothing.

He leaned in closer. "Somebody got a bootleg copy of a security tape of you. In prison. Shows you running 40s in the dark. Alone. All of them clock you in the 4.5s. A couple in the 4.4s." I said nothing. He sat back. "Then there's the thing that's got everybody salivating. It's video of you throwing with a guard and you make a fifty-something-yard rope-of-a-throw through some window and out into the exercise yard. Bunch of experts have studied it and say maybe one other guy in the league could make that throw. Maybe only a handful of guys ever. They interviewed the guard. Page, or Sage or—"

"Gage."

"That's it. He said you two threw every morning. Said he used to press paper cups into the fence at forty yards and you'd hit ten out of ten at thirty yards." He folded his hands together. "You really thinking of making a go of it?"

I tried to stop him before he got out of hand. "Wood, I'm thirty-three. I'm a convicted sex offender who can't get within fifty feet of children, schools, day-care centers, shopping malls, or movie theaters. I have about eighteen hours to register my place of residence before Big Brother comes looking for me." I shook my head. "I have one thing on my mind, and it isn't football."

We drank our milkshakes in silence. A couple of minutes passed. He didn't lift his eyes. When finished, he slurped the bottom. His tone of voice changed. "Matthew, we been knowing each other a long time, right?"

I nodded.

"Shared a lot."

Another nod.

"You were in there a long time."

I waited.

"Anything you want to tell me?"

"You mean, did twelve years soften me, bring me to my senses, and do I finally want to confess to something I vehemently denied twelve years ago?"

This time he nodded.

I knew he needed to do this. I also knew I wanted to nip it in the bud. "No."

"But you still can't prove that, can you?"

"We've been through this."

"What about all that footage they had?"

"Still can't explain that."

"Seven different video cameras show you leaving the fitness center with her and then stumbling like a drunk sailor up the elevator and into her room."

"I saw the video."

"And what about the other video? The one they found in the room?"

I didn't respond.

"Rocket, it's video. The smoking gun."

"It's not me. I never did that."

He sat back. "Even your wife admitted it looked like your body shape." Wood leaned in. "You remember what she said, when they made her watch it before the jury?"

I did. "Yes."

"It's still your word against hers, and, look, you've been locked up, you don't know. Hers is a lot more valuable than yours right now. Maybe more than yours ever was."

"So you want me to tell them I did it just so they'll stop hounding me? So this will all go away?"

"A confession would get you a better shot at a tryout than a continued denial."

"I don't want a tryout."

"Explain the DNA?"

"Can't."

Wood paused. "Man, seriously. All that video, two other eyewitnesses—"

I corrected him. "Two Asian prostitutes who spoke no English. Everything they told the jury was through an interpreter and the questions were all leading."

Wood interrupted me. "They both pointed to you in the courtroom when the judge asked who they woke up next to at the hotel room."

I interrupted him again. "That's because they did."

"You don't deny that."

"'Course not. They were there when I woke up. I was just as surprised as they were, but that doesn't mean I did what they said."

He continued. "One of them wasn't even sixteen. The other barely seventeen." He held up his finger like quotation marks. " 'Underage prostitutes' are still underage."

"Wood…"

"What about the way"—he pointed at the speaker above us—"she sat up there and told the story. Where'd she get the detail? She knew stuff that only Audrey could know. And she had no reason to lie. I don't..."

"Wood, the trial ended twelve years ago. You want to reopen the case?"

He pointed down the highway. "The trial in that courtroom ended, but the one taking place in the court of public opinion is just getting cranked up." He shook his head. I let him finish. "You realize that in *Webster's*, under the definition of 'guilty as sin,' sits your picture."

"I know."

He continued, but at this point he was piling on. "Look up the word 'deviant,' and you'll find the same picture."

I frowned.

"And you're okay with that?"

"Didn't say I was okay with it. Said I understood my situation."

During my trial, the nail in my coffin had been a grainy video that, though kept under tight security, had somehow been leaked to the press who called it "irrefutable." The first time Audrey saw it, she said, "It's like watching my soul die."

I finished my milkshake. Wood was about to speak when I interrupted him. "At the end of the documentary, what was the last film clip they played?"

He nodded and looked away.

I prodded him. "How many snaps have you and I taken together?"

"What?"

"How many times have you put the ball in my hands?"

"Including practice?"

"Yes."

"Thousands."

"And of those, in how many did we run motion away or counter?"

He weighed his head back and forth. "More than half, easy."

"And why did we do that?"

"'Cause you at one time could read defenses better than anybody maybe ever, and you saw something nobody else did or could."

"Even if that was true, I had to have a reason, so what was that reason?"

"Misdirection."

I leaned in. "There's a difference between what you see and what is."

"Even if what you're saying is true and she made all this up—which, while she's good, nobody is that good—the only way to get your life back is to get her to admit, before a judge, that she lied, and your chances of that happening are about zero."

"I'm not after her, Wood."

He leaned in. His neck was turning red. "Newsflash, Rocketman—you may not be after her, but you need to realize that while you've been away, people have not forgotten. And they certainly haven't forgiven."

"You want me to walk back to Wiregrass and knock on the door? See if they'll take me back?"

"Might be easier for you." He fiddled with his car keys on the table. "You may not be interested in the truth, but let's assume for three seconds that you actually find Audrey, and you can bet your throwing arm that she is. Sooner or later, you're going to have to confront that."

He was right and I knew it. I rested my head in my hands. "Got to find her first."

CHAPTER SIX

Two hours later, Wood drove into Gardi. The rain fell steadily. Rippling along the roadside. He pulled over by the railroad tracks just before town and cut the engine. He wouldn't look at me. "I want to get you over for dinner, but Laura just needs some time…" He shook his head. The admission was painful.

I put my hand on his shoulder. "She's protecting you. You should listen to her. I'd probably do the same." I stepped out. "Thanks for today."

"You got a plan?"

"Well…" I chuckled. "I have no money, no home, no car, no career, no wife, no family, and, to my knowledge, only one friend who half believes what I'm telling him."

He pointed down the tracks. "I knocked off the cobwebs. Stacked some wood. Canned foods in the pantry. Some eggs in the fridge. Propane's full. Window unit's busted so sleeping should be a real joy, but the ceiling fan works. You might have to tape up a few cuts in the screens to keep the mosquitoes out. And if you're looking for some clothes, when Audrey disappeared, I gathered up what was left of your stuff and put it in that old cedar trunk on the porch. Right next to that old trail bike. It sputters, but it'll get you where you need to go."

Wood's great-grandfather farmed shade tobacco on several hundred acres contiguous to St. Bernard's. The business peaked under his grandfather, then slid into oblivion with his father. When hard times hit, Wood could never bring himself to sell the acreage, making him cash poor and land rich. I'd always admired him for keeping it when his own business tanked. In addition to shade farming, his grandfather had a penchant for moonshine, which he cooked out of a cabin he built on site. The block of property sat, oddly enough, a short walk from the tracks. The cabin lay near the middle of the property, and the dirt road leading to it was gated. On Friday nights, after games, a lot of us piled in there on sleeping bags next to the wood-burning stove. I smiled. "Thanks."

"It should offer you some privacy. Keep the paparazzi at bay." He chuckled. "And speaking as your attorney, 'cause I know you can't afford one, it's legal in terms of distance from the school."

"That's comforting."

"Oh—" He raised a finger and shook his head. "You might should steer clear of the barn." He handed me an official-looking letter from the stack of papers crammed between the dash and the windshield, which I had a feeling doubled as his mobile desk.

I scanned the letter. "What's this?"

"About six months ago, the school busted some kids in there smoking dope. To deflect attention from their dope-addicted kid, one of the parents made a stink about the barn's condition. The county investigated, agreed with the parent, and told me it was a lawsuit waiting to happen." A shrug. He spoke almost to himself. "If they wouldn't trespass, it wouldn't be a hazard, but despite the fifty obnoxious yellow NO TRESPASSING signs hanging everywhere, somehow I'm responsible for their kid's trespassing and dope smoking."

I laughed.

He continued. "To make sure they got their point across, the county sent me a—" He gestured to the letter in my hand. "CYA note via certified delivery informing me that I should bulldoze it before I get sued and lose my land. I get a new one about every other month."

"That thing still standing? It was a hazard back when we were running around."

"Evidently, the county would agree with you, and given its proximity to the school, and knowing that kids have a penchant for hanging around it—"

I smirked. "I have no idea what you're talking about."

"They keep telling me it's got to come down."

"What's the holdup?"

He sucked through his teeth and weighed his head side to side. "It's complicated."

"What do you mean?"

"You'll see when you open the door. And for the record, I had nothing to do with what you find there. Neither did Ray. It all just appeared a couple years ago and every few months something new pops up. It's like that scene in *Jeremiah Johnson* where the Indians leave stuff at his old house where the crazy lady now lives. Nobody sees them coming or going, stuff just appears." He sat quietly a moment, wrestling with something on the tip of his tongue. Finally, he slid a sheet of paper off the dash and handed it to me. "Laura did some digging. There's no record—at all—of an Audrey Rising in or near south Georgia or north Florida." He glanced at me and then looked away. "She checked under 'Audrey Michaels,' too." A single shake of his head.

The rain felt cold on my shoulders. I tapped the top of the car. Not knowing quite what to say. Rare is the friend who will stick by you when most think you're a deviant. Rarer still is the one who believes. "Wood, thanks."

His eyes welled up. "You'll find out soon enough that I haven't helped you any." He waved his hand across a town oblivious to my return. "If you thought they loved you then, wait until you see how they hate you now." He put the car in drive but kept his foot on the brake. "My office is in the old Mater building. Second floor. I do—" He shrugged. "Bail bonds." He wouldn't look at me. "I can see the jail from my window." Another shrug. "It pays the bills. Or most of them." He reached into his pocket and handed me a small wad of cash. Dirty twenty dollar bills. "You'll need this."

Based on his appearance, whatever he was giving me was a lot. Maybe all he had. I waved him off. "I'm good."

He offered it a second time. "Come on. You need—"

I raised my hand. A stop sign. "Laura's right. Be smart. Stay away from me."

He tapped his chest. Eyes welling. "When I close my eyes and think back through the worst and toughest times of my life, I see you looking back at me. Telling me that I could do what I never thought I could do." A pause. "No matter what I do, I can't bring myself to hate you." He shook his head and stared at the national championship ring he wore on his left hand. He and I won seven championships together—four in high school and three in college. The one he was now wearing was our last.

The memory returned. A good one. Late in the third quarter, we were down by thirteen. We needed to cross the goal line twice and they were killing us, both on the line and in the coverage. The nose guard was pushing Wood around like a rag doll. I stood in the huddle asking myself what to do. He'd never asked or told me what to run, but in that second Wood just got mad. He stuck his face in front of mine and grabbed my jersey. "When I snap the ball, follow me."

"Wood, he's been eating your lunch all day."

Determination sprinkled with rage spread across his face. "You just hold on, and I'm gonna push this country boy back into his lineage."

And he did. When he snapped the ball on the six yard line, I tucked my head and he plowed a path to the goal line. Carried the nose guard, both tackles, the weak side linebacker, and the free safety with him. You could have driven a truck through the hole. It wasn't until after the game that I learned he'd broken his left arm—in the first quarter.

Wood had always had a high pain threshold, and sitting in the front seat of his Suburban, he was in pain. He wiped his nose on his shirt sleeve. "I think back to the trial and—" He pounded the steering wheel. "I cannot reconcile the man I knew in the huddle with the man they put on trial."

That made two of us. I waited, saying nothing.

A tear spilled down his cheek. "Matthew, these people are going to rip your head off your shoulders, pour gasoline down your neck, and light your body afire."

I nodded. I knew that.

"You're either the worst kind of man who lies to his wife and friends and self. In which case twelve years wasn't enough, never will be, and God alone will deal with you. Or somebody, for reasons I can't fathom"—his giant paw pounded the console between the seats—"did this to you. Stole what you had and everything you were ever gonna have." He wiped his face on his sleeve. "And I'm not sure which scenario hurts worse." The pain had spread across his face. "I've had twelve years to think about it, and I'm no closer to figuring it out." His voice rose. "Today certainly hasn't helped. Seems like five minutes ago, you threw that backside pass to Roddy in the end zone. I carried you on my shoulders around the field. People were holding signs that read ROCKET FOR PRESIDENT and ROCKET, WILL YOU MARRY ME? Moms were naming their kids after you. Ninety-six thousand people were screaming—" His voice fell to a whisper. He stared out through the windshield and into our shared past. " 'Rocket! Rocket! Rocket!' " He closed his eyes. Finally, he looked at me. "Call me a fool. Call me gullible. Call me the town idiot. I been called worse. I was your friend then. Am now. And will be."

When he drove off, one taillight burned out. I heard myself whispering, "How I love that man."

CHAPTER SEVEN

T he town sat a block away. I could see the flashing BAIL BONDS sign of Wood's office. Thirteen years prior, the city council had passed a resolution declaring the first day of college football season "Matthew Rising Day." They had also commissioned a sign to be built in my honor. And because they were so proud of one of their own, they'd sought to do so with permanence. The base was brick and the sign was the size of a Ford truck. It read:

HOME OF MATTHEW "ROCKET" RISING
THE WINNINGEST, MOST-DECORATED QUARTERBACK IN THE HISTORY
OF HIGH SCHOOL FOOTBALL
TWO-TIME HEISMAN TROPHY WINNER
THREE-TIME NATIONAL CHAMPIONSHIP WINNER
THREE-TIME BCS MVP

Mounted on an impenetrable and permanent foundation, the sign climbed some twenty feet in the air. To further embarrass me, and at considerable taxpayer expense, the town had commissioned the casting of a larger-than-life bronze statue that depicted me in midthrow, just before I released the ball. Including the base, the statue stood ten feet tall and weighed well over a ton.

On the day of the unveiling, surrounded by the media and most everybody who lived in or around Gardi, the mayor had handed me a gold-plated key to the city and asked me to say a few words. That night, Audrey and I climbed up the back of the sign and sat on top, our feet dangling across the top of the T in Rocket, and ate raspberries.

The shine wore off quickly.

During the trial, someone had spray-painted #1 PICK IN THE NFL DRAFT AND CERTIFIED SEX OFFENDER. After my conviction, the city council was faced with a dilemma: what to do with the sign. And given the graffiti, the situation couldn't wait. In reaction, the council voted to remove the sign, but an argument ensued regarding the statue. Both sides agreed that I'd embarrassed the town, but one half felt that, due to the expense, the town should simply rename the statue in honor of "the football player" and sell the idea as a faceless testimony to the greatness of the game. Make lemonade, so to speak. This argument won, so the losing side quickly gave the winning side what they'd asked for. Under the cover of dark, somebody hooked a chain to the statue. But given the zeal with which it was cast, it proved far more stout than believed; so when the truck sped away, the chain tightened, the body did not give, and the chain snapped off the head. By then, people were sick of talking about it and nobody really cared if the statue had a head or not. Most thought it fitting, so they left it.

Over the years, vandals had spray-painted their dissatisfaction with me across various portions of my body. Further, someone had returned with a chain and snapped off both my throwing arm at the shoulder and my balance arm just above the elbow. To finish me off, someone had taken a cement cutter or chainsaw or something and cut deep grooves and gashes in the torso and legs. A fitting depiction. As I stared at my headless, armless, stubby, carved body, a gentle rain began to fall.

Welcome home, Matthew.

The town of Gardi grew up and around shade tobacco—cigar wrapper leaf. Flourishing in its exportation, the growing season began in May where young plants were tied to guide wires that lead the plants outward and upward. Cloth tents made from gauzy cheesecloth were then spread over the plants to increase humidity and protect them from direct sunlight. Doing so created a more stable climate for the plant but a brutal environment within which to work. Farmers and their workers spent the summer tending the plants, pulling off shoots and tobacco worms, then harvesting in late summer. Once gathered, the leaves were sewn together so that they could be strung on a series of laths and hung to cure in the rafters of huge barns that were on average fifty feet wide by a hundred and fifty feet long. Wood's family were also cattle operators, as the manure was used to fertilize the shade. To feed the cattle, they planted corn and peanuts and fed the cows inside the barns where he used the peanut hulls as bedding. On average, three hundred tons of manure would cover about twenty acres of shade.

Shade farming peaked in the 1950s and '60s, with the last hurrah being 1961. Squeezed between foreign competition and severe drought, most farmers went broke—including the Jacksons—leaving only the land.

And Wood's barn.

When tobacco died, two opposing forces remained. The first took up residence at Amen Corner, or the intersection of Main and Church Streets, where the First Baptist Church, Main Street Methodist, Christ Church Presbyterian, and the Gardi Church of

Christ sat facing and quietly arguing with one another. The opposing force, or the redheaded stepchild, took up some fifty acres on the outskirts of town—adjacent to Wood's property.

St. Bernard's of Clairvoux was a church, school, orphanage, monastery, and convent that lay relatively sequestered and forgotten behind a twelve-foot-high brick wall until about twenty-five years ago, when one of the priests decided to give the orphans an outlet for all their energy and field a football team. The balance of power at Amen Corner remained relatively unchanged and undiscussed for about three years until the Saints of St. Bernard's starting winning. And win they did, so much so that the good neighbors at Amen Corner quietly pitched in, helped build a stadium at St. Bernard's, and became rather vocal supporters of a good Catholic education. We used to sit in history class and marvel at all the wars fought in the name of God and religion when all the world needed was a grassy field, a few sweaty boys, and a piece of pigskin to garner the peace. And while there was much disagreement as to the Blessed Mother Mary, the actual nature of the elements during communion, the role of the sacraments, what happened during baptism and the "correct" way to perform it, who would end up in heaven, and where God resided on Sunday morning, there was unanimous consent as to where He spent His Friday nights. And on those Friday nights, those blue-haired beauties from the Baptist church, those sans-a-belt-slack Methodists, those teetotaling Presbyterians, and those non-clapping, non-singing, quiet-as-a-church-mouse Church of Christ members got along fabulously with the Mother-Mary-adoring, rosary-reciting, bead-counting, genuflecting, Jesus's-body-eating-and-blood-drinking Catholics.

Between St. Bernard's and Amen Corner sat the relatively inconsequential courthouse. That is, until my four-week trial put Gardi on the national map. While Judge Black held the gavel, the jury of my peers—most of whom I'd known a long time—looked down their noses at me and the courthouse dispensed the justice that the country was calling for. And while the members of Amen Corner heard from God and supported the verdict, the balance in power did not shift. As long as the lights lit up on Friday night, the Catholics held the power—all given to them by a group of smash-mouth boys with dreams in their eyes.

Wood's property shared one border with St. Bernard's, the other with a government-owned junkyard that covered another almost fifty acres called "the graveyard." The government stopped dropping junk there twenty years ago, but prior to that it had been in use for nearly sixty years as a final resting place for broken-down and discarded vehicles of any type. Everything from huge cranes once used to build skyscrapers to World War II planes to dump trucks, tractor trailers, old Chevys, fire trucks, and barges; we even found a tank tread when I was a kid. When the government ran out of lateral space, they began stacking vertically. Over the decades, that stacking created a maze of thousands of cars and equipment, piled on top of one another. In some places, the piles stood thirty and forty feet high. During the construction of one of the federal highways, the government used the property as a dump for fill dirt. That left a scalable mound mixed with bumpers, hood ornaments, truck bumpers, and old Fords that became affectionately referred to as "Rust Bucket Mountain." Or simply "the Bucket." The back side was too steep to walk or run up. It had to be climbed hand over hand—literally stepping from fender well to door handle—while the front side was the length of a highway on-ramp, only about three times steeper. And other than the NO TRESPASSING—VIOLATORS WILL BE IMPRISONED signs, it made for a magical playground. I, along with countless other boys, trespassed daily, sometimes several times a day, and climbed all over that hill. From the top—with an elevation of maybe a hundred and fifty feet—you could stare down on the football field and get a decent view of the game.

Which we did.

I pulled the hood of my sweatshirt up over my head and walked the railroad tracks west. Most mornings during high school, I'd wake before class and go for a run. And on most of those mornings, I'd run these tracks. Knowing I needed to increase my foot speed, I made myself step on every railroad tie. Quickly. Lifting my knees, forcing me to take short, quick steps, only landing on my toes. Then, in an attempt to lengthen my stride and gain some strength and endurance—sort of another gear—I'd step on every other one. Lastly, when I was trying to put some spring and explosion in my calves, I'd hop every third. This repetitive, monotonous torture drilled strength into my stomach, power into my arms, neck, and back. I did this for miles at a time.

Hence, I knew these tracks pretty well.

I climbed up the bank and was met by the smell of creosote and spent diesel. Slowly, I began stepping from railroad tie to railroad tie. Feeling my way. Pretty soon, I was jogging. The muscles in my legs and core, the ones I'd once pounded into submission that grew up under the stress and strain of constant testing, remembered what freedom and power and joy felt like and sprung to life.

I ran hard, bumping up against but not crossing my redline. As I did, my body woke, my lungs opened wide, and the memory of running without fences returned. Having starved so long, my body feasted on air and space not dissected by razor wire. Sweat soaked me, flung from my fingertips, and the miles clicked by.

After an hour, the moon had climbed high and full, throwing a shadow across the Bucket and the light poles of the stadium that spiraled up out of the pines lining the tracks. Dark, unlit, silent sentinels, they stood guard over a quiet field, waiting for somebody to throw the switch and flash them to life.

I slowed to a walk, my heart pounding, lungs and muscles burning, smiling over the thought of a blister on my right foot and left heel. Given different circumstances, I'd have described my feeling as euphoric. I scurried under the fence, rattling the NO TRESPASSING sign, and wound my way through a maze of hundreds, if not thousands, of junk cars to the mountain. Looking up, little had changed. Grass and weeds and even a few small trees grew up out of the cracks and crevices. I climbed up the back side, picking my way, hand over hand, over old Cadillacs, worn-out Chevrolets, and forgotten Fords. We used to stand up here, sing along with David Wilcox, and dance on the graves of "tail fin roll locomotives and rusty old American dreams" because after their owners were done with them, this is where they'd all come to die. When I reached the top, I stared down on the dented and mangled hood of an old Buick where we huddled as kids. We had poked holes in it to let the rain drain where our butts sat. "Rising Field," so named during my tenure in college, spread out before me, and the breeze lifted to me, bringing with it the smell of cut grass and the memory that I once had dreamed.

CHAPTER EIGHT

I stared down on the field where my dad brought me as a kid. Late in the afternoons, after he clocked out. Grease packed beneath his fingernails. He managed mechanics, had a desk in the front office, but he wore his name on his shirt and couldn't resist getting his hands dirty. He hated that desk, and he'd much rather show you how to do something than tell you. Several days a week we'd rumble up here in his old F-150 and play catch on the field.

This is where he taught me a buttonhook. Fly. Post. Down and in. Fade. Hitch and go. And this is where he taught me to throw. *Grip it like this...Left hand pointed at the target. Come over the top. Look at the target, or where your target's going to be—not at the ball. Rip the left arm straight down and follow through. If you hear footsteps, either tuck it or get rid of it. Get back up when they knock you down. And*—I remember him laughing. His head falling back. Teeth showing. *They're going to knock you down a lot. It's part of the game. Might as well get used to it.* Then we'd throw. Back and forth. Thousands of times. Over the weeks, the distance between us increased but the bond grew stronger. Pretty soon, he was running routes and I was throwing. Once I could manage the throws, he inserted my first major hurdle—an imaginary defense. This meant that not only did I have to know his route, and how and where to throw to him when he ran that route, but now I had to think through the fact that there were several imaginary men running around out there with varying assignments—and I had to know those as well.

It was glorious fun.

Dad explained defenses and began using words like "zone," "man," "Cover 2," "Cover 3," "goal line," and "nickel defense." Each code explained assignments and responsibilities for several of the defensive players—primarily the safeties, but it also included the inside and outside linebackers. Just as every man on the offense had a specific individual assignment, so did every defensive player. With every trip to the field, he added another defense, stuffing my brain with exponential possibilities. This meant that as a quarterback calling the play in the huddle, I had to think through— beforehand—what would be open, or might be, and where the other team's players should be if they executed their assignments. In short, my job was to know the defense as well as my offense.

I don't remember exactly what route he said he was going to run or what defense he had called on the other side, but one day, all my wires got crossed. The x's and o's merged into alphabet soup and I lost track of pretty much everything. Dad stood waiting on me to snap the ball but all I could do was tuck the ball under my arm, shrug, and say, "I have no idea."

He jogged over to me and waved his hand across the field. "This is nothing but a chess match, and you're just moving pieces around the field. Take your time. Think it through. We're not in any hurry. You control the clock." He smiled. "Worst thing that can happen is a delay of game. No biggie. The ump backs us up five yards and we start over." A chuckle. "Only with more field to work with."

78

"What if they—" I looked away, afraid to voice every quarterback's fear.

He interrupted me. Raised both eyebrows. "Take you the other direction?"

I nodded.

"You play this position long enough, and it's not a matter of if, but when. Might as well get over that now. What matters is not the fact that some defensive player intercepts you. What matters is what you do when you get the ball back in your hands." He waved across our imaginary opponents, chuckling. "They can't beat us." A smirk. "They're good, but they ain't that good."

While that day tested the capacity of my brain, it was grammar school recess compared to the paradigm shift I had coming.

It was late afternoon, sun going down. Dad stood on the left hash, his pants tucked into his boots. Grease stains on the back of his hand. I was standing in the center of the field, ball in my hand. He'd line up wide left, and we were playing against a defense that was lined up in Cover 1—which meant the imaginary cornerback across from Dad was playing man coverage, two yards off and one inside, forcing Dad outside and taking away the quick slant. I visualized how that imaginary guy in front of Dad would be in his back pocket the entire time he ran his route and knew my throw could not be off more than a few inches or it'd get intercepted.

Having thought it through, I moved to snap the ball to myself.

"Blue forty—"

Suddenly, Dad lifted his head and began pointing wildly at the cornerback and then the entire defense. "Change Cover 2! Change Cover 2!" He shouted.

I hesitated, raised an eyebrow. But we'd already called the play. So I continued my count. "Blue forty-two—"

Dad began jumping up and down and pointing at the defense and shaking his head. Finally, I motioned time-out to the imaginary referee and called Dad over. He was breathing heavily. He turned away from the defense and spoke in a low tone. Hands on his knees. "Cover 1 was a decoy. The farther you get in your count, the more they start backing up to Cover 2. If you throw that deep ball"—he smiled—"that I know you're itching to throw, that strong side free safety will time your throw, intercept it, and run eighty yards the other direction."

This made no sense to me whatsoever. It violated all the rules he'd taught me. "But, Dad, they've already called the defense. They can't change it just before the snap."

He smiled and his head tilted just slightly. "Hate to break it to you, sport, but yeah, they can." He leaned in closer. "They can change it anytime they want."

The weight of this revelation was more than I could bear. I almost sat down. "But that's not fair . . . How do we beat that?"

He put his arm around me. "It's called an audible."

Incredulous, I just looked at him.

"It's when you get to change the play at the line of scrimmage."

The tectonic plates, which once formed the foundation of what I knew to be the game of football, shifted inside my head. I pointed a few feet behind me. "But what about the play I just called inside the huddle?"

"You can change it. You're not locked in. An audible is an if-then statement."

I had no idea what he was talking about. I looked at my dad as if he'd grown three heads.

He explained. "*If* the defense does one thing, *then* we do another."

I motioned to my offense. "Great, but how do I tell those ten guys without"—I pointed at the defense—"those eleven knowing?"

He snapped his fingers. "Pick a word."

"What?"

"Any word. Something catchy."

I said the first thing that came to mind. "Matthew."

"Good word. But how about 'Mike,' 'hot check,' or 'Rocky'? Words that are easy to say and hear. The word itself doesn't matter. It's a verbal bell—a way to get their attention. That's all. It's your way of telling your offense that you're changing the play at the line of scrimmage. Their job is to always listen to the sound of your voice—for that one word—and make adjustments as needed. Your job is to read the defense and know what play will work, given what the defense is showing you."

We agreed on hot check.

But that only solved half the problem. I scratched my head. "But how do I tell you what route to run?"

"We assign routes to words. In this case, when the defense shifts from Cover 1 to Cover 2, that opens up the slant and maybe the hitch and go. So if you want me to run a slant, you say, 'Bomber.' Want me to run a hitch and go? You say, 'Razor.'"

That meant that as a quarterback I had to know our offense as well as all the defensive possibilities we might face and the audibles for changing our offensive play at the line when the defense shifted cover. In that moment, football became chess played in 3-D, with a little cardiovascular challenge thrown in for good measure. Not to mention the marauding horde.

Dad grinned. "Ready?"

I called the play in the huddle, and we walked up to the line of scrimmage. I stood under my imaginary center and Dad lined up wide left. In my mind, I returned the defense to its rightful place and began my count, "Blue forty-two. Blue forty-two..." With the stands in my mind full of people screaming and waving towels and shaking penny-filled milk jugs and the scoreboard showing we needed a TD to win, I scanned the field and watched as the defense began shifting—changing coverage. A giant hand moving the pieces around the board. I shouted and pointed at the same time. *"Hot check! Hot check razor. Hot check razor."*

Dad nodded once, smiling. He knew I couldn't resist throwing that long ball.

Dad gave me a closed fist behind his back to let me know that he'd heard my "hot check" and knew his new route.

Hut-hut-hut. I snapped the ball, dropped five steps, read my primary receiver, who had been stuffed at the line, faked to a back in the flats to draw the safeties in, and then turned, ducked under the nose tackle who'd beat my center, rolled right to evade the outside linebacker, and threw the ball deep into the corner of the end zone—where Dad wasn't yet but would be in about a second. The ball spiraled, turned nose down, and Dad caught it over his left shoulder in the end zone. The crowd went wild.

That's where my dad taught me to dream.

My anklet had rubbed my skin raw, but I ignored it. I sat on the rusty hood of that Buick, stared down at the cut grass, and tried to remember my dad's face. But it had faded. I could hear his laughter, feel his hand resting gently on the back of my neck as we walked back to the truck, but his features were blurry. My dad saw me play one high school game when I was a freshman and died that night in his sleep. I had given him the game ball. Mom said he never uttered a word. He just died—holding that ball.

Mom did what she could. Worked a couple of jobs to put me through school. I remember her ironing other people's clothes at midnight when she had to be up at four to open the coffee shop and bakery. When my trial came along, she mortgaged the house to pay for my defense. When we lost, something in Mom cracked, and she died my second year in prison. Given the possibility of children under the age of eighteen at the funeral, the state filed an injunction and wouldn't let me attend the service until everyone had departed. I walked up the aisle in the empty sanctuary—my chains rattling and scraping the marble—and stood next to her coffin. Then I hung my head in my hands and soaked the floor with my tears.

I have known wonder and majesty and unadulterated joy in my life. I've also known some pain.

And I'm not sure which was greater.

The field spread out before me, the memories continued to flow back. My last game there returned. The end of my high school career. Twenty thousand people in the stands. Over a hundred college scouts. Radio. TV. To say our town was enthusiastic would have been an understatement. *USA Today* had ranked us number one in the country and covered the entire front page with a picture of the team. The number two team was on the field warming up. They'd brought busloads. The visitors' stand was a sea of black and purple and noise. Jim Kneels had waited outside the locker room. When I walked out, he held out the microphone and, with doubt in his voice, said, "Lot of pressure on one so young. Think you can handle the weight of it?" I remember staring out across those stands and wondering the same thing. One second. Then two. Finally, I shrugged. "Guess we're about to find out."

Ever the skeptic, he smiled, dropped the microphone, and said, "Yes we are."

We made our way to the end zone, where the fog machine poured smoke around the paper banner the cheerleaders had made for us. It'd been raining. Falling steadily all day. The field was soaked, as were we. A breeze filtered through my face mask and dried the sweat across my face. Cut grass. Fresh paint. Sweat. Anxiousness. Nerves waiting for an outlet. Our stands were colored with garnet and black. Painted faces and proud moms waved towels, and dads with swollen chests told half-true, worn-out stories. The lights shone down on the pom-pommed cheerleaders, with their faces painted and hair in ponytails, and a shiny brass band.

The team had asked me to run out first, but I'd declined. I never ran out first.

"Guys, I been looking at Wood's butt for four years. I don't think we ought to change things now."

They laughed. The tension-breaker was needed. When the speakers started blaring "Lunatic Fringe" by Red Rider, Co-Captain Wood, ever the clown, burst through the banner and the fog attempting a back flip gone awry, followed by Roddy who performed fourteen backflips in a row—in full pads—ending in a split. The other team got the message. One flip for each win, including that night.

The crowd went berserk.

I stood in the corner of the end zone, waiting for my name to be called. One last time. The end of one career and the start of another. 59–0. Tonight would, or could, make a perfect 60. Something that, according to the record books, had never been done in high school football. Every interview this week was the same. Even the national networks. *Can you pull it off?* Each interviewer wanted to make this about me, but it wasn't. It was about us.

Big difference.

I stood surrounded by guys I'd sweated and bled with—guys that were as identified with their numbers as with their names. Mikey was bouncing on his toes, alone in the corner, racing downfield in his mind, wondering if this last game would soothe the thing with his dad. Kevin was sizing up blocks, over the middle grabs, and what girl would fill his imagination after the whistle blew. Ronnie had taken a knee, envisioning over-the-middle, bone-jarring tackles and wondering if and where he'd play college ball. Roddy was staring across the field, seeing himself breaking through the line, downshifting into that gear that few have. He was *Street & Smith's* number seven. Its scouting report said, "He is one of the greatest combinations of strength, speed, agility, and sheer athleticism most recruiters have seen in a receiver in a long time." The rest of the guys were milling around the end zone.

Finally, there was me. I wore number 8, for no other reason than

I always thought it a good number for a quarterback, and *Street & Smith's* had ranked me number one.

My left ankle felt stiff due to a few extra layers of tape. The week before, a guy named Thompson, the outside linebacker for the Bulldogs, held onto it while I dragged him into the end zone. He didn't like that so he torqued it beneath the pile. It was the worry of all the interviews. It'd be okay. Early in my junior year, Coach had handed me the reins of the play calling. Thompson either didn't know this or didn't care. So on the following series we ran the option up his nose. Kevin crack-blocked him—breaking two ribs—and Roddy went forty-seven for the go ahead.

My left hand was throbbing; it was slightly swollen and felt like somebody was hitting it with a hammer. Fortunately, the broken bone had not broken the skin. The ER doctor wanted to operate on it the night before, but I wouldn't let him. With or without surgery, he said it'd take weeks to heal. Wood and Audrey knew about it—and the events surrounding it—but they'd never say anything. There was a fourth person who knew, but she had her own reasons for keeping quiet. I knew if I could make it through the next forty-eight minutes without reinjuring it, that it would eventually heal.

What I didn't know was that the events that caused it would not.

Audrey stood at her seat on the fifty yard line. The cameras were pointed at her as much as they were at me. Sixty-seven teams had offered me Division I scholarships, and the reporters felt she knew where I intended to go to school. We'd told no one. She guarded our secret closely.

She'd painted her face. Wore my freshman jersey. Was shaking a milk jug. Screaming. Her eyes were glued to me. National Signing Day wasn't until February, but everybody was pressing both of us. Wanting to know. A few commentators were actually tossing back and forth the idea of my skipping college altogether. Straight to the draft. Petition the league to make an exception. *He's that good.*

I wasn't about to skip college.

The crowd was on their feet. Signs waving: ROCKET FOR PRESI-
DENT, ROCKET, WILL YOU MARRY ME?, and T-MINUS ONE GAME AND
COUNTING. They were calling my name.

Deep in the third quarter, we were tied and we were tired. Their
defense had put together a delayed blitz package that was wreak-
ing havoc on my offensive line. The guys were all looking at me.
Shaking their heads. Deer in the headlights. The score was 48–all
and I'd been sacked seven times by the defensive tackle. The guy
was a giant, and he was tossing Frank, my guard, around like a
sack of potatoes. I grabbed Wood by the face mask, pressed my
forehead to his, and said, "I need four seconds." That meant that
he would have to take on both the nose guard and that defensive
tackle. "That's all. Can you give me four seconds?"

He looked over his shoulder, sized them up, and nodded.

Wood snapped the ball, gave me all he had, and I hit Terry on a
post. He crossed the goal line untouched. The momentum shifted,
and we scored four more times. I threw eight touchdown passes
that night. Ran for two more. We put up almost a thousand yards
of total offense. Jim Kneels went on the air at halftime and said he
was watching a performance that may never be surpassed.

And for the first time in the history of high school football,
a small, unnoticed team from south Georgia won a national
championship—among teams we were never supposed to beat. The
team, headed by Wood, lifted me on their shoulders. I found my
mom in the stands hugging Audrey. They were crying. Laughing.

I've known some good moments in my life.

I opened my eyes. The field was dark. I blinked and saw a lone
figure tossing a ball in the air. He was thin. Tall. Several balls lying
at his feet. He'd hung three tires from the crossbar of the goalpost.

Differing heights. From this distance, he made no sound. He stood at the thirty, under center, ball in hand. On mental command, he'd snap it to himself, roll out, and throw at one of the three targets hanging from the crossbar. He was strong, athletic, and fast; he had good footwork, good hips, good speed, and his throwing motion was quick. But for all his talent, he looked confused. He looked to be wrestling with something in his head. It was working its way out in his throwing motion—and not very well. His motion was hitched. Ugly. Unnatural. And, as a result, inaccurate.

If I had to guess, I'd say some coach got in his head and told him to throw the way he thought he ought to. I watched this kid for an hour. Throw after throw after throw after throw. He was persistent, and determined, but his motion was a mess and seldom the same. And, judging by his body language, he knew it. After a hundred throws from the ten back to the forty-five, where few came near the tires, he packed up and then ran twenty hundred-yard strides, followed by a couple hundred push-ups and sit-ups, and then he left as quietly as he'd appeared. No fanfare. No entourage. Little, if any, success or improvement.

As he walked off, a familiar voice spoke softly behind me, and something in me smiled. "They say he's the next coming of you."

CHAPTER NINE

I turned and found Coach Ray sitting above me. I don't know how long he'd been there, maybe the entire time. He'd propped his elbows on his knees and clenched his pipe between his teeth. He pointed the bit at the kid on the field. "With some help, he could break your single-season record." When I stood, he stepped down from his perch and approached me. Arms wide, he never hesitated. "Thought I'd find you here. How you doing, son?"

I hugged him back. "I was just sitting here trying to figure that out."

He chuckled. "Out of one prison and into another."

"Something like that."

He put his arm on my shoulder. "You look good."

We stood, staring down and remembering. He dumped his pipe, then repacked it with Carter Hall and lit it, drawing deep and bathing us in the sweet memories and aroma. As the cloud enveloped us, we watched the kid exit the field. "His name is Dalton

Rogers. Most folks call him Dee. Got the feet of a deer. But as you can see, he's got a bit of a problem."

I nodded. "Yep."

His teeth were clenched around his mouthpiece. "His coach is an idiot."

"Well, if his coach did that to him, he hasn't helped him any."

"Coach Damon Phelps. Kids call him Coach Demon—among a few other choice names. Has a bit of a mean streak. Likes to scream and yell. Get all up in their faces." He put his arm around my shoulder. Hugging me from the side. "It's good to see you."

"You might be in the minority on that."

Another deep laugh. "I been there before."

After my arrest, the team that had picked me and hired Coach Ray had taken back all signing bonuses. Including Ray's. He never made a dime. Although he'd come with Wood to see me several times in prison, I'd never addressed that with him. Seeing him now with tattered clothes and worn-out shoes, I needed to. "Coach, I'm sorry about—"

He waved me off, blinking. "Wood and me, we measured the distance from the cabin. Got one of those little surveying deals with the wheel." He pointed to the roof of the cabin a half mile away. "You're 2,516 feet from the corner of St. Bernard's so you're good and legal. And 2,109 from the corner of the stadium. You're inside two thousand here, but . . . you're not living here." He glanced at my anklet. "Wood finally had a phone installed in the cabin so's you can register that thing when you need."

"You two've done your homework."

"It's Wood. He couldn't wait for you to get out. Jumpy as a kid at Christmas." He stood with his arm around my shoulder as we stared down on the field. A minute passed. He was skinnier. Bonier. He smiled but didn't look at me.

"School treating you okay?"

"Fine. They leave me to do my thing, and I love on they kids."

"You were always good at that."

He smiled slyly, his voice mimicking scouting reports. "I do seem to possess some talent in that area."

It'd been a while since I'd been this close to him. He used to wrap my feet before games. The image of his pained face in the courtroom returned afresh. I tried a second time. "Coach, I'm real sorry about—"

He cut me off. "You're all over the radio. TV. Everybody wants to know if—"

I didn't care about TV or radio or satellite or carrier pigeon. And because he knew me better than most, my guess was that he knew this. "Coach—have you seen Audrey?"

He dumped his pipe and slid it into his shirt pocket. "Wondered when you might get to that."

"Every time you came to see me, you were hiding something."

He chose his words carefully. "I love that girl. Almost as much as you."

"She made you promise not to tell me. Or Wood. Didn't she?"

He wouldn't make eye contact.

"You've known all along."

He studied the field. Finally he turned and began walking down the mountain. He spoke over his shoulder. "I'll be seeing you. You owe me dinner. It's the least you can do for ruining my pro debut."

"Coach?"

"Town's changed since you've been gone."

"Coach!"

He pointed his pipe at the clock tower without looking. "You should check out our new rose garden." He sucked through his teeth. "Really something." He wiped his head with a white handkerchief. "But it's the view from the clock tower that will take your breath away."

* * *

The garden was old. Two hundred years or more. The monks had spent five years constructing the wall. A twelve-foot-high brick fortress—thick enough to walk on and repel small cannonballs and words that pierced the heart. When finished, it encompassed the entire eight acres. Eight Civil War–era live oaks spiraled up, rolled, spilled, and spread out over the wall, sweeping the ground on the other side. Legend held that a Union ball lay dormant in the middle of the oldest, but no one really knew the truth. The scar had healed. Over the years, the limbs had welcomed children seeking play, workers seeking shade, Confederate soldiers seeking silence, and lovers in search of each other. Irrigation flowed from an eight-inch pipe drilled into the artesian aquifer some six hundred feet down. Exposed limestone marked the wellhead. The water was cold, clear, and, some would say, sweet. A hundred years ago, one of the monks had chiseled into the limestone:

. . . THE WINTER IS PAST
THE RAIN IS OVER AND GONE

Over the decades, the roots of a wisteria vine had discovered the rock, crept in, and entangled the base. A jealous lover's embrace.

Throughout its life, the pendulum had swung between beauty offered and utter disrepair. When worked, tilled, toiled in, sweat over, and bled in, the garden had opened itself, accepted the stiletto roots, and then emptied itself, filling the world with color and sweetness and life. But when overlooked and forgotten, the weeds rose up, choked out most everything else, and loose vines serpentined rampant.

When we were young, rumor held that the brick wall encircling St. Bernard's had been constructed to protect the nuns from the outside world. We'd also heard that some of them hadn't spoken in thirty or forty years. A vault of silence. Only they knew the truth of that, but the wall stood taller than I remembered. Thicker too.

I ran my fingers along the mortar and then scampered up the tentacled limbs of the giant live oak, spiked with rusted twelve-inch nails serving as steps and handholds, and stepped off onto the top of the wall—twelve feet off the ground.

When we played here as kids, the garden lay overgrown. A jungle of weeds, disrepair, and indifference. Because of that, we escaped here. And that night after the game, shivering in the cold, she tasted like hot chocolate and red hots.

It'd been homecoming. The wind was howling and creating an unusual windchill for south Georgia. Audrey stood outside the locker room, wrapped in my letterman jacket, which dwarfed her, blowing into her hands to keep her fingertips warm. I showered, walked out of the locker room, and she slid her hand in mine. Neither of us wanted to go home. A little while later, we found ourselves here. Huddled beneath a copper moon. Midway through the garden, she'd stopped, tugged on me, and we sat on a cold marble bench. She'd whispered, "You're shivering."

I was on fire. "I don't feel cold."

I had never been in love and wouldn't know what to do with it when I found it, but when she looked at me, my heart melted, slid out of my chest, and landed in her hands.

And that's the last place I remember seeing it.

The garden before me now was anything but disorderly and overgrown. The Masters in August didn't look this kept. Not a blade of grass was out of place. Twenty-two fig trees spilled over the wall and shaded walkways. Given my slightly aerial view, I tried to make sense of the pattern and could not. Precise vertical rows of plants marked either side, intersected by several horizontal, equally spaced rows, dotted with an indiscriminate array of colors and sizes. Roses scattered the lawn in between. Some were bunched together, almost intertwined, while others had been singled out and left alone. A scarecrow stood in the middle—aluminum foil plates spinning in a slight breeze. A few feet away, a stump rotted conspicuously out of place. Despite its apparent lack of order, something about the layout struck me as strange. It was ordered without being orderly or symmetrical. I turned my head, squinted, and scanned it again. Not able to make sense of it, I walked the rim of the wall to the clock tower, where I slid through a window and shimmied up the steps to the top. Standing beneath the bells, I studied the garden. It might have taken longer in the daytime, as the impressionistic colors would have added to my confusion. But given the moon, and the black-and-white contrast, the pieces fell together. Finally it hit me.

Audrey.

The detail was incredible. She had recreated the final play of the national championship, thirteen years prior. The last great moment we all shared. Looking through the lens of that last play, she had used the colors and textures of the garden to recreate one second in one game—complete with opposing teams crowding the sidelines, coaches, umpires, goal lines, sidelines, hash marks, goalposts, and then there were the players.

I stood in astonishment. *How long had it taken? Where did she start? And why?* It was as if she had taken a snapshot of one of the most perfect moments in all our lives and frozen it. A living, 3-D recreation. Theater-in-the-round.

I wanted to get closer, so I climbed down and walked out into the garden and onto the field among my larger-than-life teammates.

You had to know him to recognize it, but center stage, larger than life, stood Wood. She'd trained a climbing rose with finger-thick vines woven through and around each other in such a fashion that his trunklike legs grew up and out of the earth, then twisted at his torso where they fed into a barrel-like chest and giant, powerful arms. I had no idea how she'd trained the rose's vines to do that, but carefully, meticulously, over time, she'd crafted a masterpiece. She'd even figured out how to craft great effort, or angst, or struggle. His arms were intertwined—or locked with—another dominant, darker rose that grew over the opposite side of the stump. I stared up into the frame that fanned and stretched out over me. Major Hawkins. He was the linebacker who'd been eating my lunch. Jake, my right guard, had his hand—or a trained branch—hanging on Wood's shoulder, the other on the rose leaning over the stump. They were double-teaming the linebacker. And in that play, they had. They'd bought me time, and it's one of the only reasons I ever got the pass off. Crowder, the fullback and my secondary receiver, had spun out into the flats and was waving his arms at me, uncovered. He was represented by a single, squatty bush surrounded by several feet of cropped grass and two loose vines waving in the breeze. A single stray vine draped across the ground, trailing behind him. Crowder was famous for never tying his shoes, and in that play they'd come untied, which was why he tripped coming out of the backfield. I turned my attention to the corner of the end zone and stepped it off. And just like in the game, Roddy was forty-seven yards away. Audrey had planted a tall, skinny rose with long branches fully extended. I ran my fingers along the vines and laughed. No thorns. She'd either clipped them off or found a rose without them because everybody knew that Roddy didn't have a mean bone in his body. He was confident, borderline arrogant, but never mean. Everybody liked Roddy, and standing there, stretched across the sky above me, he never looked so graceful. Because he could leap like a gazelle, she had suspended him along a wire frame several feet in the air. His outstretched arms were intertwined by three roses coming up out of the end zone and climbing up his back—in that final play he'd been triple-teamed by both corners and the safety. Their limbs had been cropped short, never quite reaching his fingertips. Around us, the fans were represented by an indiscriminate web climbing up the wall on one side of the field and along a slanted wooden frame opposite—like a bleacher. Interestingly, beneath the slanted woodwork, she'd planted several small roses huddled around an even smaller stump—kids playing a pickup game. Every player, coach and referee, trainer and water boy was represented by a rose, or series of roses, except the quarterback, who was nowhere to be found.

Then the scarecrow caught my eye.

Clever.

While the rest of the garden was pristine, perfect, pruned, and not a weed in sight, the scarecrow was a patchwork of broken pieces of junk, strung-together fragments of fabric held together by twine, wire, whatever she'd found on the potting room floor. His arms and legs were made of PVC pipe. Aluminum plates, suspended by fishing line, swung from each. Each piece looked like it'd been run over by a tractor, chewed up by the mower, and then reassembled with little thought to permanence or form. A spinning copper wind vane comprised the head of the poor scarecrow. Once round like a roof vent, it had been bent and rebent and now looked more like a piece of rock candy. A thick wrapping of silver duct tape held it oddly canted atop the shoulders. A hole had been cut in the chest of the white T-shirt—right where the heart should have been.

My eyes climbed above the field and scanned the silhouette of the wall. Rising periodically above the top were six odd-shaped boxes, mounted on single rough-hewn timbers and standing just inches from the wall. They were tough to see in the dark, but from a certain perspective—like down on the field—the poles and boxes might look like the lights of an athletic field. I climbed back up on the wall and across the oak limbs along the top of the wall, approaching the first box. Squirrel-proof bird feeders. Full of seed.

Audrey might be hiding from the world, but she had not forgotten the one she came from. And she had spent considerable time—a decade or better—recreating a single moment in time.

When all the world was promise and possibility.

I was sitting, my feet dangling, marveling at the world Audrey had recreated when a squeaky, swinging gate caught my ear. The person walked briskly, not stopping to smell the roses but almost walking over them, breaking off blooms with her arms as she strode quickly by. In her hands, she carried a stick of some sort. It was tough to make out in the dark, and several times I lost her in the shadows of the fig leaves. She disappeared for a moment in the back of the end zone, reappeared beneath Roddy, across the red zone, through the defense, and toward the center of the field. Her pace was fast, determined, purposeful, and I'd seen it before.

My junior year, national championship, fourth quarter. We were down by six. Eighteen seconds on the clock. Their defense had put together a pretty good blitz scheme, and my offensive line was so confused they were cross-eyed. Their outside linebacker was a guy named Brooks who later spent a decade in the pros. But before he left for Dallas, he left his mark on me and the BCS Bowl Game. Every time I turned around that guy was in my face and I was on my back. The fourth time he sacked me came on the second-to-last play of the game. I was looking downfield, scrambling, trying to find anybody open, and when I turned he hit me blindside. I remember hearing the announcer say, "Rising down. Rising down." I didn't know what my name was, much less what quarter it was, but I knew I needed to stand up before the trainers raced out onto the field and the officials made me sit out one play. Wood recovered my fumble, allowing us one more play, which was eventually intercepted in the end zone. Not my best effort.

When Brooks stood up—and thereby climbed off me—he danced around, made some hand motions toward our fans, and then began the return to his huddle where he, as captain, was calling the plays. Before he got there, a speeding and undetected bullet shot from our sideline en route to his body. The bullet launched itself airborne four yards in front of him and intersected his vertical and celebrating body with a horizontal and knifing plane. The blow flattened him and knocked off his helmet, causing more embarrassment than harm. When the dust cleared, the umpires pulled Audrey off his chest, where she was pounding his shoulder pads with her clenched fists. The referee obviously ejected her from the game, but not before a standing and raucous ovation from 121,000 people. Two State Troopers led her, laughing, from the field, and she watched the final play from the media room, where they had welcomed her with open arms. After the game, one of the sideline reporters had used the description "Spider Monkey" and the name stuck. Brooks would later describe the incident as one of the more memorable hits in his entire football career. A year later, Audrey and I had our picture taken with him when I convinced her that he was a good guy.

In the garden, Audrey approached the line of scrimmage and without notice, she swung backhanded at what would have been Wood's gut. The dismissive blow bent the well-trained vines of Wood's stomach, swaying the branches but doing little harm. He'd live to play another day. Unphased by Wood, she approached the scarecrow, which stood innocently staring down the field, its plates spinning slightly. Its head turning with the direction of the breeze. Within arms' reach and without any verbal indication, she stepped, loaded, and swung like Hank Aaron, completely removing the scarecrow's already tilted head from its drooping shoulders. The blow sent the wind vane sailing into the bleachers, where it banged off the brick and came to rest hanging in the thorns about three rows up. Reloading, with short, quick blows, she broke off the right hand, shattered both arms, and removed both legs with a vicious swing accompanied by a belly-deep groan. Standing over the pieces, she then began chopping downward, smashing the small pieces into even smaller pieces. Not content to just chop it to death, she spoke to the pieces—grinding them into the earth as much with her words as the stick in her hands.

She used to fight for me with the same intensity.

Having dismembered the scarecrow, removing him from the field of play and doing a pretty good job of telling him what she thought of him in the process, she walked to a bench along the wall just below me, dropped her weapon to the ground, and leaned back, breathing heavily. If I'd had a raspberry, I could have dropped it on her head. A minute passed. Followed by another. Finally, she pulled her knees up into her chest and sunk her head in her hands. At first the sobs were muffled. Then she came unhinged and the angry cries echoed off the brick and clock tower above us.

The last time I'd heard that sound it occurred in the courtroom. It bellowed from her soul and exited her mouth without restraint. Then and now, the sound cut me.

Off to the left, the lights of the school and the male and female dorms—just a few hundred feet away—shone through the trees. The pressure of the collar on my ankle spoke to me.

I slid over the side of the wall and dropped onto the grass just feet from her. Doing so startled her. She looked older; her eyes were cold, almost lifeless, and the years had not been kind. Her hair had been cut boy-short and looked gray. More silvery white. Entirely. Her eyes were shadowed by circles, and she was skinnier. She wore no wedding ring. Audrey had always reminded me of Angie Dickinson. Penetrating eyes, high cheeks, defined lips, ample curves, sultry voice. I couldn't speak for her voice, but despite the color of her hair, little had changed since I'd last seen her.

I'd been in prison six months when a guard fetched me and told me that I had a visitor. I grunted. "They got a name?"

"Audrey Michaels."

Using her maiden name was a bit of a sting. I took a seat and waited. Audrey walked in, arms folded across her midsection, holding herself. I stood, wanting to reach through the glass, my chains echoing off the walls. She'd lost a good bit of weight. Gaunt. She'd not spoken or communicated with me since the trial. She perched on the edge of the chair, angling away, not looking at me. I wanted to say something, anything to ease her pain. But Audrey wasn't here. Just her body. She sat there maybe ten minutes. Finally, she glanced at me out of the corner of her eyes, then returned to looking at the floor. She said, "Why?"

What answer could I give? Would one more denial satisfy? The first ten thousand had not.

I said nothing. I wanted her to look in my eyes but she would not. She stood, paused, wrapping her arms tighter around herself, as if she were keeping her insides from spilling across the floor, and walked out.

It was the only time she ever came to see me—eleven years, 187 days, and nine hours ago.

I reached down and picked up the stick. Hefty, it was a worn and gnarled hardwood, well oiled from sweat and use. She stood, a cold resolve returning. Three feet separated us. I held out the stick. An offering. My voice cracked but no words came.

I guess we were past words.

She stood and took the stick out of my hand. At first it just dangled while she considered it, then she spun it in her hand and propped it on her shoulder. Finally, when the ice water glazed over her eyes, she extended the stick and touched me on the side of my cheek and jaw, holding it there several seconds. Her bottom lip trembled. She opened her mouth to say something, closed it, then gritted her teeth and pressed the stick to my temple. For several seconds, she held it there, looking more through me than at me. After a moment, she began shaking her head and gripped the stick with both hands. I looked into her eyes and knew that if my wife was in there, she was buried beneath a world of pain. Gathering herself, she tucked the stick under her arm like an umbrella and returned through the way she'd come.

I watched her disappear across the field, leaving me alone in her garden. It wasn't until after she was gone that I noticed the tears dripping off my cheeks and chin.

CHAPTER TEN

Sometime before daylight, I awoke sweating in Wood's cabin while the fan spun noisily above me. The outside world was quiet. In the distance, I heard a train horn, hollow and haunting. After a workout in the junkyard, I showered and stood in front of the sink, shaving, remembering the sight of Audrey's face. Wood stuck his head in the door. He nodded toward the junkyard. "You don't look like you've lost much. The way you scampered up the hill out there, I'd say you still got some juice in your legs. You sure you don't have some plans you want to tell me about?"

I shrugged. "Some habits are tough to break."

"You thought about today?"

I glanced at the clock on the wall. "I've got about four hours to register before people in uniform come knocking."

He glanced at a cheap digital wristwatch, which was not the Rolex I'd bought him just before the draft. "You better let me drive you to town."

*　　*　　*

The sign out front simply read SHERIFF. I waited in line while those in front of me posted bail or requested to see someone locked in jail. The lady dispensed of the guy in front of me in about two words and then craned her neck and raised her eyebrows at me. Several people were milling around so I tried to speak softly. I leaned across the counter, "Ma'am, I need to register as a...an offender."

She scratched her beehive head with a pencil. "Say again."

I spoke slightly louder but still kept the conversation between the two of us. "Ma'am, I need to register as a sexual offender."

Her expressionless face spoke with great volume and clarity, and when she added words people passing on the sidewalk outside could have heard her. "You need to register as a sexual offender?"

All eyes turned to me. I nodded.

She mimicked me with half a nod, speaking with increased volume. "Does that mean yes?"

"Yes, ma'am."

"You wearing a sexual offender anklet?"

I lifted my pant leg around the side of the desk so she could see it. Using a handheld scanner tethered to her computer that looked like something at a grocery store checkout counter, she scanned it. My prison mug shot taken a day before my release appeared immediately on the screen in front of her. She spoke without looking. "Full name?"

"Matthew Tate Rising."

She took off her reading glasses and stared at me, sort of chewing on one side of her cheek. "Son, I'm not here for your jollies. Now you either speak up—" She pointed over her shoulder at several uniformed officers milling around the coffee pot. "Or you can have this conversation with them."

I said it again, this time loud enough to be heard.

"Confirm your date of birth."

"11-3-1981."

"Driver's license or identification card?"

"I don't have either."

"Social security card?"

That had been in the documents they returned to me when they released me from prison. I handed it to her.

"Employer information?"

"I'm not employed."

She spoke without looking. "Unemployed?"

I thought that's what I just said but figured it better not to bring that up. I dropped the ma'am. "Yes."

"Do you have any identifying tattoos?"

"No."

Her fingers moved with the speed of hummingbird wings. "Scars?"

I had two. One about four inches long next to my belly button and the other over six inches long just above my right hip. "Yes."

"Are they in private areas?"

"No, I can show them to you."

She held up a camera tethered to her computer so I lifted my shirt and she took several photos of each.

"How did you get them?"

I paused and waited. I knew I was losing this verbal joust but I had everyone else's attention in the room, I might as well have hers. She did not look at me but tapped the keyboard impatiently. Finally, a quick glance at me and then back at the screen in front of her. "A man stabbed me in prison."

She never hesitated. "Do you possess a passport?"

"I did, but I haven't seen it in about thirteen years." I shrugged. "I imagine it's expired by now."

She looked at me over her glasses. "You get cute with me and you can sleep it off next door." She pointed her pen at me. "You understand?"

"I wasn't intending to be—"

"What's your phone number?"

I turned to Wood and he recited the number for her.

She spoke without looking up. "Wood, he staying at your daddy's cabin?"

"Yes, Betty."

"How tall are you—" She leaned forward, pretending to read my name on the screen. "Matthew?"

She knew my name. "Six four and a half."

She eyed her screen. "Says here you're six five."

"Okay."

"I told you not to get smart with me."

I didn't respond. One of the officers walked in carrying his coffee, stood over her shoulder, and stared at me.

She continued, "Confirm your social security number."

I had just handed her my card and we'd just been through this, but I let it go and confirmed it for her without sarcasm.

"Will you be staying anywhere other than Wood's cabin?"

"No."

"If you intend to stay anywhere other than that cabin for more than seven days you must notify this office or any other law enforcement office in the area where you will be staying. Do you understand?"

"Yes."

"Do you own a vehicle or will you be using one?"

"I do not own one and, as of this moment, don't have any plans to."

Wood spoke up behind me. "Betty, I've got an old dirt bike that I'm gonna let him use. I'll bring you the registration later."

She clicked a few keys, glanced disbelievingly at Wood, then up at me. Finally, she looked back at her screen and scanned the information in front of her. She spoke to Wood without looking at him. "2005?"

"Yes."

"Is it orange?"

"Yep."

"125cc?"

"Yes."

"You got insurance?"

Wood handed her his insurance card. She received it and spoke to me without looking. "I don't suppose you have insurance."

"Not yet."

She returned the card to Wood, tapped her front teeth with a pencil, and then opened an ink pad and positioned it next to a thick piece of paper possessing ten labeled boxes. She stood, took my hand in hers, rolled my left thumb in the ink, and then rolled it onto the first box on the paper. She repeated this nine more times. Wood watched in silence as Betty did her job. Finished with the fingerprints, she handed me a bottle of Windex and a paper towel and then returned to her desk. Next, she pulled on two rubber gloves. Wood chuckled. She said, "Stand here, open wide. I am required to swab your mouth." I did and she paused, speaking loud enough for everyone in the room to hear her. "Open wider." I did as instructed and she circled the inside of my mouth with the cotton swab. When finished, she deposited the swab in a Ziploc bag. She picked up a pair of scissors. "I need to trim a section of your hair. Lean over this bag." I obeyed and she cut my hair, letting it fall into the open bag. Sealing the bag, she returned to her keyboard, pulled off her glasses, and folded her hands in front of her. "You need to listen carefully, as I'm only going to say this once."

I leaned in closer so she knew she had my full and undivided attention. As if on cue, the officer behind her inched forward, set down his now empty cup and ran his fingers along the inside of his duty belt. She spoke through tight lips. "You may not live or work within two thousand feet of a school, day care, movie theater, or any place where children under the age of eighteen may frequent.

Violate any of these conditions and the DA will send you back to prison. In most cases, the sentence is twice that of time previously served. Knowing the location of Wood's cabin, I doubt it qualifies, but you can rest assured that we will measure it this afternoon. If it does not, we will notify you and you will immediately seek another place to live."

I swallowed.

"Do you understand these conditions as I've laid them out for you?"

"I do."

She handed me a small USB scanner. "You will use this to check in daily. Scan it and then confirm registration. It's your job to make sure your scanner is working and that we receive confirmation, not ours. We're not your parents, not your babysitter. You understand?"

I was ready to be finished with this. "I understand."

"Sign here."

I signed on the electronic keypad.

Without looking up, she said, "You are free to go."

I turned, took a step, and the anger in me that had bubbled up since I walked in here foamed over my edges. I leaned back over the counter and spoke softly. "I don't feel free."

She set down her pencil, folded her hands, and let out a breath through her nose. Disdain covered her face. "Mr. Rising, you should have thought about that thirteen years ago. And if you violate the conditions of your freedom, the State will gladly return you to your previous home, where sick and twisted deviants like you belong." The officer behind her smiled and rocked on his toes and heels.

Having been put in my place, and realizing I should have kept my mouth shut, I turned to leave and found Wood waiting at the door in the hallway that led outside. I couldn't see the steps, but judging from the look on his face and the noise, something wasn't right. "You might ought to consider an alternate exit."

I could see multiple media trucks parked outside. Obviously, someone inside the Sheriff's Office had ratted me out. Given my experience with the media, I knew that if I didn't feed the sharks now, they'd circle until I did. "Probably best just to get it over with."

He stepped aside and pulled off the Costas that were pushed up on top of his head. "You might want these."

I slid them on and stepped outside to flashes, microphones, and voice recorders. Their voices were loud and intrusive, as were the questions.

Matthew, what's it feel like to be a sex offender?

Have you found a place to live?

What will you do?

Will you be attending a combine?

Have any teams contacted you?

Will the anklet affect your play?

Have you had or do you intend to have any contact with the victim, Angelina Custodia?

I was holding it together pretty well until the last one. The word "victim" shot up my spine like a steel rod. I stared at the reporter. "No."

How about the other two girls?

I imagined my fist breaking the jaw of the bottle-blond reporter, then I eyed the pool of reporters. "I'd like to make a statement."

They pushed in tighter, pressing me against the door and extending the microphones to within inches of my face.

I decided to skip any preliminaries. "No, no teams have contacted me, and I have no plans of attending a combine or attempting to play any type of organized football." I paused. One of the reporters tried to speak, but I cut him off. "The specific conditions of my parole would prevent me from doing so."

Dissatisfied with the newsworthiness of my responses, the feeding frenzy continued.

Where will you live?

What will you do for work?

Will you stay in this area?

I had decided that my interview was over until one question rose above all the rest. The voice was familiar, as was the face. Audrey stood behind the reporters, her voice booming. Given the severity of her question, the other reporters paid her no notice but rather waited for my response. She screamed above the fray: *Mr. Rising, what was it that made you betray your wife? What did she not offer you that two underage girls did?*

It was *the* question. The question killing Audrey's soul. I saw that. The gaunt look, thin cheeks, and hunched shoulders all betrayed the depth of it.

The question quieted the crowd; the reporters were almost licking their lips waiting for my response. We'd just traveled from the ho-hum pressing of a has-been to sensational in one question. Audrey didn't wait for the answer but backed out of the crowd and began walking around the courthouse. Between the scarf and the sunglasses, I doubted if even Wood recognized her.

The crowd stood between me and her, but if I didn't move now, I'd lose my chance. I elbowed my way through, sprinting out of the crowd and following her. She was stepping into a van with ST. BERNARD'S printed on the side when I stopped her from closing the door. Several cameras appeared around us.

The reporters quickly reassembled en masse around the front and sides of the van. Between the courthouse steps and here, the number of microphones had doubled. She pulled on the door, but I stopped her. I said, "My plan is to find my wife."

Realizing that the life of anonymity she lived behind the walls of St. Bernard's could well change in the next few moments, she bit her lip and gathered her composure. She tugged on the door I wouldn't let her shut and spoke through gritted teeth. "And when you've done that?"

"I'll tell her that I love her. Always have. She's all that matters. All that's ever mattered."

Another tug. "There were witnesses. Video. Little girls were... hurt."

"Aud—" I dropped my head. Still fighting a battle I lost twelve years ago. "I told the truth."

Her face grew tighter. She stepped out, staring up at me. The reporters were in a frenzy to catch every expression. Every intonation. A scuffle broke out between two cameramen vying for position. Her bottom lip trembled. The she reached out and pounded on my chest with her fist in the same way someone small might bang on a giant door. Seeing her in the daylight exposed the frailty. The anger. The torment of the years. And the sight of it pained me. "The jury was unanimous!"

"That doesn't make them right."

She stamped her foot and was nearly screaming at the top of her lungs. "After all this—" She waved her hand across the circus around us. "Are you still going to stand here and lie to me?"

For twelve years I'd envisioned this conversation, but this wasn't how. My voice rose. "I've never lied to you."

I saw it coming but didn't move. She reached behind her, twelve years back, through all the cold, sleepless nights, and struck me in the face with a closed fist. The acrid taste of blood filled my mouth, but I felt the sting in my chest.

"You're nothing." Not satisfied with her first punch, she reached back into the same bank of years and slapped me with an open palm. Doing so sprayed blood and saliva over the first row of reporters. She then spit in my face. "Always were." She gathered her composure and spoke with mock enthusiasm. "Your fans are awaiting your long-anticipated and much-discussed return." She pulled harder on the door, this time whispering, "Let go."

"Aud—if I never played again, let it go forever, how long would it take for you to believe me?"

"Never."

I wedged myself between the door and the van. "Think about it. If I did. Gave it up. Never took another snap." I waved my hand behind me. "Even though all these people are screaming for my return and you, you of all people, know in your heart of hearts that I could. That I can. That I'm still good enough. Wouldn't it cause you to think that something isn't right here? That maybe I never lied to you? That maybe someone that's not me is lying?"

We hadn't said this much to each other since shortly after my arrest. Given the evidence, the story Angelina had spun, doubt had crept in and Audrey had distanced herself from me. Everyone had. The words she spoke here were words she wished she'd said in the courtroom, to cut herself from me. And knowing that I was facing a minimum of twelve years, I don't blame her. Twelve years is a long time when you're staring it in the face. If it would have helped ease her pain, cut the cord between her heart and mine, then I wish she'd said it then. Maybe the last decade wouldn't have hurt her so much. Problem was, she hadn't. And as much as she hated me now, and no matter how she'd tried to forget me, and even though she'd quit wearing a wedding ring, and even though she'd only come to see me once in prison, and even though my anklet would follow me the rest of my life, and even though I couldn't make her believe me, she couldn't deny that her heart was still tethered to mine.

Her words were mocking in tone. "Play the martyr. I don't care if they bury you beneath the fifty yard line." A stiletto finger poked me in the chest. "Your heart lied to mine."

"Football means nothing without you." She slammed the door, cranked the engine, and roared off. I spoke to exhaust, tail lights, and smirking reporters. "Always has."

Wood stood next to me. Eyes wide. Mouth open. Watching the

van disappear down the street, he shook his head. "She was here all along. Right under our noses." He turned to me. "I had no idea."

"She wanted it that way."

My sensational return to town was covered by the networks. Jim Kneels, who had departed daily reporting years ago to anchor a weekend-only show, came out of semiretirement to host a special. Somebody in the Sheriff's Office leaked the location of Wood's cabin, and within an hour, three broadcast boom trucks were parked at the gate. Several inspectors and state officials were brought in to measure the distance between the cabin and school grounds. Several school administrators were interviewed and much was made about "protecting the children." I don't blame them. If somebody who was like they thought I was shacked up half a mile from their children's school, and he'd actually done what I'd been convicted of doing, I'd have chaired the committee to run him out of town. But this was me they were talking about. And I knew me. Various measuring instruments were used, including satellite and GPS imagery, all of which confirmed that I was, in fact, entirely legal. "But," Jim Kneels said with raised eyebrows, "just barely." Jim concluded his report. "Mr. Rising's insistence that he has no intention of playing professional football begs the question, 'What then, Mr. Rising, are your plans, and why, of all places, would you choose to live where you are living?'" Jim shook his head and folded his hands. "When a man is accustomed to winning, as Mr. Rising is, it is difficult to accept losing. You can take the man out of football, but taking football out of the man? Well, that's another thing entirely."

I clicked off the TV, stared out the window through the trees in the direction of the shade barn, and nodded in silent agreement.

CHAPTER ELEVEN

The barn door squeaked when I pushed it open. I turned up the flow of gas on the lantern and walked in. When the light from the brilliant white mantle showered the inside of the barn, I stood back in wonder.

A shade barn was designed to hang and dry shade tobacco. On average, barns were fifty feet wide by a hundred and fifty feet long and fifty feet high—nearly the same size as a basketball gymnasium. They were vented on the sides, top and bottom, by hinged doors that ran horizontally along the length, intended to control the heat and humidity. Inside the barn, rafters crossed the entirety of the interior. Five feet apart, each ran the width of the barn, spanning its entire length from front door to back. Overhead, the rafters started just overhead and climbed every four feet like ladders to the roof. The inside of the barn looked like a laundry rack for tobacco leaves, and a monkey would have had a heyday. For Wood and me, it was better than Disney World. We would climb the ladder to the first rafter and then pick our way like Spiderman all the way to the far end without ever touching the ground.

Given the decline in shade farming, few barns remain in the South. You can find a few in Connecticut, but most have been disassembled board by board and sold for the value of the heart-pine lumber. Heart-pine is a unique feature of pine trees. Turpentine, a natural product of the tree—which is farmed and refined into kerosene or Pine-Sol or a thousand other things—resides in the fibers of the wood. It's the sap. When cut, the sap remains, leaving a natural fire starter in the wood with almost the same ignition qualities as gasoline. On cold nights, I have dug up more than one pine stump out of the dirt, peeled away a small section of bark with my knife, lit the raw, exposed end of the root, and watched it burn like a torch for hours. And if you find the true heart of the pine, where the thickest sap resided, it will create a blowtorch sound when lit.

Given that the barns are constructed of what is essentially fire starter, it's no wonder that when one of these barns catches fire, it makes quite an impression. There's a very short window to stop it before it gets out of control. Within seconds, it can turn into a raging blaze. Best thing to do is back up and watch the show. You'll seldom see its equal.

The aroma of manure, tobacco, earth, and turpentine, delivered in the suffocating packaging of humidity and heat, filled and reminded me as I walked in. It'd been a long time. And while the memories were sweet, they paled in comparison to those hanging inside.

Filling one third of the barn were posters, awards, plaques, game balls, jerseys, newspaper articles, every form of memorabilia ever associated with my career had been found, bought, uncovered, purchased, or stolen and hung on the inside walls, where it was accessible and viewable by absolutely no one other than Wood and Coach Ray. I climbed the rafters, rising in the heat, and hung the lantern. Thirty feet off the ground, I straddled the beam and viewed in amazement my own private hall of fame. One wall was covered in the WELCOME TO GARDI—HOME OF MATTHEW "THE ROCKET" RISING sign stolen from the city limits. On the ground below me, covered in dirt and manure, lay the head of my bronze statue, along with pieces of arms and elbows. I had no idea where this stuff had come from, who had collected it, and had never seen most of it, but sitting there I felt thrust back into a world from which I'd been banished and that I'd tried to forget.

I climbed another twenty feet to the top of the rafters and stared out the vents. The world around me was dark. Quiet. In the distance beyond the cabin, a train sounded. One of the things I'd always loved about Audrey was her resolve. Relentless and unwavering. But now that resolve was aimed at me, and rather than fighting for me, she was fighting me.

Below me, the door squeaked. A tall figure stepped into the lantern's umbrella of light. He looked up and found me hanging in the rafters. "Mr. Rising? Sir?" The voice was young, deep, male, and I didn't recognize it. I climbed down and dropped onto the dirt before him. Nearly eye level with me, his large hands held a well-worn football. He asked again. "Mr. Rising, sir?"

He was dressed in the uniform of St. Bernard's. White button-down. Shirttail tucked in. Belt. Dark-blue pants. Tie. A good-looking, handsome kid. His skin color suggested that one of his parents was black and the other white. His features were distinct, chiseled, not much fat on him, pretty muscled.

He extended his hand. "Sir, my name is Dalton Rogers."

I shook his hand. "Matthew." His grip was strong, firm, and calloused.

He got right to the point. "Sir, I need some help."

I glanced out the barn door. "Kid, they can put me back in jail for having this conversation."

"Sir, I'll sign a waiver or whatever. You can put me on video saying that I came to you. Do whatever. I just know that I need to fix a few things and Sister Lynn, she always said—"

"Sister who?"

"Sister Lynn. She always said that if you weren't in prison, you'd be the best coach I could ever find, and now that you're out and, well—"

Audrey's middle name is Lynn.

I glanced down the road leading back to the cabin and on through the gate where the boom trucks were parked. "And what would you have me do for you?"

He mimicked a throwing motion with his right arm. "Help me."

"Why?"

He tried to find an answer and couldn't. "Sir, I'm—I don't know. I just—I'd like to play in college and, since last season, things have gone from bad to worse, or even real bad. I can't seem to—"

"I can't help you."

He looked confused. Like the person he was talking to didn't match the image that someone else had created in his head. "But you said—"

"I said what?"

"You said you'd love to coach one day."

My eyes narrowed. "When?"

He looked up above me, then at me. "After the Texas game, your sophomore year. And then when you beat Louisiana in Death Valley. You said after your pro career, or if one didn't pan out, that you'd—"

He was right. I had said that, but the interviews he spoke of were fifteen years old and films of them weren't just lying around. "Where'd you see these interviews?"

He pointed toward the school.

It wasn't out of the ordinary that St. Bernard's would have film of me. I wouldn't be surprised if they still had all my high school films, but that's high school. Not college. There'd be no reason for them to have film of me that contained both the game and post-game interviews. Unless someone donated them.

"You've watched film of me?"

Not feeling the need to say more, he simply nodded. "All your high school games." Another nod. Followed by, "And college."

"You've seen a few of my college films?"

He shook his head. "No. All of them." A pause. "Maybe a hundred times."

"You've seen my college films a hundred times?"

He nodded matter-of-factly. "Yes, sir. Sister Lynn and me. She—" He chuckled at what he thought was an embarrassing admission. "She loves football, and knows a pretty good bit about it too. She lets me into the archive at school and she's even watched them with me, but she doesn't let me check them out. She makes me watch them right there."

After that one visit at the prison, Audrey disappeared, along with everything we owned—including the $27,000 left in our checking account. I had always assumed that she had emptied our house and pitched my belongings, including my film library, in the nearest Dumpster.

"You two have watched my films together?"

He nodded matter-of-factly.

"For how long?"

He held out his hand, level with the ground, about waist high. "Long as I can remember."

I tested him. Starting off easy. "Who did we play third game of my freshman season?"

"Mississippi State. 42–20. You threw six TDs."

"Junior year, what play did we use to start the fifth game of the season?"

He smiled. "Quarterback sneak. The safeties were playing twenty deep, so you audibled at the line and went eighty yards. 52–0."

"Last play of my career?"

"*Twenty back fade storm deep sticky weak.*" He held up a finger. "Except Roderick Penzell ran a fade and not a post, which there's no way for him to know that unless you read it in the defense and called it at the line, but the film doesn't show that too well."

He's right. I had called it but not at the line. Only Roddy, Wood, and I knew the truth.

He continued. "Mr. Kneels asked you about that pass in your last interview before your arrest. And Sister Lynn—" He dropped his eyes and wouldn't look at me. "Your wife." He made eye contact. "She talked about it, too." He turned, almost embarrassed. "And so did Roddy in a later interview, after you'd been locked up and he was playing with the Steelers."

"You've done your homework."

"Sister Lynn isn't really a sister, but that's what we all call her. She made me promise not to tell anyone about her, and you, 'cause...well, she just did and I never have. That is, until just now." He tucked the ball beneath his arm. "Will you help me?"

I wanted to. I really did. I lifted my pant leg.

"Can't." I walked out in front of him. The thought of him living in my shadow for one second longer bothered me. I turned. "Can I give you one piece of advice?"

"Sure."

"You'd do well to remember that I didn't make me. All that stuff—I was just being me."

He smirked. "You said the same thing to Jim Kneels."

"True then. True now. Good luck to you." I left him alone in the dark of the barn and returned to the cabin, where I kept looking over my shoulder. I laid awake a long time.

CHAPTER TWELVE

It was four a.m. when the boards squeaked on the front porch, followed by a petite figure opening and closing the door. The figure remained silent for several minutes, staring over at me. Then, she tiptoed to the side of my bed. I was awake because I'd never gone to sleep. Audrey's light footsteps betrayed her, as did her breathing, the angle of her shoulder, the lines of her cheek, and the silvery reflection shining from beneath her sweatshirt hood.

I broke the long silence. "Hey."

My voice had not startled her. She stood over me. Breathing down. Hands in her pockets. "Dee needs your help."

I sat up. The only light in the room came from a streetlight. "Sounds like he's got pretty good help."

"I've done all I can. He needs you."

"Honey, I can't help that kid."

She paused. Her tone changed. More venomous. "I'm not your honey."

121

I let it go. I lifted my ankle. Even in the dark, the protrusion of the anklet was visible. "Even if I wanted—"

She crossed her arms. "Sure you can."

"You do it."

"Can't."

"Why not?"

She slowed her speech. "I don't know how. His throwing motion is a mess, and it starts in his head."

"Based on what little I've seen, you're correct."

"So you've seen him?"

The surreal nature of this discussion struck me. "Audrey, after twelve years in prison, there are a few other things I'd like us to talk about before we take up the case of Dalton Rogers."

"Answer my question."

"Yes, I've seen him. Ray and I watched him from top of the Bucket."

"So you'll help him?"

"If I get anywhere near that kid, they'll put me back in prison for the rest of my life."

"Nobody will ever know."

"So you want me to lie?"

"You're pretty good at it."

"Aud—"

"I want you to help Dee's dreams come true."

"What about mine?"

She stepped back, distancing herself from me. "Yours are dead. His don't have to be. He's got a legitimate shot."

"I cannot do this. I won't. I'm not going back in there."

She stepped closer. Leaning down over me. Inches from my face. "I don't know what you thought would happen when you got out. That you'd waltz back into my life and we'd settle down? Pick up where we left off?" She held up her ringless left hand. "Your life with me is over. Finished. We're done. Has been since the trial. Since the draft."

"Audrey—I'm here for you. Not Dalton. Not anyone else."

She cut me off. "You can't have me."

"Then why should I help you?"

"He was four when I met him. His mother dropped him off and never looked back." She turned, quartering away. "He's the son you never gave me." She turned back. Facing me. Eyes narrowed. "Matthew, I'm not asking you, I'm telling you. You owe me."

"Even though spending one second with that kid of my own volition will land me back in prison?"

"Even though."

"Why'd you never divorce me?"

"Doesn't really matter."

"I spent twelve years lying on my back, rotting, waiting for anything. A phone call. Letter. Visit. Divorce papers. I wondered every time the mail cart squeaked down the ward if today would be the day. But that day never came. So yeah, it matters. Why didn't you ever contact me?" My voice rose. "Nothing. No contact for twelve years. I saw the videos. I get it. Even I would've thought it was me. But no matter what you think of me, I deserve more than your backside walking away."

She chuckled and almost said something but snuffed it at the last minute.

The silence moved in. Neither spoke. She began to mumble under her breath, carrying on a conversation with herself, and both sides were angry. Slowly, she reached up and pointed. "You want redemption?"

"Yes."

She said it again. Slower. "Do you want redemption?"

"Yes."

She walked to the door, opened it, and stood, her back to me.

"Help Dee." She took a step, then stopped. "We're done. Have been. But maybe by helping him, you can salvage something of what remains of your pathetic excuse for a life. And in the process, maybe he can become what you never were." She looked over her shoulder. "You owe me that. And ... you owe you that."

I stood, speaking softly, "Will he listen to me?"

She had not expected the sight of me in the moonlight. My body in boxers. My scars evident. Her eyes quickly fell to them, then her resolve returned and the steel rod reinserted itself into her spine. "He'll do everything you tell him." She paused. "And more."

I stopped her. "One condition."

She waited.

"You're present at every workout. You don't show ... I don't coach."

A question surfaced on the tip of her tongue. Something she'd wanted to ask. Her eyes quickly glanced at my scars, then back at me. "You were ..." Her voice faded. "Stabbed?"

"Twice."

A pause. Another glance. "Were you scared?"

"I don't really remember. It happened pretty fast."

"Did you suffer?"

"Not as much as being there."

She stood several seconds, finally speaking. "Matthew—" Her eyes were cold and tired and the window to her soul was closing. "They gave you twelve years. That's all." She shook her head. "I got life without parole."

Turning away, hiding her face, she stepped through the door and pulled it closed.

I stood in the shadows and peered around the bleachers. He walked onto the field at daylight. Audrey stood alongside. I knew I'd better make this quick, so I pulled the hood of my sweatshirt up over my head and jogged onto the field. He saw me coming and met me on the twenty yard line. Before he said a word, I started. "We work out twice a day. Six and six. You've got eight weeks until the season starts, and we've got a lot of work to do." He nodded and smiled. "But before you get giddy, a couple of rules."

He stopped tossing the ball in the air.

"You do what I say, when I say it, every time I say it, as soon as I say it. Got it?"

He nodded.

"You give me any flack, argue with me, or offer me some lame excuse and—" I pointed at the trail leading back through the trees to the junkyard. "I'm gone. And 'please give me another chance' won't bring me back." I pointed at the ground on which we stood. "This is your chance right here."

He nodded again. "Yes, sir."

"And stop this 'yes, sir' crap. I'm old enough to be your dad, but you don't have to rub it in."

"Yes, sir."

Whatever that is, that ability to respond quickly and do exactly the thing I'd just told him not to do—but do it with jest and a fun amount of playful disrespect—great quarterbacks need that. And he had it in spades. It's a built-in level of self-assuredness and self-confidence that you can't coach. They also need to be able to roll with the punches. Coach Ray once said the same is true with all the great racehorses—it's either there or it's not. The trainers' job is to take a fast horse with all the tools and make him faster. And every now and then you find a horse that has all the tools, and all the possibilities, and then you add some honest self-confidence bubbling just beneath the surface, and, well—I liked this kid from that moment. I turned to Audrey. "Can I ask a favor of you?"

Her lips moved but there was no emotion in it. "You can ask."

"You mind running by the Army-Navy?"

She shook her head. "I don't mind."

"You know his shoe size?"

She nodded.

I turned back to Dee and lifted my sweat pants, exposing my ankle. "I need your word that you'll never tell anyone, not a soul, that we're doing this. You do and they'll put me back in prison. I'd like to avoid that."

"You have my word."

Audrey stepped up alongside. "He won't. I'll see to that."

I stepped closer to him. Inches from his face. I pointed at Audrey. "Just so we're clear, I'm here for her. Not you. She's your ticket. I don't care how much you beg me, if she's not here, you're on your own."

"But that's outside of my control."

I turned and started walking away. "Life's like that. Better get used to it."

He tossed the ball and hit me square in the back. "I've got a question for you."

I stopped but didn't turn. I was starting to like this kid even more.

"How do I know you're still any good? How do I know you can help me?"

The sun was just breaking the tree line. Standing on the twenty, I picked up the ball, dropped two steps, and launched the ball toward the far end zone. While Dee watched the ball spiral through the air, I whispered to Audrey, "Just because they let you out, doesn't make you free." The ball split the uprights midway up, some ninety-two yards away. Dee's eyes grew to the size of Oreos. I shoved my hands in my pockets and began walking away. "And we can't work out here. I'm not allowed to step foot on this grass." I pointed at the junkyard. "Don't be late."

In all this time, Audrey's eyes never watched the ball. Her eyes never left me.

CHAPTER THIRTEEN

It was a Thursday night. Two weeks shy of Christmas. The ring-throwing issue with Ginger had faded and, while still red, the scar above my eye had healed. In characteristic tenderness, Audrey had smiled and said, "Chicks dig scars."

With the state championship on the line the following night, the team had practiced in shorts under the lights, run through formations and special teams, and then watched some game film. After practice, a couple of us had gone out for burgers and then I'd dropped Audrey off at her house. My mom had gone to bed so I was sitting in our den studying game film when the phone rang. It was Wood, and judging by the background noise, he was not at home.

"I need your help."

Something loud passed near or behind him. The phone crackled and drowned him out. I read the clock on the wall. "Where are you?"

"Pay phone. Near the old Apiary warehouse. Get here quick."

"What are you—"

"I'll explain when you get here."

The phone clicked, and I grabbed my truck keys. Eight minutes later, I pulled off the hard road onto a gravel path that led out behind the old warehouses backing up to the railroad tracks on the outskirts of town. I mumbled to myself, *The only thing out here this time of night is trouble.* Wood saw my headlights, walked out of the bushes, and flagged me down. Just behind him, a hundred or so yards in the distance, I could see the reflection of lights in the warehouses, which was unusual given that nobody had used them in a few decades.

When Wood got in the truck, he was sweating and looked genuinely scared. He pointed. "That way."

I shook my head and put the truck in park. "Wood, what in the world is—"

"Ginger. She's in trouble. Or about to be. Called me and wanted me to pretend to be her boyfriend. Real muffled tone, slurred words, trying not to be heard. I parked over there and snooped around enough to know that I'm not walking in there by myself." At the time, Wood was six foot three and 285 pounds. If he didn't want to walk into an abandoned warehouse, I didn't either.

"What's in the warehouse?"

"Bunch of guys in this alternative-punk, heavy-metal, paint-your-face-and-chew-the-head-off-the-neighbor's-dog band. All of them look closer to thirty than twenty, like they've been partying hard for as long as we've been playing ball. Lots of tattoos—couldn't see a square inch of skin that didn't have ink on it. Maybe the band is a front for crystal meth or coke or whatever. Anyway, she said she met the lead at some bar. He told her they were filming a music video here tonight. Said there's going to be one heck of a party after. Wanted her to"—Wood made quotation marks with his fingers—"'star' in the video." Wood frowned. "From what I saw, they're planning on doing some videoing, but it's got nothing to do with music. They got a good bit of white powder on a table in there, and I saw a guy holding a needle. Seemed like he was explaining to Ginger why she should try it." He paused. "She's not dressed, and they're being pretty rough with her. One guy has a pistol shoved in his waistband."

I looked Wood squarely in the face. "Is everything you're telling me true?"

He held up a hand. "God's honest."

"Did you have anything to do with this?"

"I dropped her off."

"Have you done anything illegal that I need to know about before I stick my neck out?"

"No."

"You sure?"

"Yes."

I climbed out of the truck, stepped into the public phone booth, and dialed 911. When the operator answered, I said, "This is Matthew Rising. I need to speak with Captain Roberts. Ring him at home if you need to."

"Hold, please."

Captain Roberts had a son named Kerry who was two years ahead of me and had been my tight end during my freshman and sophomore years. Kerry and I had spent some time on the field throwing routes and patterns, so I knew him well enough to expect his dad to know me and take my call. Two seconds passed, the phone clicked several times, and Captain Roberts picked up. He was not in a good mood. "Matthew, it's late."

"Sir, you need to send several officers down to the old Apiary along the tracks. And, sir, I need them right now."

His tone changed. "You want to tell me what this is all about?"

"I will when you get here, but in short it involves a good bit of drugs and some guys doing some stuff to a girl that she doesn't want done to her."

"Who's the girl?"

Kerry and Ginger had gone on a couple of dates so I had an idea he'd know her. "Ginger."

"Are you in any danger?"

"No, sir. Not yet."

I heard a door open in the background and he muttered something to someone. "Where are you?"

"In the pay phone, where the hard road turns to dirt."

"Give us ten minutes."

I hung up, returned to the truck, cut off all the lights, and sat there. It didn't take me long to realize we might not have ten minutes. I slid the stick into gear and slowly idled down the road. Wood asked, "What's your plan?"

"Don't really have one."

Wood looked at me, somewhat dubious. "I know you're you and all that. And everybody knows you, and you're getting pretty used to folks rolling out the red carpet for you. But these guys don't care who you are. They're hard core."

"I believe you."

We pulled up to the warehouses and parked just out of earshot. I quietly shut the door and Wood stood alongside. I could hear several male voices, a female voice laughing, and another female voice that did not sound like she was having fun. I whispered, asking Wood, "Ginger?"

He nodded. All I could see was the whites of Wood's eyes. "You going in?"

"Well, I'm not about to sit here and listen to that."

Wood slapped himself in the face twice, shook his head, rolled up his sleeves, and jogged up alongside me. He put his hand on my back. "If pushing comes to shoving, don't hit anybody with your right hand."

I nodded. "Good advice."

Wood and I had been in a few scraps together but most had been in football games. Nothing like this. We were high school football players, not heroes. We approached from the railroad tracks, which turned out to be in our favor because when we rounded the corner all of the lights of the stage, or loading dock, were facing from our direction and into their eyes, which gave us a few seconds' advantage. I counted five guys. A girl. And Ginger. Only two of them had their clothes on and not much at that. Ginger had slid off a dirty couch and was lying on a blanket on the floor. Some guy was sitting next to her. Rows of white powder covered one table along with various needles, a lighter, and a piece of rubber tubing. Judging by the look in Ginger's eyes, she was flying in another stratosphere.

She was also scared.

I didn't like Ginger. Never had. She'd always annoyed me, so I kept my distance. Add to that the eyebrow-splitting sucker punch seven weeks prior and I had reason enough for not being there. Regardless, a quick look around told me that she was in way over her head and couldn't talk her way out of this one. I strolled in with a smile on my face, rubbing my hands together with my best nerd I'm-just-here-for-the-party impression. "Hey, guys."

The friendly tone of my overly excited voice caused them to question whether I was here to party or cause trouble. I knew it wouldn't last long. The first guy—the one sitting on the ground with a smear of white powder under his nose—stood up directly in front of me. I pointed at Ginger and tried to laugh. "Looks like the party's already started."

They looked confused—both by what I was saying and by not being able to place my face. They knew they knew me, they just couldn't get the pieces to click amid the fog of the drugs. Ginger held out a hand, but her eyes weren't really looking at me nor did the smile on her face make me believe that she was enjoying herself. Wood managed a big, stupid, goofy-looking, Three Stooges smile and reached out a hand to Ginger. "Hey, baby."

Ginger stood. "Heyyyy, Woooooodyyyyy."

Off to my left, a muscular, bald-headed guy, obviously the leader, began a brisk walk in my direction. He was about five ten, and real fit. He'd pumped a lot of iron and probably consumed a lot of steroids to stay that way. He wore only a pair of tattered blue jeans and his chest, neck, and face were almost entirely covered in tattoos. The most striking was a series of flames—some of which looked like long, slender hands with veins—rising up his chest and neck and onto his face. One of the flames wound up his cheek, around his temple, and then fanned out over one ear and behind the back of his head. He looked like Queequeg meets the Incredible Hulk. Wood had been right; the pistol was tucked in his waistband for all the world to see. Judging by the speed of his walk and the look in his eyes, he was the one individual in this group who had not consumed any of the hallucinatory drugs. He was crystal clear and not buying my pocket-protecting, white-tape-around-the-glasses routine.

He stepped between myself and Ginger and was about to put a hand on Wood when I decided our best defense was to play offense. In a game, it's called a "quick count" and it's where you snap the ball before the defense is ready. I never said a word. I put my legs into it. The kinetic chain started in my toes, and I hit him as hard as I could in the left side of his face with my left hand. When I did, he crumpled and I felt a bone break both in his face and in my hand. The guy with the white powder feathering his nose watched me knock out his friend, swigged from a whiskey bottle, and then tried to stand. But he couldn't find his balance and fell back over the couch.

Everybody else was too stoned to react, so Wood picked up Ginger in one arm, her dress in the other, and fireman-carried her to the truck. When we got her in the front seat, she started crying and hanging all over me and saying how she was sorry. I didn't understand most of what she was saying. I shoved her off on Wood and we spun gravel and mud all the way back to the hard road where Captain Roberts was just arriving with five cars. Between the warehouse and the corner, my hand had swelled to the size of a catcher's mitt.

Given my growing local celebrity status, the Brunswick emergency room came to life as I carried Ginger through the sliding glass doors. When I set her on the bed and attempted to leave, Ginger clung to me and refused to let go while they examined her. The doctor obliged and nurses moved around me. It took only seconds to learn that Ginger was too stoned to understand her own medical condition. Hence, the doctor entrusted that information to me. An hour later, reading from a toxicology report, he said she had enough drugs in her system to kill a small horse and, in fact, that among an indiscriminate cocktail of other drugs, a horse tranquilizer had been used.

I looked down at now-sleeping Ginger. "Horse tranquilizer?"

He nodded. "Inexpensive and common, black market date-rape drug. Seeing more of it weekly." He went on to explain that the drug was most often used by guys who wanted to knock a girl out for about twelve hours and cause her to forget the events of the evening. He said they're in a class of drugs called 'amnesiacs.' Victims woke groggy with no recollection or memory of any of the events that had occurred. He said someone had probably slipped Ginger the drug in a drink or something liquid, and he doubted she'd have any memory of that night's events. Further, he continued, depending upon the dose, the drug could even erase memories that occurred prior to consuming the drug. Meaning, Ginger would wake in the hospital tomorrow morning and possibly need an explanation as to why she was there. As he was finishing writing notes in Ginger's chart, he looked at my hand. "How's the other guy?"

"Sleeping."

He nodded. "I believe it." He set down his clipboard, and I tried not to wince as he examined me. When finished, he glanced up at the clock on the wall and then at me over the top of his glasses. It was after midnight. "You starting tonight?"

I nodded.

"Any chance I could convince you to sit this one out?"

I shook my head.

His squinted one eye. "How tough are you?"

I answered honestly. "Not as tough as everyone thinks."

He pointed at my hand. "I've got to set this or—" He gently touched places on the back of my hand with a sterile probe. "This bone will affect that artery and that nerve, which will in turn greatly interfere with your ability to one day hold your wife's hand, open a door, or zip up your pants." I didn't like where this was going. He continued, "So I can either put you to sleep, fix it in a few minutes right now and you can wake up rested and happy tomorrow morning with a few pins and screws in your hand, in which case you won't be playing anything tomorrow night, or you can be stupid, I can set it right here, and you can take your chances tomorrow night and hope you don't injure it further."

"If you operate tonight, how long am I out?"

He weighed his head side to side. "Four to six weeks."

"And if I take my chances?"

He frowned. "If you injure it tomorrow night, the pain will be more than you can probably stand, and you'll be back here tomorrow night begging me to do what I'm telling you I should do now."

"And if I don't injure it?"

"There is a chance, albeit slight, that the bone can heal and you'll make it to college without my having to cut on you."

Wood was sitting about three feet away, and he started shaking his head. "Matty, don't be a hero. Let him operate. I'll call your mom. Don't jeopardize college. We've got Squeezey and we'll be fine."

Squeezey was our backup quarterback. I liked Squeezey. He

had the potential to be a good quarterback but he was not at that time, and if we tried to play Friday night with him as starting QB, we'd lose. Badly.

Apparently, Wood—feeling guilty for involving me in something that now had real consequences—had already called Audrey, because at that moment she walked into the room. She took one look at my hand, slid her arm in mine, and leaned forward. "Doctor, don't do whatever he tells you."

I looked at the doc. "Set it."

The rest of the night was not fun, and I didn't get much sleep.

The hospital kept Ginger overnight. Miraculously, Ginger appeared at the game the following night—in her cheerleading uniform. We heard via the gossip grapevine that she had no memory of last night's events. I wasn't sure whether that was true amnesia or convenient amnesia. Regardless, she didn't say anything to me prior to the game. Through all four quarters of the game, she cheered as if nothing had happened. Wood worked himself into a frenzy protecting me and more importantly my left hand. I didn't need it to throw, but he felt guilty and he didn't want the story of an injury to jeopardize college. After the game, I walked out of the locker room. I had slid my left hand into the large front pocket of my sweatshirt—both to protect it and because I had it wrapped in ice and I didn't want scouts or anyone else to see it and start asking questions. Ginger stood off to one side, in a shadow, which was unusual as she loved the spotlight. Audrey was walking toward me. Ginger approached first and slid her arm in mine. She then slid her hand down my left arm and into my pocket and the bag of ice. She held it there, watching Audrey approach. "You love her, don't you?"

"I do."

"Is it real?"

I nodded.

She turned to me, looking up. Audrey was twenty feet away. She whispered, "Any chance you'd share that?" She glanced at Audrey. "She'd never know."

"Ginger, I'm sorry about last night. I feel for you. And I'm your friend, but—"

"Tainted goods?"

"Naive? Yes. Tainted? I wouldn't say that."

"So you disapprove of me?"

"It's got nothing to do with approval."

"What then?"

I shook my head.

Faking a smile, she pulled herself closer, brushing against me. "What!"

"Ginger, I think you have a tendency to make some bad decisions and want what's not yours."

She gripped my arm, but rigidity replaced feigned tenderness. "Then why'd you show last night?"

"Because Wood called me."

"You do whatever Wood asks?"

"He's earned my trust."

She recoiled further. "Do you trust me?"

"No."

She nodded, a frown spreading across her face. Audrey was almost within earshot. Ginger squeezed my hand with a catlike strength that surprised me. The pain was intense, shot through me like a knife, and nearly buckled my knees. "Who's naive now?"

The smile fell off her face, her eyes turned a steely cold, and whatever life had been there drained out.

Ginger turned her back to us and disappeared into the crowd. Audrey reached me, gently locked her arm in mine, and we watched in silence as Ginger worked the crowd. Audrey shook her head. "That girl is poison."

I nodded.

Audrey turned me toward my truck. "How about I buy you a cheeseburger and you tell me just exactly what is going on here."

"I'll tell you what happened, but I'm not sure I know what's going on."

A week later, for reasons unknown to us, Ginger dropped out of school and disappeared.

Four years would pass before I'd see her again.

CHAPTER FOURTEEN

Ray and I sat on the cabin porch, drinking coffee, and he filled me in on Dalton Rogers. A rising senior, Dee was six foot three, 195 pounds, 4.5 speed. He had not been invited to any camps and no schools had expressed interest in him. He threw five touchdowns in one game his freshman year, and midway through his sophomore year he was on track to surpass my single-season sophomore yardage totals. While not undefeated, he'd shown moments of real brilliance. He was winning, in some cases by a lot. Ray hovered over his coffee. "Folks around here are beginning to think they might have someone they can believe in again."

"You mean, someone who will erase the memory of me."

Ray blew the steam off his coffee. "Exactly."

Dee's trouble started when he returned to camp his junior year to discover that the newly hired coach of St. Bernard's, Damon Phelps, had bumped him down on the depth chart and decided that his son, Marcus, would start.

"Nothing like playing favorites," I said.

Ray nodded. "You don't know the half of it." Ray lit his pipe and began drawing on it. "Prior to Coach Demon's arrival, Dee could sling it. I'm talking about a pure Div I, SEC-screamer of an arm. The kid had it. Then the Demon spends a few"—Ray held up his fingers—" 'weekend coaching sessions' with him and alters his throwing motion. Told him he was 'making a pro-style quarterback out of him.'" Ray spat. "That man wouldn't know a pro-style QB if he bumped into him. He took that kid, changed his motion, and now we're left with two problems: the one in his arm and the one in his head."

"What'd he do to his motion?" I asked.

Smoke rose out of Ray's mouth. "He cut it in half and put this quick hitch in it." He paused. "It's like this: if Dee is Secretariat and his average stride is, say, eight yards long, then some genius of a trainer named Damon comes along and shackles his feet with six-yard chains. God made that horse to cover eight yards. Not six. He's got a body made to do one thing and a coach requiring him to do something else. Now he can't run, or throw, worth squat. His body is all cattywampass and his mind is just as axle-wrapped. Boy's got chains hanging off his feet and mind." I loved the way Ray talked about football. "If you want to help that boy—" Ray tapped himself in the temple. "Break the chains on his mind and the ones on his feet will follow."

We sat, enjoying each other's presence. And the quiet. Something prison had done for me and age had done for him. After a few minutes, I said, "Ray?"

His eyes moved. His head didn't.

"What happened to Audrey? I mean, really."

He chuckled. "You happened to her."

"No, I know that. I mean...she's not the same." He nodded knowingly. "You've been watching over her. I know that. And she loves you. Always has. It's part of the reason she's here."

Ray chose his words. "The trial broke her. Didn't eat for weeks.

Ended up in the ER on IVs. I brought her home, fed her chicken soup for about two weeks, and when she got her strength back, I told her this foolishness has got to stop. Convinced her to go see you in prison. That she owed you that much." He sipped. "If Ginger succeeded in one thing, it was in causing Audrey to question you. She'd never done that. And once the seed of that question took root, no power on earth could uproot it." He shook his head. "The testimony, witnesses, video, all too damning. She needed irrefutable evidence to the contrary, and you didn't offer it. Didn't come through." He pointed toward the school. "That garden? All that digging in the dirt? That's just her hands trying to work out what her mind can't." He thumbed over his shoulder toward the barn. "Your own private hall of fame? That's her digging through your past trying to find the answer to her future." He shook his head. "How many times has she watched you lead a fourth-quarter comeback?" He answered his own question. "Dozens. And yet when it mattered most, you didn't do it. Couldn't. In her mind, you're good at winning when it comes to a bunch of sweaty guys in a huddle, but when it comes to her and her heart, you failed. Lost. Plain and simple."

I let out the breath I'd been holding since I walked out of prison.

He continued. "Rocket, I'm gonna tell you something, and you may not want to hear it but here it is…beneath her anger—and believe me there's lots of that, I can't tell you how many times I've helped her patch that dang scarecrow back together—there's a grain of hope. It's small but it's there. And try as she might, she can't kill it. Can't snuff it out. Can't get past it."

"Hope in what?"

"You."

"How?"

"'Cause you haven't gotten her out of this mess yet. I know that's backwards, but a woman's heart don't always make sense."

"After all this time? You really believe that?"

He raised an eyebrow. "Boy—we're talking 'bout Audrey. You need me to remind you? They don't call her Spider Monkey for nothing." He waved his hand across an imaginary field in front of us. "When you got hurt, she bled. She bleeding still." He looked at me. "Only one thing stop that."

"But I can't make that happen."

He weighed his head side to side. A tear trickled down his face. "I once watched a boy play ball out on that field. Watched him do things I didn't think possible. Despite what all the newspapers and magazines and talk shows say, he became great because he did one thing better than all the rest." A single shake of his head. "He never walked off that field with anything left in his tank. Left it all out there. Emptied himself." Silence followed by a slow, knowing nod. His eyes turned to me. "I remember carrying you from the sideline to the locker room because you couldn't physically stand up. That's the Rocket I remember." He sucked through his teeth. "I don't care if you ever play another down, and I don't care what you're up against, but I do care what happens to that girl." He tapped me in the chest. "You owe it to her to try." He blinked, pushed out the rest of the tears, and tapped himself in the chest. "And you owe it to me."

I love that old man. I put my arm around his neck, pulled him to me, and hugged him. He patted my hand, and I kissed his head. "Yes, I do."

Audrey and Dee showed at daylight. He held his cleats in one hand, helmet in the other, and the ball was tucked under his arm. I walked outside wearing a sweatshirt, sweat pants, and an old pair of black army combat boots. No ball. He looked confused. Audrey handed me the bag draped over her shoulder. I reached in the bag and handed him the new pair of black boots that matched the older pair on my feet. He held out his hand. "You serious?"

"Are you questioning me?"

He sat quickly, started lacing them up, and chuckled to himself. "Didn't know I was joining the army."

During high school, Wood's folks had given him a street-legal 125cc Honda trail bike that we used around his property. While Dee pulled on his boots, I rolled Wood's bike up next to Audrey, she swung a leg over it and kicked it started. I took Dee's helmet from him and said, "Not yet. The position of quarterback starts in your feet. So let's go see what's in them."

He lifted his feet, testing the weight of the boots, and eyed my older but matching pair. "Not the lightest things I've ever put on."

"That's the point." I pointed to Audrey. "Blame her."

"There's probably a story behind this, isn't there?"

"I ran in them in high school because I thought the additional weight would make me faster, which it did. When I got to college, I kept it up until I won the Heisman, and maybe my head swelled a bit because that's the year I quit wearing them and we lost in the national championship." A shrug. "The morning after, Audrey changed my workout schedule to avoid the media, had Roddy waiting on me at the field, and—" I eyed the boots on my feet. "Had these next to my bed when the alarm went off at three a.m. I wore them in every workout, and my speed picked up."

He smiled. "And you threw that backside to Roddy in the corner. Forty-seven yards. Three defenders. Made *SI*'s top ten plays of the decade."

"Well…" I paused to look at Audrey. "Without ten other guys, and one woman, that never would have happened."

Dee set the ball down next to his helmet, signaling he was ready to go. I picked up the ball and set it back in his hands. "For the next eight weeks, this doesn't leave your hands. If I catch you without it either in your hands or just having thrown it, you'll wish I hadn't caught you."

He smiled. "Yes, sir."

"I'm talking about eating. Sleeping. Going to the bathroom. Only one place you're allowed to set it down. Work. Agreed?"

"What about the shower?"

"Hold it above your head."

"Man, you're hard core."

"I'm just getting warmed up. Let's go."

We jogged down the dirt road that led from the cabin to the railroad tracks. Audrey trailed alongside or behind us in the dirt—just idling in second gear. To say she was skilled on the dirt bike would not have been true, but she'd put hundreds of miles on it doing the very same thing with me so she didn't need instruction.

Dee copied my every move. I climbed up the embankment and began jogging, my toes hitting every railroad tie. We did this over a mile. Then stretched it to two. Dee did likewise. Mirroring me. At mile three, I stretched it out and Dee again followed. As we ran, I talked to him about defenses, offenses, reads, audibles, and possible down-and-distance situations against various defenses. I wanted to know what he knew. I also wanted to know if he could process and communicate under physical stress.

He could. The kid was smart. And all the hours Audrey had spent watching film with him were evident.

At four miles we turned around. Given the extra few ounces of weight, my anklet was digging into the lower part of my shin. Before we started running, I'd taped it and laced the top of my boot around it so it wouldn't bounce around as much, but by the time we turned around at mile four, it'd pretty well worked its way loose. At mile six, we slowed and started skipping from tie to tie. Then we started crossing left foot over right, right foot over left, skip one, then skip two. Left foot over right, right foot over left, skip one, then skip two. At first, he bobbled it, even tripping. But once he found the rhythm, he fell in step with me.

Audrey was never far away, and as my eyes were glued to the tracks in front of me, I couldn't see her face. I just knew she was close. Her body language suggested she was interested in Dee and disinterested in me.

When we left the tracks, he was breathing heavy but not slowing, so I pushed him farther. We ran across the yard through rows of cars and out to the edge of the lot to the foot of the Bucket. I pointed to the top. "Every workout ends up there." He followed me every step. Tired and gorging on air, we left Audrey at the bottom and began sprinting up the hill. After the first slight hump, he faltered just a bit. I slowed, put my hand on his back, and gently pushed. He caught his breath and regained his stride. So I stretched him again and pushed farther. Three-quarters of the way up, he'd redlined. Which was good. I needed to know his limits. I also needed him to know that he could push past them, so I stretched him farther and upped the tempo one last time. He dropped a step or two behind me. I slowed and ran alongside him. My shoulder bumping his. "Nope. Not now. You want to be something other than what you are, then run up here alongside me. I know you're tired, and I don't really care. You can breathe when we get to the top. You want to become better? Then this is where it starts." He gave me all he had and never offered an excuse. When he reached the top, he bent at the waist trying to catch his breath but he didn't take his eyes off me. He was waiting for the next call—the next play. Every quarterback, sooner or later, will face a point in a game where all hades has broken loose and very little, if anything, is in his control. It usually comes somewhere in the fourth quarter when he's tired and hurting, when his body is bruised and battered and his mind is screaming at him to lie down and quit. To make the bad man stop. Audrey believed in Dee and that told me a lot, but I needed to know what was in him. How deep was his well. Could he respond to me when his mind was screaming at him to quit? And how much did all of this matter? I needed to know if he was enamored with the idea of *being a quarterback* or *playing quarterback.*

The difference matters.

My punishment of him the first morning out may seem insensitive but I didn't want to waste my time or his. So I pushed him until his body cracked. That very moment is what I wanted to see. And when I did, when his body had done all it could, his eyes and ears were trained on me.

And you can't coach that. This kid wanted to play quarterback.

After he caught his breath, we jogged down. At the bottom, he was strapping on his cleats when I stopped him. "Not now. Get some rest."

He smiled, relieved. "What? I wear you out, old man?"

I laughed. "Go home. Eat. Protein first. Start with what's easily digestible. Like eggs. And I don't care if you like them or not. Eggs are your new best friend. Then complex carbs. No sugars. No white carbs. And drink. Lots of fluid. No sodas. No milk. Water primarily. Something with electrolytes. And stay away from dairy. Dairy is not your friend."

He sat down and then lay on his back, laughing. "Dude..." He pointed to the tracks and then the mountain. "I'm going to need more than electrolytes. I'm going to need a stretcher and a surgeon."

I turned to Audrey. She wasn't looking at me so I waited until she did—which she didn't want to do. "I can't coach an engine that's tired or running on fumes. I need you to make sure he's sleeping enough and eating and drinking what he ought. Chances are good that he's never done to his body what I'm about to ask him to do to it." She nodded, devoid of emotion.

I didn't need to explain this to her. She knew this. And I knew this. And she knew that I knew that she knew. I said it for his benefit. To let him know that what I—we—were doing was twenty-four hours a day. The position of quarterback didn't stop when he or I walked off the field. What he ate, when he slept, how much he slept, how much he drank, what he put in his system, everything mattered.

He was still lying on the ground. Sprawled out. I knelt next to him. "You got a girlfriend?"

He smirked. "Maybe."

"It's a yes or no thing. Like being pregnant. You either are or you aren't."

"I like her."

"Does she know this?"

"I'm still trying to—"

Audrey interrupted him. "He has yet to ask her out."

"When you do, curfew is ten p.m. Not a minute later. If I find you out after ten, you won't enjoy the following morning. Time is precious. You can waste yours but not mine. And I've got a good bit less than I once had."

He nodded.

"Nodding isn't good enough. I need to hear you say it."

He spoke through closed eyes. His stomach rose and fell inches with each breath. "Have you always worked out that hard?"

"Yes, but you're changing the subject."

"I got it. Ten p.m. Not a minute later."

"If she loves you, she'll understand." For the first time all morning, Audrey's eyes focused on me when I peeled the tape off my anklet, exposing the sight of my own blood. Dalton eyed the red stain that covered my sock. "Dude, does that hurt?"

I ignored his question. "One more thing."

He sat up. "Audrey and Ray have both told me about you. Told me how you'd like to play in college. But what they say doesn't really matter if you don't agree. So what do you want?"

He took his time. He stared through the trees at the field in the distance. "My freshman year, we won district." He pointed toward the field just beyond the trees. "Then we lost in the semis. It may not seem like a big deal to some, but I'm a senior. Or about to be. I'd like to take these guys back." He looked at me. "Farther, if possible." He turned the ball in his hands. "After that?" A shrug. "I'd like to know if I could play at the next level. Most guys at this point in their career have verbally committed. I threw five interceptions in the one game I started last year." Another point to the far side of the field. "I'm not in the position I'd hoped to be in. I've got to change some perceptions, and I'd like to do that early and often." He paused, nodding honestly. "I'm competing against the coach's son. He's pretty good, and I think he's juicing so he's getting bigger and better—fast. He's been to a bunch of camps this summer and I've heard the scouts are impressed. He's got his own website, and they've uploaded a bunch of film. Sister Lynn's been telling me that I've got to be so much better that Coach can't not play me. And I've got to be that good out of the gate."

I kept peeling the tape. "First"—I tapped my temple— "quarterbacking takes place here. And"—I tapped my heart— "here." Then I mimicked injecting drugs into my arm. "Not here." Removing the tape had peeled off the caked blood and reopened the cut. A bright red line trickled down my ankle. "Second, the question is not whether you can play at that level. You can. You need to accept that right now and change the way you think about you. The question before you is, are you willing to do what is needed when the critics tell you that you can't?"

He nodded.

"And are you willing to fight through circumstances you can't control and are not in your favor?"

"Yes."

I shrugged. "Well, we're about to find out." I put my hand on his shoulder. Other than the gentle nudge I'd given him running up the Bucket, it was the first time I'd touched him since we'd met. "Some things we can control. Some we cannot. Don't get axle-wrapped on what you can't. Focus on what we can. I can't make the coach play you, but we can make his decision a lot tougher. Your job is to focus on every opportunity. Make the most of them and the fans will pull you off the bench if and when steroid-boy falters. Agreed?"

He smiled. "Agreed."

"You got a job?"

He nodded matter-of-factly. "Mason's." He looked at Audrey, then back at me. "But I've got some money saved. I can pay you."

I chuckled. "I don't want your money." Mason's was the family-owned grocery. "Bagging groceries?"

"And stocking shelves."

That meant he'd be standing on his feet all day. "Rest when you can. Eat wisely. Drink lots of fluids. See you tonight." I tapped the dirt. "Right here, six p.m."

"Um—"

"What?"

"I don't get off till six."

I chuckled. "Okay. Soon as you get off. If you're going to be late, you let me know."

"What's your number?" he asked.

"Don't have one."

"You don't have a cell phone?"

"No."

"Then how do I get in touch with you?"

"You want to be a quarterback? Figure it out. I don't care if you have to send a carrier pigeon, it's your job to find me and let me know."

He smiled. His honesty was disarming. "Anybody ever told you that you can be a bit demanding?"

"Yep. And the last group of guys to register that complaint are all wearing rings that say 'National Champion.'"

He stood up and placed one hand behind his back. "Mr. Rising, would you like paper or plastic?"

I laughed. "That's what I thought."

Dalton and Audrey turned and began walking away. Audrey brushed by me, her sleeve touching my arm. When she looked up, one eyebrow was raised above the other. She didn't voice it but her mouth said it loud and clear. *Told you so.* And she had. He'd done everything she'd said he would. And better. I could see what she saw in him. Plus, she'd always had a thing for quarterbacks. I watched her walk away—the sun on her face, the angle of her shoulders, the small of her back, the shape of her legs, the sun glistening on her hair.

Prison numbs desire, it doesn't kill it. And being around her, while it was what I wanted, was difficult.

Our time frame was short. Eight weeks wasn't much. Following my run with him, I was less concerned about his physical skills and strength as I was unwiring or uncoaching what had been imprinted into his mind. I'd never met Coach Damon, and he might have been a good man off the field, but he had not helped Dee. And based on the quarterback competition with his son, I'd bet he knew that. My job, and the reason Audrey had invited me into this, was to undo bad coaching. To complicate matters, we had to do everything in secret. We couldn't set foot on the field in daylight hours, and we couldn't use his receivers. We also did not have a lot of time, so I had to cram as much as possible in what time we had, and that process was going to make smoke come out his seventeen-year-old ears. If we were to pull this off, Dee would have to be more than a senior in high school. He was going to have to rise above himself, and he may not like me during the process.

I had to tear him down before I could build him back up.

The questions I wrestled with were twofold: Would he follow me far enough and trust me long enough to let the process run its course? And more importantly—would Audrey? Could she force herself to believe in me while I tore him down? The future of Dalton Rogers hung on a fragile peg—could she trust me with what she loved when she didn't trust me?

I had my doubts.

CHAPTER FIFTEEN

Wood and Ray appeared midmorning in Wood's Suburban. His ring-around-the-collar dress shirt was soaked in sweat, meaning the AC had quit working again.

I was tinkering with the trail bike, trying to stop the sputter. Wood said, "My phone's been sort of busy today."

"Yeah?"

"Lot of folks been asking about you."

"And?"

"I had three calls yesterday from teams asking me if I still represent you."

"And?"

"I told them I didn't know and that I needed to ask you."

I held up my fingers, making quotation marks. "The word 'represent,' suggests a future. A career in football. As in, I'm headed toward one."

Wood nodded. "That would be correct."

I straddled the Honda, started it, and let it idle. It sounded better. "Then no. Not in a professional capacity."

"That's what I thought, but I figured I'd better check." I waited, sensing there was more to his statement. He put his hand on the throttle, gave it some gas, and listened as the engine wound up and then returned to idle. Nodding, he said, "I guess you don't want to hear how all three are offering to pay you for the chance just to evaluate you. Seems your prison video is making the rounds."

I cut the engine. "Wood, I'm done."

"That may be, but a couple of the news stations are carrying a story about how the commissioner said he'd be willing to work with the authorities to get you permission to travel, and then, if need be, get you reinstated into the league. Said that given the fact that you served your sentence, he'd be willing to help you work around whatever limitations they put on you."

I pointed at my leg. "What's he plan to do about that?"

"I spoke with NFL legal this morning. Their team has looked into jurisdictional requirements, and they believe they can work with the various locales in which you'd be playing since the limitations placed on you are local and subject to state law. You've already complied with federal law by registering, and because you're not living in the stadiums where you'll be playing, only working, they believe your chances are pretty good. He also said that the league would be willing to ensure the fans' safety by requiring and supplying a law enforcement escort every time you boarded a plane, dressed in a locker room, gave an interview, or left home. Essentially, twenty-four-hour protection."

"That sounds oddly familiar."

Obviously, Wood had been doing his homework. He continued, "The league believes the law will look at you in much the same way it looks at long-haul truckers whose workplace is the roads and highways throughout the country. Or maybe a self-employed handyman who works out of his home and does home-improvement work in another jurisdiction at other people's homes. Truckers, handymen, and others are allowed to work wherever they want as long as they provide information concerning the places where they'll be with whatever specificity is possible under the circumstances. Like travel routes or the general areas in which you would be working, i.e., stadiums and practice fields."

"And the hotels where we'd be staying before games?"

"The law says you have to provide information about any place in which you're staying when away from home for seven or more days, including identifying the place and the period of time you're staying there. The league says that, in your case, they would work to ensure that you never stayed anywhere longer than seven days. In the rare event that you did, say the playoffs or something, they'd work with authorities and register you where appropriate. Even flying you home for a night, if necessary."

I leaned against the van, "Let's say, just for the sake of conversation, that they can overcome the legal hurdles. What about the hurdle where the fans hate someone who's been convicted of committing deviant acts with a minor? All of which he filmed and photographed for his later viewing pleasure. Oh, and let's don't forget the drugs he dumped into their systems to force their compliance. The commissioner say anything about that little detail?"

"No." Wood kicked the gravel with his toe. "We never really talked about that."

"Let me know when he does." Ray was following our conversation with eager eyes. "Look, guys, even if I tried out, and even if, by some miracle, I made some team as probably the oldest member on their roster, every female in the stadium or watching on television would loathe my very existence, boycott team events, and sign petitions to install day cares next to locker rooms just to keep me from playing."

Wood countered, "ESPN, CNN, FOX—all took polls. Thirty-seven percent of the people say you've paid your dues. They say,

'Let him play.' Fifty-three percent are willing to let you back into the league if you start some foundation for battered and abused women or become a spokesperson for children who are the victims of sex crimes. Something showing you've learned your lesson."

"And what lesson might that be?"

"The one where you're repentant. Sorry for your crime. Hat in your hand."

"And what percent wanted my head on a platter?"

Wood paused. "I'm just relaying your options."

"If they call back, I currently possess no professional representation. Nor do I intend to seek it." Wood's deflation was visible. "But chances are pretty good that I'll still need an attorney."

Wood scratched his head. "I'm not sure you really want me to do that. Other than the occasional divorce, writing of a will, or sale of a house, legal work's been thin for several years."

"And agenting athletes hasn't been?"

Wood shrugged.

"I'll need you to be my attorney before I'll ask you to talk to a team."

Wood frowned. "You gonna let me in on what you're planning?"

"On the other side of that hill lives a girl. A girl hiding in a garden in a convent surrounded by kids and a school because she's ashamed of her past."

Wood turned to Ray. "You knew?"

Ray lit his pipe.

Wood shook his head. "I thought we were friends." He stared through the windshield, talking to himself. "What'd I ever do to her?"

Ray spoke through a gentle cloud of smoke. "You were his friend."

Wood shrugged in agreement. "Well, yeah, there's that."

The night, or morning, I was arrested, I woke for my workout at four a.m. as usual, dressed, and stepped onto the elevator headed to the fitness center in the lobby. That's the last thing I remember. I have no memory of the twenty-four hours that followed. Only that I woke up in a hotel room that was not my own surrounded by three women who were not Audrey. In truth, I can't remember waking up, dressing, or getting on the elevator. The only reason I know that timetable is because the prosecution recounted it for the court during my trial. My last memory stopped an hour or so earlier with Audrey. "She probably doesn't trust you any more than she trusts me."

He poked Ray in the shoulder. "Oh, but she trusts him."

I shrugged. "Evidently."

Wood still couldn't believe I'd found her. "How's she doing?"

"Surrounded by a twelve-foot wall, but those twelve feet are nothing compared to the wall around her heart. When I get within a few feet, her skin crawls. I had hoped maybe things would be different when I got out. Maybe time had healed something. Anything." I shook my head. "It hasn't. My presence is painful. Like pulling off a scab, twelve years in the making. The only tie between us is this kid Dalton Rogers. She wants me to help."

Wood nodded. "There's always Canada—"

"Dunwoody, it's a game. She's not. Let it go."

"So you're really done? Like, it's really over? All this working out, and that throwing-in-prison thing had nothing to do with ever playing again?"

I paused. "You remember the last meeting in New York the night before the draft? The one where they were rolling out the red carpet, promising me the world."

He nodded.

"And what'd I tell you when they left the room?"

Wood looked away.

"Come on."

Wood spoke slowly. "You said that as long as you can remember, you've had a football in your hand. It's your lens. Take away the football and you might as well stick an icepick in your eyes."

I prodded him. "But..."

"But compared to Audrey," he shook his head, "it's nothing."

"And?"

"And if you were ever forced to choose, she wins."

"And right now, I'm choosing. Audrey doesn't trust me. Doesn't believe in me. The only way I can get to her heart is to give up what she knows I love. To lay it down."

"But that doesn't make any sense."

"Wood, everyone, you included, thinks I betrayed them. None more so than Audrey. You want me to get over it. Move on. Break more records. But Audrey is broken and she doesn't care about records. I love the game. Love it as much as ever, but if I choose the game now, then I lose her forever. Somehow I've got to show her that I love her more than this game."

"But this is your window. You're getting older. Not younger. You're on the bubble now. Besides, what on earth are you going to do to make money? You're not fit for regular work, punching a clock."

I held up my hand. "I have no plans to ever play again."

He dropped his head. Dejected. "I guess maybe I thought you'd serve your time, get out, and make a go of it. Pick up where you left off. Lot of the guys were." He tried one more dig and left it dangling. "The Rocket would have."

I stood and wiped my hands on a rag. "Wood, prison killed the Rocket. He's dead. Buried beneath cell block D."

We were quiet a few minutes. Finally, he spoke. "I'm not sure I want to know the answer to this, but what's the story with you and Dalton Rogers? You said Audrey wants to help him, but being within fifty feet of a kid is a parole violation. And it's a one-and-done. No leniency."

"I've agreed to train him. Help him get better."

"You don't need me to tell you that that's a real bad idea."

"I know. That's why I need you."

"And you don't care?"

"Didn't say that."

"But you're training him anyway."

"Yes."

"Why?"

"Only way to my wife's heart is through that kid's arm."

"Even if that's the arm that hands you over to prison authorities?"

"Even if."

Wood exhaled, letting out the breath he'd been holding since they released me from prison. "Hope you know what you're doing."

"Never said I knew what I was doing. Just that I was doing it."

"Yeah, that too."

CHAPTER SIXTEEN

Aided by a public that had tired of high-profile athletes living above the law, my trial had been short, swift, and judicious. Georgia's State Attorney, Ron Able, an undefeated litigator who could smell a political career following my successful conviction, requested and was assigned to the trial. *Where,* he had promised, *it would be vigorously prosecuted.*

And it was.

Given the sensational nature of the charges and testimony, my complete and absolute but rather weak-sounding denial—which I kept repeating and sounded like, "I did not do this. Any of it"—was dubbed by the tabloids ROCKET'S LAME EXCUSE. The sensationalism grew, and more than fifty cameras covered the trial, conviction, and sentencing. For three weeks, I essentially had my own channel. Early in the process, I was offered a very public plea deal, but to Able's great delight, I had refused, demanding a trial by jury.

And I got one, too.

Judge D. S. Gainer, who had more than forty years on the bench, a flair for history, and an understanding of its events that rivaled the tombs of Alexandria, presided over both sides as well as a jury of five men and seven women. My mom mortgaged her house to pay for my defense. Stephanie Walsh, a well-respected defense attorney out of Harvard with ten years of successfully defending professional athletes, accepted my case. For about twenty-two hours we thought we had a legitimate chance at a defense, and I tried to comfort Audrey. Then the prosecution revealed the evidence.

The State charged me with capital aggravated sexual battery, sexual battery on a minor, lewd and lascivious conduct, lewd and lascivious conduct on a minor, drug possession with intent to traffic, and intent to record such conduct—as in, make a video.

After viewing the video, my team and sponsors promptly dumped me, Audrey quit coming to see me and refused my calls, and Judge Gainer denied bail. My trial started eight months later. During that time, other than my mother, my attorney, Ray, and Wood, I had no visitors.

The trial was covered by every major news network and lasted eight days. I watched the proceedings with a numb, I-can't-believe-this-is-happening-to-me look spread across my face. Ginger was the last witness called by the prosecution. Following her story, and the pounding of the nails into my coffin, Stephanie attempted a rather short cross-examination that went nowhere, which Ginger seemed to enjoy and control. In truth, Ginger ate Stephanie's lunch and looked smugly at me in the process. Stephanie uttered the words 'No more questions, Your Honor' and sat down licking her wounds. Judge Gainer called for a recess, followed by closing arguments the next day. When both sides rested, the judge instructed the jury and sent them out.

While we waited on the verdict, the judge tasked a clerk with reminding me that a plea deal had been laid on the table. He, too, could see the writing on the wall, and sending that clerk was his way of telling me that the end was near.

I declined a final time.

During the trial, and given the explicit nature of the video, Audrey had kept her distance—from me and everyone else. She was not present in the courtroom as the prosecution laid out its case, nor as Stephanie defended ours. She showed minutes prior to the reading of the verdict.

The jury deliberated two hours.

When the sentence had been read, Audrey was sitting on the far end of the pew, four rows back. The only communication I had with anyone during my trial had been with Stephanie Walsh and my mom—whose heart was as broken as Audrey's, though not quite as bitter—and an occasional word with Ray and Wood. Mom fell ill during the trial and never really recovered, dying my second year in prison. Ashamed and broken. Stephanie Walsh kept me at arm's length, never met alone with me, and when we did, she talked only of the trial. After my imprisonment, Stephanie sued my mom and collected payment for the balance of her defense from my mom's life insurance.

I was convicted on four accounts and found not guilty of "intent to traffic." The four guilty counts carried with them mandatory sentencing totaling twenty years with the possibility of parole after twelve. While the jury had found me guilty on four of the five, the court of public opinion had found me guilty on all charges—plus several hundred more. As the bus drove me through the double gates covered with razor wire, more than a thousand people stood outside screaming. One sign read BURY HIM UNDER THE PRISON!

Walking into that prison, I stood as the angriest man on the planet. Even my sweat reeked. As the weeks melted into months, the tap root of my hatred for the woman now known as Angelina Custodia had shot downward, grown upward, blossomed, and spread, poisoning me. Audrey wasn't the only one with a seed. After a year, it consumed and crippled me. I didn't sleep. Didn't eat. Didn't talk. Most nights I went to sleep imagining the repeated sound of her neck snapping beneath my hands.

It wasn't difficult to imagine.

From my first day in prison, dozens of defense attorneys had offered to handle my appeal, but even I could read the writing on the wall. They weren't concerned with my acquittal, and much less my innocence. And they certainly weren't concerned with my marriage to my wife. They were concerned with their image and what my popularity could do for them.

And because hatred is no respecter of persons, I grew to hate them, too.

At night, deep in my cell, I flipped back through the mental images of the twelve members of my jury. Ron Able. Judge Gainer. The bailiff, Mr. Castor. The court stenographer, Ms. Fox. The fifty-plus media members in attendance. The woman who brought water bottles for members of the jury. The paralegals who aided the attorneys.

The faces of each were seared in my mind, and I hated every last one.

Those around me could smell hatred. Anger oozed out my pores like garlic, and the bars of my cell were toothpicks compared to those inside me. After two years, I could hate no more. That doesn't mean I quit hating. It means I had exceeded my own capacity. I was full and my cup was running over but drinking from my cup was killing me.

One afternoon early in my third year, Nate Roberson—a giant of a prisoner serving life for any number of crimes—paid off the guards, followed me into my cell, and attempted to put me in perpetual submission when they locked the door behind him. To give you a sense of how far I'd fallen, I remember smiling when the door locked. Given a target, I opened the valve of my hatred and in his face, I saw the images of every person in that courtroom. In the end, I'd been stabbed a couple of times, requiring stitches, while he lay unconscious on the floor, with multiple internal and external injuries and several broken bones. Blood, both his and mine, covered us and most of my cell. He'd required more than eight hours of surgery to reconstruct his face, elbow, shoulder, and knee. When they rolled him off, barely alive, I screamed at the top of my lungs. Told everyone who would listen. Come one, come all. Unlock every door and send the whole prison at once.

No one wanted any part of me. Including me.

Given his several-month stay in the hospital and the guard's testimony that I, in fact, was the intended victim and simply defending myself, word spread and I served out my time in relative obscurity and silence. Even the gangs left me alone. That meant I lived alone in isolation with memories and emotions and whispers that sought to kill me. Close to the four year mark, when the realization of who I'd become and who I'd never be hit me, I spilled off my bunk and shattered on the floor. I cried for days. Roaring in my cell. At the top of my lungs. What hatred I had not sweated out my pores came spilling out in my tears. Out of my cries.

Somewhere in there, life gutted me and my soul broke down the middle.

I had been there 1,507 days—four years, one month, fifteen days—when Gage Merkel knocked on my cell. "You the Rocket?"

I didn't look at him. He was tossing a ball in the air—something I'd not touched since they walked me in.

"First time I ever watched you play, you threw for over six hundred yards. Not bad for a—" He turned to look down on me and whispered, "Freshman."

The strings he was tugging at were connected to raw, painful, and violent anchors buried beneath time and the residue of anger. I was gurgling.

I stared up at Gage and the memory shot back.

My dad had bought me some new cleats, helped me lace them up, then strapped on a helmet that was so big I could barely stare out through the face mask, and then he'd taught me how to throw.

Turns out, I was good at it.

Real good at it.

When I got the hang of it, he shook his head, smiled, and tapped me on the chest. "Football is not played with strong arms and fast feet, it's played with heart. Grow your heart and your arms and feet will follow." My dad was not a good, or even skilled, player, but love for the game is not only given to the gifted. He paused. A knowing look. "You play long enough and you might find yourself in a place where your arms and feet fail you." He smiled and nodded once. "That's when you find out what's in your heart."

I sat in my cell, staring at twenty years, my father's voice echoing off hard, concrete walls. Time in prison is like being slowly filleted alive. The knife is not greedy. It only cuts enough skin for that day, leaving enough to stretch out across the remainder of the sentence. That left me to sit in my cell and rot.

Gage spoke softly, "Maybe . . . we could throw sometime."

I sunk my head in my hands. Who I'd become was killing me. I couldn't live with me anymore. I nodded. It was all the response I could muster. On the wall, inches from my face, my predecessor had etched these words into the concrete: WELCOME TO HELL—YOU ARE NOW SITTING IN THE GRAVE OF YOUR DREAMS.

The next morning, at daybreak, he appeared at the door to my cell. Tossing the same ball in the air. He knelt, his head inches from mine. "Tell me what you love?"

I didn't answer.

He inched closer, pressing his forehead to the bars. "Come on. One thing."

A long pause. "My wife."

"And?"

I glanced at the football in his hands.

He smiled. "We can build on that." Then he whispered into a shoulder-mounted microphone. My door unlocked, and he nodded. I rose from my bed and stepped out into the ward, where he held the ball hovering over my outstretched hand. He eyed the cameras aimed at us. "You do anything other than catch this and throw it back, and they'll put you back in that cage. Understand?"

I nodded.

He swirled his right index finger in a circle. "Eight cameras." He leaned in, whispering. "A mile down the street, there are some smug people in suits, sipping triple lattes, watching you on the monitors on the wall. Wondering what you'll do. A few of the has-beens and never-weres have placed bets, saying you've lost it. The rest say you never really had it to begin with. So . . . let's prove them wrong."

He placed the ball in my hands. My fingers read the laces, the leather's texture and tackiness, the weight of the ball, and my chest let out the breath it'd been holding since they'd arrested me five years prior.

My voice cracked. "Understood."

We threw one day. Then two. A week passed. Then another. Every few passes, a new memory would surface. So I crawled into my memories, into the games I'd played, the plays I'd called, the defenses I'd read, and into the sound of the woman who once loved me.

Remembering who I had been was the only way I could combat who I'd become.

I spent days replaying entire games, living within the memories and emotions. I crawled so far inside myself that I seldom returned to my cell. My body may have been there, but my mind was long gone. And if I wasn't replaying games in my mind, then I was preparing for them. Every morning I threw with Gage. And when I wasn't throwing, I was working out. Several times a day. Sometimes all day. Push-ups. Sit-ups. Pull-ups. Squats. Leg raises. I even jumped rope with an imaginary rope. I ran sprints. Lost count of the number of down and outs. Ran in place. Squat jumps. I sweated and sweated and sweated, all in an effort to both remember the past and forget the present.

To kill time.

My mind had become a battleground. On one side stood the cesspool of memories of my arrest, the courtroom, the accusations, the testimonies, the experts, the closing arguments, the cinching of the handcuffs, the reading of the verdict, Audrey's screams as they led me out in shackles. And on the other stood a boy with a football in his hand who loved a girl.

The months ticked by and the guys in the cells around me, at meals and out in the yard, said I'd gone loco. Lost my mind. I don't disagree. It probably looked that way. Be it weakness or strength, I was fighting for my soul, trying to remember that I once loved a woman and that she once loved me.

Some days were better than others. Some not. All taught me the same thing—hatred and anger does not kill hatred and anger.

CHAPTER SEVENTEEN

Dee arrived at five minutes to six p.m. Audrey was nowhere to be found. He had this look on his face like he knew something I didn't and he didn't want to be the one to tell me.

"While we wait on Audrey," I handed him one of two jump ropes, "you're always moving. When I'm talking, you're jumping. You will be in constant motion unless I tell you otherwise. Your feet and hands will be moving. It might seem silly, but this will force your mind to work while your body does something else." He still wouldn't look at me, and he had yet to lace up his cleats. "You all right? What's up?"

"She's not coming."

I glanced toward St. Bernard's. "I know."

"You want me to go?"

"Why?"

"No Sister Lynn no workout."

I wasn't about to send this kid home. "Why? You don't think you can hang with the old man?"

"No, I can hang—"

"It's okay. You can tell me the truth."

"You're playing me, aren't you?"

I smiled. "Yes, Dee. I'm playing you. Get your shoes on."

He sat and began lacing up his boots. "How'd you know?"

"Had a feeling."

"Really?"

I nodded. "She's pretty strong willed."

Dee stood and began jumping rope while I pointed at the two walls of cars around us. In front of him, I'd hung four ropes with eight tires. They ranged in distance from eight yards to forty. Different distances, different angles. The line of scrimmage was a line I'd drawn in the dirt. I emptied a bag of balls at his feet and pointed at his targets hanging in front of us. "Given that we can't use real people, I've given you a few receivers." One by one, I named them. "That Michelin hanging over there is your go route. Behind it, that B.F. Goodrich is a slant. That retread with the steel radials curling out of it is your sideline bump and run." He started smiling. "That bald thing there, or 'baldy,' is a secondary read, a hitch and go. Over there, that big tractor tire, that's John Deere and he's your back out of the flats. That MINI Cooper tire is your fade. Pirelli is a post. Goodyear is a streak." I ran my hand along the wall of cars on our right which made impromptu sidelines. "You see that red station wagon right there?"

He nodded.

"You see that open window just above it?"

"Got it."

"That's a Chevy Impala. Or what remains of it. The window is your sideline route." I turned him to the left. "That window there?"

He nodded.

"I'm not sure, but I think it's a Volkswagen."

"Left sideline. Got it."

I tossed him a ball, and he dropped the jump rope and caught it. I knelt in front of him, a dozen balls at my feet. "When I snap you the ball, I want a three-step drop—starting with a strong first step— and while you're doing that, I'm going to call your receiver. Got it?"

His eyes ran through the hanging tires. "I think so."

"You ready?"

He smiled. "No, but I'll get there."

I snapped him the ball. "John Deere."

A quarterback's throw starts in his feet. They are his anchor. His foundation. They get him in position to throw and they start the power transfer or kinetic chain. At the snap, Dee's first step was big and backward, covering about three yards. His next two were short, choppy, and quick—that's good footwork, and I'd bet it was natural and no one had taught it to him. Guys either have it or they don't. His eyes were quick to read his receivers and check off one or two—which would buy him a half a second or so from the safeties—before he committed to John Deere. Then came his throw.

If you could call it that.

"Wow." I scratched my head and tried to make sense of what I just saw. "What was that?"

He chewed on his lip. "Yeah. I have a bit of a problem."

"I'll say. Did you always throw like that?"

He shook his head.

"Who did that to you?"

"Coach Damon."

"I know he's your coach, but if you want to improve you'll never listen to another word he says to you when it comes to your throwing motion. Just nod, smile, say 'yes, sir,' and then disregard every word that comes out his mouth. The delete button is now your best friend."

He laughed. "That go for you, too?"

I smiled and shrugged. "Well played."

In its simplicity, the throwing motion is a simple transfer of energy. One seamless symphony of muscles and memory. In its complexity, it's an incremental buildup of leverage, finally released out the fingers.

Think of a medieval catapult. Stored energy rests high in a structure. A decision is made, a lever is thrown, and that energy is released straight down, where it is driven through some mechanism that utilizes other levers to convert that energy into a swinging arm, which, as a result, launches a projectile. The more energy stored, the more available to be released. The more released, the farther the projectile is hurled. Distance is a function of two things: energy stored and the efficiency of the structure to transfer that energy into the object.

A football player is the catapult. Energy is stored in his body. At given intervals, like when a receiver is open or going to be open, the QB's mind tells his body to release stored energy that is then channeled along a kinetic chain. It starts in his toes, rises up through his legs and hips, and then narrows through his core. All the while, it is multiplying exponentially. Then it courses through the shoulders, arms, and finally off the tip of the index finger on his throwing hand.

Simple, right?

Well, yes and no.

When released into a football, that energy can be measured in such units as release velocity, launch angle, and spin rate. Scientists, coaches, players, even armchair quarterbacks, get really axle-wrapped in this. So difficult is the act of getting the ball into the receiver's hands without a defender getting to it first that it's been called "threading the needle"—and a moving one at that.

Good quarterbacks can put the ball in the same place five out of ten times. Great quarterbacks put it there ten. Greatness wins games. Consistent greatness wins championships. Consistency is king.

The problem with Dee's throw was simple. Somebody had monkeyed with his catapult. For a quarterback, his nonthrowing arm is as important as the throwing arm, because what you start in the nonthrowing arm is finished in the throwing arm. It is commonly agreed that the most efficient and accurate throwers come over the top. Meaning, the ball is released somewhere above their ear. In order for an over-the-top release of the right hand to happen, the left arm must come straight down and back along the torso. That forces the right arm, or throwing arm, to come over the top. If the left arm swings wide, like a helicopter blade, then as a matter of sheer physics the right arm will swing wide as well, causing the thrower to sidearm the ball. There are exceptions to this, but they're few. Sidearm quarterbacks are not known for their accuracy, and their careers are rather short given that the shoulder is not designed to handle the torque produced by a sideways throw. In short—for a right-handed quarterback—left arm straight down and back is good as it causes the right arm to come up, over, and forward.

Every time Dee threw, his left arm swung wide. As a result, his right arm did, too. To make matters worse, he was dropping his right elbow to compensate for the torque put on his shoulder. Ray was right, doing this to Dee was like taking a Derby-winning racehorse and tying a rope between his feet, shortening his stride by a foot or two. The kid had all the strength in the world yet maybe only half his available power made it out his arm, and his accuracy was sporadic at best. And he just didn't look comfortable. As a result, he was throwing ducks.

It was bad all the way around.

But it was also fixable.

Very fixable. Problem was the rope between his feet also rested in his mind.

Dee dropped back, checked off his read, and fired the football, missing his target by about three feet.

I'd seen enough. I said, "Follow me."

One of the unique features of the maze of cars within which we were throwing is that in some places the stacks of cars were twenty feet high and piled in tight rows. The aisles between were two- to three-feet wide and a man of average shoulder width had to turn slightly sideways to walk between them.

Dee and I walked down one of the aisles. When separated by about fifteen feet, I said, "Now, throw me the ball."

He laughed. "You're joking."

"When it comes to throwing a football, I never joke."

He pointed to the pieces of rusted metal protruding from the walls. "I'm not sure my tetanus shot is up to date."

"You arguing with me?"

He brought the ball up and tried to fire it toward me, but his left arm brushed the crushed car next to him and the ball went tumbling and bouncing off the sides like a pinball machine. I threw it back to him. "Only one way to throw in here. Over the top."

He caught the ball. "How'd you do that?"

"Think about it. The problem is in your left arm. Pull it straight down. For now, keep your left arm in constant contact with your body. That will change as your motion improves, but right now I want you to overaccentuate."

He tried again. More pinball.

I demonstrated in slow motion. "Left arm down. Right arm over the top."

He gathered himself and threw. Left arm came down, right arm over the top, and the ball came straight to me before the wobble pulled the ball right.

"A little wobble is good. A lot is bad. Too much can take a ball five yards off target at thirty yards. Again."

We spent the afternoon playing catch between rusty crushed cars, throwing a couple hundred balls.

When we emerged from between the cars, his arms were scratched and right knuckles a little bloody but he was smiling and shaking his head. And his throw had shown improvement. "How's your arm feeling?"

He rotated it in its socket. "Tired, but good."

"Ice it. Ice is your new best friend." I turned to him. "We can't undo in a day what a coach imprinted over two years. It'll take time. But it's doable. So hang in there."

He looked at me suspiciously. "Are we done?"

"Finished."

"What?"

" 'Done' is what happens in the oven. Out here, we're either finished or we're not."

"You sound like somebody else I know."

"She's the one who taught me." I pointed up the hill. "And no, we're not finished. You know the drill."

He smiled. "Race you to the top."

I reached down and grabbed both of the harnesses. "Wearing this."

His head tilted sideways as he traced the lines of the harness I'd handed to him. It was tied to a tire. A large tire.

He pulled on the harness, leaned into the tire, and groaned. "Dude...your old-school coaching is killing me."

I sprinted past him. "Come on. That pain you feel is just weakness leaving your body."

"Yeah, I've heard that before."

"Where?"

"It's painted on our locker room wall."

"That's 'cause I painted it there."

He mumbled behind me. "Figures."

A few minutes later, we stood at the top, staring down over the field in the distance. A coach stood on the field blowing his whistle and shouting orders at a quarterback and several receivers. The quarterback was muscular and looked more like a weight lifter than a football player. The coach was animated, screaming loud enough for his echoes to be heard atop the Bucket, and the throws, while powerful and fast, were acutely inaccurate. Not only was he inaccurate, he was prone to fits of rage that I can only guess he picked up from his dad. While we watched, he screamed and pointed at his receivers. We couldn't hear what he said, but his body language suggested he was blaming them for balls they didn't catch. "I guess that's your coach and his son?"

"Yes," he spoke slowly. "That would be them."

We watched as more and more balls sailed wide and high. With each successive throw, his body language grew profane, as did his fathers'. "Wow. That guy has a temper."

"You haven't seen anything. He's just getting warmed up. Wait till he starts throwing the ball in their face while they're standing in the huddle. Or when the coach smacks them across the face mask with the clipboard."

I chuckled. "I can't hear what he's saying, but I'm pretty sure those receivers aren't having any fun."

"Coach Damon says fun is what happens when you win."

"I certainly had more fun when I won, but it wasn't limited to that."

He paused purposefully. "Can I ask you a question? And will you give me an answer even if the answer hurts me?"

I heard the echo of my wife in that question. "Did Audrey tell you to phrase the question that way?"

He smiled. "Yes."

"Sure. Go ahead."

"You've seen enough of me now to know whether or not I can fix what needs fixing and play both"—he pointed at the field—"down there and at the next level." He waved his hand across the earth stretched out before us. "So can I?"

I unclipped both tires, turned them on end, and sent them rolling down the hill, where they bounced and crashed into a stack of cars some four hundred yards below us. Coiling the rope from the harnesses, I asked, "You want to?"

"Yes."

"Then what I think doesn't matter."

"'Course it does."

I shook my head. "Nope. Only thing that really matters is what's—" I tapped him in the chest. Above his heart. "In here." I nodded down at the field. "Look, we might as well get this on the table right now. Much is made of quarterbacks and their skills. Who's got the strongest arm. Fastest feet. Best vision. The media constantly gets this wrong, and yes, at one time, I got all hung up on that, too. To some extent, all that is needed. And yes, if you need to hear me say it, you have all those tools. Maybe more than most any kid I've seen in a long time, and certainly more than that rock-'em, sock-'em blockhead down there. But in truth, the best quarterbacks aren't the guys with the greatest skills but the biggest hearts. The question you need to ask yourself is not, 'Am I better than steroid boy,' but, 'How deeply can I love.' "

He looked confused. "What?"

"For a quarterback, football is not a game about how great you are, but how great you can make others." I pointed at the receivers. "Take those five guys. Right now, would they take a bullet for steroid-boy or use him as a human shield?" He laughed. "The guys in your huddle don't care what the statisticians say. Or how you rank in some bean-counters lineup. They want to know how deep into your well you're willing to dig when everything in your body is telling you that you can't or won't. And when you do, they want to know if you'll do it again."

"What if I don't get the chance?"

"Don't get axle-wrapped bout what you can't control. You'll get your chance. Your job is to make the most of it when you do. You might only get one. And you want to make such an impression that Coach Clipboard," he laughed, "will lose his job if he doesn't play you again." The wind dried the sweat off our faces as more shouts and screams erupted off the field. "When the whistle blows and you're in a war down there—and make no mistake about it, it's a war—the guys in that huddle need to see in your eyes something that can't be measured. Can't be coached. And it isn't made better with steroids. The five greatest words to ever come out of your mouth are, 'We can win this thing.' Those guys down there want someone they can believe in. And I'm pretty sure they don't believe in that guy. The answer they're looking for doesn't come from your arm strength, forty-yard-dash time, good looks, or the fact that your daddy is the coach. It comes out of here." I tapped myself in the chest.

We watched the bodies run routes on the field. A ball left the quarterback's hand and flew wide right. I spoke both to him and me. "It's a great game, maybe *the* greatest. I had a lot of good memories on that field."

"You'll come watch me play this year?"

I squinted one eye. "Sure. But not from down there. Maybe you can use Audrey's cell phone and call me at halftime."

"You don't own a cell phone."

I pushed him sideways, knocking him slightly off balance. "For you, I'll figure something out."

As we turned to jog down the Bucket, something caught his attention that made his eyes grow larger and wider. I turned and found Audrey walking toward us. She'd climbed up and was carrying her scarecrow dismantling stick on her shoulder. She didn't look too happy. She marched up to me, pointed her finger in my face, and whispered through gritted teeth. She spoke slowly and articulated every syllable, "You don't dictate anything to me."

I had a feeling she wasn't finished, so I waited.

She hefted the stick in her hand. Eyes welling. Her last word was barely audible. "Ever."

Having spoken her mind, and decided not to crack open my skull, she turned and left. Dee watched her leave. He leaned in. "What'd you do?"

"Made her mad." A pause. "Again."

He whispered almost to himself, "I've never seen her like that."

Audrey disappeared as dark surrounded us. A couple of mosquitoes began buzzing our ears. We started walking down, and I patted him on the shoulder. "Tomorrow morning. Same bat time. Same bat channel."

"What?"

"Nothing. Before your time. I'll see you in the morning. Right here. Same time."

I turned and started walking off toward the cabin. "Coach?"

I'd not heard him say that before. "You better call me Matthew, or Matty."

He stepped close enough for the streetlight to create a shadow across his face. He picked at the cleats in his hand. "Did you—did you do what—" He nodded over his shoulder. Into the past. "All that stuff like they say you did?"

"Why?"

"Just…" He shrugged.

"Dee, why should you believe anything I tell you?"

He shrugged again.

"Innocent or guilty, I can't prove it."

He shook his head. "I'm not asking you to prove it. I'm asking you to tell me. Straight to my face."

"You've no doubt done your homework. What do you think?"

"I think if you did, then you got what you deserved. And"—he glanced over his shoulder in the direction of where Audrey had disappeared—"you're still getting it. And if you didn't, then…" He lowered his head, then looked back up at me and shook his head. "I'm real sorry."

"I think it's best if you and I keep our eyes on the ball. I don't know how long we're going to get to do this, and if I dodge your question, like I'm doing now, and we don't talk about it, then when you're asked about your relationship with me, you can answer honestly. Might make things easier on you in the future. You can tell them I said this. Agreed?"

"Can I ask you one more thing?"

"Sure."

"You still love Mama Audrey?"

The name surprised me. "You call her that?"

"She says that when she first met me…" He paused to calculate in his mind. "I guess this would've been a few weeks after you went to prison. She was sleeping in the room with me at night 'cause I didn't like being alone in the dark, and somewhere in there I got scared and called out, 'Mama.' Her face always showed above my bed. I guess she didn't feel right about me calling her that around the other Sisters so she added 'Audrey.' Now that I'm older, I call her Ms. Audrey or Sister Lynn around them and in public. But when it's just us…she's 'Mama.' "

I crossed my arms and stared in the direction of St. Bernard's and the convent, turning my head slightly so he couldn't see my face. I had yet to answer his question.

I'm not sure why he continued with his story, other than it was comforting to him and I had the feeling that he felt it would be comforting to me. Which told me a lot about Dalton Rogers. He chuckled. "She used to put me to sleep with bedtime stories about great quarterbacks. Countless. Each one led to another that led to a rivalry or another championship. She knew how to string it out and stretch the tension. I couldn't get enough of them. 'One more,' I was always asking. I had no idea they were true until I got older. For a long time, I didn't know you two were…Somewhere in the seventh grade, we were watching a video of one of your high school games, and when she didn't turn it off quick enough I saw her and you after the game." He shrugged. "I put two and two together." He pressed me further. "Mama says you love this game more than life. More than her."

I nodded. "I do miss it."

"So why aren't you trying out? Making a go of it."

I weighed my head side to side. "It's complicated."

He pointed through the trees toward the convent. "She's pretty sure you're packing up any day and flying out on some team owner's jet for a tryout. Keeps telling me not to get my hopes up about you sticking out the summer. To get what I can and not get attached."

That was her pain talking. "Dee, I'm not flying out on any jet."

The complexion of his face changed from innocent curiosity to honest admission. "I spent some time on the Internet yesterday."

He was baiting me. I waited. "And?"

"Old articles. Video clips from your trial."

More silence. More bait. I played along. "And?"

"That woman, Ms. Custodia, she was…convincing."

"Her name is Ginger, and the jury agreed with you."

"It's tough to tell, but it looks like you on the video."

"That's what the jury said."

He shook his head. "I don't believe her."

"That'd put you in the minority."

He looked over both shoulders. "In case you haven't noticed, I'm half white and half black. Grew up with the nickname Oreo. I been of the minority my whole life."

I chuckled. His quick ability to poke fun at himself was refreshing. It also suggested confidence. "I'm sorry about that."

"That's not why I'm telling you."

"Okay. Why're you telling me?"

"'Cause I appreciate what you're doing and don't want you to think I'm out here using you for all the ways you can help me while looking at you through the lens of you're-a-sick-pervert."

"What lens then?"

"I think you may be, or could have been, one of the greats to play this game, and I consider myself lucky to be standing here and you standing there."

"Dalton, there are going to be people who, if they find out about you and me, will see my standing here and your standing there as my sick attempt to persuade you. To cause you to believe in my innocence when even my own wife doesn't believe me. And you need to understand that. The closest person to me on the face of the earth believes I'm a liar and that I betrayed her in the worst way. Add to that, my best friend and one of my former coaches don't really know what to think. If you and I are caught—found out—folks will call you gullible and impressionable and they'll call me worse stuff than before. What's important is this: if you want, and it's your choice, I'll coach you—whether you believe in my innocence or not."

He smiled and tapped his chest. "I feel you, dog."

There it was again. I pressed him. "You sure you understand what's at stake?"

He cracked a smile. "I'm a big boy."

"Well, take your big boy self on home. Get some dinner. Drink plenty of fluids, and I'll see you here in about ten hours."

He trotted off through the woods. I hollered after him. "Dalton?"

He stopped, turned, trotted back, and raised both eyebrows. "I think it's best if you call me Dee."

I chuckled. "Okay, Dee...what if you're wrong about me?"

He flexed his muscles and smiled widely. "When I get bigger, I'll come back here and beat you like you did that guy in prison."

"You read about that, too, huh?"

"Yep."

He trotted off and I hollered after him again. "Dee?"

He stopped, turned.

"Yes, I still love my wife. More than this game we're playing—and I'd give my left arm right now to lead a team the length of the field on a Sunday afternoon. Or," I smiled, "Monday night."

A big smile. "Thought so."

He disappeared through the trees, and I heard myself whispering after him, "Kid, I'd say you're big enough already."

To our left, along the tree line I caught a flash. Like sunlight on glass. Or a lens. I squinted into a dark shadowy space in the trees, and I thought I saw two limbs separate and then return but, given the half-mile distance, it could've been the breeze. Or it could've been nothing.

'Course, it could have been something, too.

I walked into the cabin, then quickly out a side door that could not be seen. I circled around through the woods, making my way to the fence where I thought I saw the reflection. By the time I got there, I had convinced myself that it was nothing and I was just being paranoid. Empty coffee cups, footprints in the dirt, a half dozen cigarette butts—one still smoking—convinced me otherwise. From their vantage point through the fence, they had a pretty good view of both our practice inside the junkyard and the real field below. Given the older butts piled a few feet down the fence and the matted grass, it was probably practices. If they'd had a camera, like one with a telephoto lens attached to it, they'd have had no problem counting the hairs on my face or the serial number on my anklet. The trail out led to the railroad. I heard an engine crank, so I took off running after it. When I reached the road, all I saw were red tail lights fading into the distance. Below me, a dark-red oil spot stained the dirt, suggesting a leaky transmission.

Damon and his guys had been working out at the same time as us. Someone had been watching, and possibly recording, either the team's workout, or ours.

CHAPTER EIGHTEEN

I had given a good bit of thought to this morning's workout, so I was ready when Dalton showed with a smile on his face. He looked at the yard and everything I'd spread around us. He squinted one eye. "Looks medieval."

"I pulled a few tricks out of my bag."

He surveyed the torture apparatus around us. "Definitely older than old-school." He pointed at the rear axle and gear housing of an old three-quarter-ton Ford pickup. "What do you expect me to do with that?"

"Throw it over there."

"Then what?"

I pointed. "Throw it from there . . . to there."

"And I suppose we keep doing that until you get tired."

"Exactly."

He stared down at a tractor tire five feet in diameter. "And that?"

"Flip it over there."

"How many times?"

I shrugged.

He scratched his chin. "This is going to hurt, isn't it?"

I squatted and placed my hands beneath the tire, readying to flip it. "I won't ask you to do anything I don't do first."

He nodded. "That's what I'm afraid of."

Over the next ninety minutes, we hopped, skipped, ran ladders, pulled sleds, flipped tires, swung a sledge hammer. I took him through various foot speed drills, single leg explosions—some weighted, some not. I strapped a harness to an old Honda Accord that had been stripped of most everything but the tires, and we pulled it back and forth across the yard. Forty yards one way, and forty yards the other. The entire time I was talking in his ear, "Can you sustain power for four, possibly five, quarters of football?" When he started to get tired, I pressed him. "When your primary is a go route, and your secondary is a slant, but they line up in cover 3 with the free safety cheating and the middle linebacker is screaming at your slot receiver, 'Inside,' what's your throw?"

He leaned into the harness, sweat pouring off his face. "Back out of the flats."

He was smart and he thought well under pressure, so I pressed him further. "Unless?"

"Unless my go route is really fast."

I smiled. "Good."

Once his legs got good and tired, I wanted to activate his shoulders so I unhooked him from the harness, strapped the rope to a tractor trailer tire, and then pulled it with arms out in front, holding the harness in my hands. A functional shoulder press with leg press thrown in. It's a killer. Somewhere in here he gagged and showed the first signs of throwing up.

I took the harness from him and began pulling the Honda the opposite direction. I said, "You can puke if you want to." He gagged again and put his hands on his knees. "But right now your body is telling you what it wants to do." I lifted his chin and then stepped back into the harness. "What we're doing is training it to do what we want it to do." He swallowed and choked it back, stepped inside the harness, and began pulling.

After sleds, I stretched four long ropes out in front of us. They were old ship anchor ropes, each about twenty-feet long, three inches in diameter, heavy and cumbersome. I held one in each hand and explained. "This activates the shoulders." I smiled and began waving my arms out in front of me, which created a wave in each of the ropes. When one arm was high, the other was low. I did this for twenty to thirty seconds. "I hate these things, but this, and pull-ups, are the secret to the long ball."

Hands on his knees, he shook his head. "Then I should just love them."

We ended with a run up and down the Bucket followed by abs: Superman sit-ups, Superman sit-ups with tire toss, bicycles, bicycles with rotation, crunches, planks, wipers, scissors, and finally, one-armed and one-footed planks. Over the entire ninety minutes, we never stopped moving.

When I said, "That's probably enough for today," he collapsed and his face landed in the dirt. He lay there a few seconds, breathing, then stood without ceremony, walked in a slight circle, then stopped and took a deep breath. Then, as if shot from a canon, he arched his back and hurled from his toes. Much of the fluid he'd drunk since we started ended up on the ground around him, splattering his legs and feet. After a pause, I was about to say something smart and ask him if he was finished when he started round two. After that exorcism, he sunk to his knees, wiped his mouth with his shirt sleeve, and stared around and then up at me. His face was a mixture of both relief and incredulity. He said, "Wow." He fell back, a snow angel in the dirt. He shook his head. "I don't believe I've ever felt this bad in my entire life."

I looked down on him. "I'm surprised you held it in that long."

He shook his head. "You're a sadistic and mean man."

"I've heard that before."

He rolled over and stood up. "Yeah, I'd just never believed it until now."

I laughed, we fist-bumped, and Dee stumbled home.

I straightened up the cabin and then drove the trail bike to town. In the twelve years I'd been locked up, a lot had changed. The way people dressed, the music they listened to, the way people communicated. I felt as if I were walking on Mars.

I parked in the Walmart lot, perused the aisles until I happened upon the stuffed animals, and dug through them until I found what I was looking for. At the checkout counter, the woman asked me, "What's that?"

She was in her late thirties but looked midforties. High mileage. Tried to cover up the bags beneath her eyes with too much makeup. Thickening around the middle, her leathered skin was starting to sag in places, but her smile was kind and inviting. Her hair was pulled back, exposing the skin of her neck and high cheekbones. I think she had been pretty at one time. The thing in my hand was about two feet long and real fluffy. "It's a spider monkey."

She raised an eyebrow and lay the change in my hand, letting each coin drop slowly. "Looks cuddly. Like you could just wrap your arms around him and get lost for a while."

I stared at it. "I think it's a she."

She smiled. "Even better."

I didn't realize it until after I'd walked out that she was trying to pick me up. I cranked the motorcycle and started talking to myself, *You've been in prison too long.*

In my playing days, I experienced a feeling—or a rush of emotion—after a touchdown pass or score that is best described as jubilation. We've seen this countless times on instant replay. It's expressed by a look on the face, something screamed in triumph, a dance, a jump, a fist pump. It is the culmination of hundreds, if not thousands, of hours of mental and physical work, of a strategy defined and executed, of eleven guys gutting something out. It's a powerful release of emotion seldom, if ever, equaled in my life. Driving through town, the slide show in my mind began ticking off passes and scores, and with each picture I remembered, even tasted, the sense of jubilation. Of happiness. When I looked at the speedometer, I was driving twenty-seven in a fifty. And my knuckles were white.

A horn behind me, followed by an angry passing vehicle and a driver who told me that I was number one in his heart, brought me back to that seat and the handlebars. So many times, I'd thought about walking out of prison. Of unlocked doors and freedom. Of the ability to go and come as I wished. And the belief that all of that would be accompanied with that fist-pumping sense of jubilation.

I was wrong. It had not. Didn't even come close.

While my hands cramped from squeezing the handlebars, the painful reality of my life set in. In prison, the possibility of what could be fueled my hope, and the impossibility of acting on my anger kept me safe. Out of prison, what I saw waged war with what I hoped. And churned inside me.

Given that my helmet hid my face, I detoured to Wood's office. When I peered through the window, he was leaning back in his office chair listening to talk radio. I pushed open the door and stepped into his office. The sound was turned down, but I could hear Ginger's voice. When he spun in his chair and looked up, I said, "Really?"

A shrug. "She's talking about you. A lot of people calling in."

Her tone of voice betrayed her smile. She was enjoying every minute of this. She clicked between callers with the speed of a court reporter. Those in support of me were quickly silenced. Those who wanted to nail me to the barn door were encouraged to express their feelings. Their emotions. In her time on air, she hadn't lost a step. She led this dance, and she could give Jim Kneels a run for his money.

Wood and I listened as one caller spouted, "I don't know where he is, but that pervert needs to be deported. Exported. Ported somewhere. He made us believe in him. We bought his jerseys. Shouted his name. Made us think he was all that and turns out he wasn't. He wasn't nothing. That's the worst kind of man. The kind that says he's one person, but inside, he's another. And another thing is this…" The person's voice rose and you could hear a chair squeak in the background. "People have a right to know where he's living. Don't he have to register or something?"

Ginger clicked over to another call. "Mary from Ellaville, you're on the air with 1-800- R-U-A-VICTIM."

"Angelina, I can tell you right where he's living." The sound of paper being unfolded or crinkled echoed over the phone line. "2122 Whiskey Still Road. Just outside of Gardi, Georgia."

Wood's eyes lit and he sat up straight. Both palms landed flat on his desk. "They just gave out your address over national radio."

Ginger interrupted the caller. "Thank you, Mary. For those of you listeners who don't know, convicted sex offenders are required by law to register where they will be living for any period of time greater than seven days. This information is public and Mary is correct. Matthew Rising registered three days ago, and his address is listed as 2122 Whiskey Still Road."

Wood stood out of his chair and pointed at the radio. "She just said it again."

Ginger continued. "You can find Mr. Rising's registration online at—" She rattled off the web address as if she knew it by heart.

Wood sat back down, scratched his head, and began talking out loud. "Did you lock the gate when you left?"

I nodded.

He shook his head. "Won't take them long to find it."

"I know."

"You might should take the back way home."

And he was right. I should have.

It was a quarter to six when I rode up to the gate. The sign was six feet long and maybe four feet tall. White background. Big black letters. Hung between two four-by-four posts. It had been professionally stenciled. It read:

CONVICTED SEX OFFENDER MATTHEW RISING LIVES HERE.
HE WAS CONVICTED OF KIDNAPPING, DRUGGING, SEXUALLY
ABUSING, VIDEOING, AND RAPING ONE WOMAN AND TWO GIRLS
UNDER THE AGE OF EIGHTEEN.
HE IS NOW FREE ON PAROLE TO VICTIMIZE AGAIN.

There's no way on earth someone commissioned and/or printed that sign following the announcement on the radio. The owner of that sign had been waiting for this moment and—although I can't prove it—I'd say the broadcasting of my address had been orchestrated long in advance. The word "victimize" was the signature.

The gate was still locked, but the support beam had been bent by something big and heavy like a bumper. I unlocked it, rode through, and locked it behind me en route to the cabin a half mile down the dirt road. I idled along, swinging wide around the corners.

I was right to suspect something.

Most everything I owned or Wood had left for me was strewn about in front of the cabin. Somebody had pulled my mattress out of the house and, given the smell, yellow stain, and brown pile, had both urinated and defecated on it. Across the front of the cabin someone had spray-painted the words, RAPIST, PERVERT, DEVIANT, FREAK, and CHILD MOLESTER with a few other choice words thrown in for color. On the front door, somebody had sprayed, YOU WILL BURN IN HELL in red lettering.

I put down the kickstand and was sitting there reading the walls when Dee appeared. He was early. Out of breath, he'd been running. "You okay?"

"Yeah."

"I overheard some folks at work talking about that stunt the lady pulled on the radio."

I nodded.

He held up his phone. "You want me to call the police?"

I shook my head once. "I don't think it'd do any good."

"You want some help?"

The only bright spot in the whole thing was that I didn't have much to begin with, so cleanup wouldn't take long. "That'd be great."

When we finished twenty minutes later, the only thing remaining was the mattress. His nose curled. "What about that?"

It lay in the middle of the yard, surrounded by dirt, so I grabbed the kerosene can used to light the wood-burning stove, doused the mattress, and threw a match on it. The kerosene caught and spread across the mattress. The flames had climbed fifteen feet in the air by the time we tied on our boots and started jogging.

I began jogging the opposite direction from the gate, across what were once fields covered in cheesecloth that shaded the tobacco. The Bucket loomed behind us. Soon, the sun would set behind it. He'd never been this way. "Where we headed?"

A mile in front of us sat a tree line. I pointed. "The river."

"What's there?"

"The solution to your sidearm."

The Altamaha River drained southeast Georgia to the Atlantic. It started out in a narrow stretch of cypress swamp many miles northwest of us. By the time it got to us, it had turned into a tannic, ice-tea colored river that meandered its way south, feeding into several crystal-blue springs before eventually dumping into the Atlantic. Flow depended on the rain. In times of drought, it could become a snake-infested mud hole. In rainy season, it flowed with a two-to-three-mile-an-hour current. Filled with catfish, bream, carp, bass, and bellowing with alligators, it teemed with life. Average depth was a few feet while some holes were ten to fifteen.

Afternoon rains had swelled the river. I'd been counting on this. We neared the edge and watched the current rolling south. "Wow," he said. "Had no idea this was back here."

"Pretty, isn't it?"

Off to our left sat a covered area. Wood's grandfather had built a tin-roof shed over the work space for his still. Dirt floor. No walls. Vines had snaked in and were climbing up the support poles and the wind had blown off one of the tin panels, but I found what I needed. Twenty years ago, some log cutters had left two empty butyl tanks that had been used to fuel their cutting torch. The tanks were eight feet tall and maybe sixteen to eighteen inches in diameter. The volume of air inside each was enough to float two people so, eighteen years ago, we'd used them as a modified log roll. They'd been here ever since.

The tanks stood on end beneath the shed. Dee helped me lower them and roll them to the water's edge. I tied a rope from end to end, allowing them to spin independently yet stay oriented toward each other. I pushed off on the first one, straddling it like a horse, soaking my legs to the knee, and said, "Mount up."

He stood on the bank, pointing. "You want me to stand on that?"

I stood, balanced, and slowly rolled the tank beneath my feet. I motioned for him to toss me the ball, which he did. "I want you to stand on that and play catch with me. And do it quick before the snakes and alligators eat me."

He pushed off, tried to stand, slipped, and went for a swim. Head first. When he came out of the water, his eyes were wide and he was moving a bit faster than when he went in. I started laughing, couldn't stop, messed up my rhythm, and followed him head first. The sound of his laughter was good medicine, and I needed it.

We climbed back up on our "logs," balanced, and, once he'd found his sea legs, I tossed him the now-wet ball. He caught it and threw it back. The reason this works is pretty simple. In a situation where extreme balance is required, your body instinctively knows what will throw it off balance. Our internal gyro knows without being told. So when Dee caught the ball, he threw it back to me. Perfectly. Granted, it was a weak throw and lacked any zip, but the motion was good. His left arm ripped down. Right arm came over the top. It even surprised him. Proud of himself, he pointed into the air where the ball had just been. "Did you see that?"

Over the next hour, we talked through his motion. A few times, his arm slipped sideways and so did his body, sending him back into the water. But as the hour played out, he fell less and less. And pretty soon, we were just two guys playing catch.

We finished with a jog back to the junkyard and then three times up and down the Bucket. Walking down the last time, Dee spoke without looking at me. "I, um…take out the trash at night, all around school. It's how I pay for my meal plan and books.

I drive this golf cart around, and, anyway, last night I was making the rounds near the garden, near Mama Audrey's little cottage, and—I heard her crying." He paused. Looked at me. Then looked away again. "And not just a little bit." A shrug as he stared over the smoking remains of the mattress. "Just thought you'd want to know."

CHAPTER NINETEEN

Lunchtime. I was sitting in the Laundromat minding my own business when the caravan of black Mercedes, Range Rovers, and one giant black bus came roaring into town. The stardusted ANGELINA was obnoxiously billboard-big. Curious, I packed up and followed them to town, where they set up shop on the courthouse steps. They parked, taking up most of spaces around the courthouse, the bus's robotic arms protruded like a transformer and leveled the rolling sound studio. Within moments, dozens of people—mostly dressed in black—all wearing secret-service earpieces, exited the vehicles and began a dizzying, antlike procession around the grounds. It'd been a long time since I'd seen so many people scurrying to and fro for one person. Reminded me of me.

I parked the bike and observed the festivities in mute amazement. And even some enjoyment. Talk about a well-oiled machine. I'd seen cartoons that didn't develop this quickly. The traveling *Angelina Custodia Show* had taken Gardi by storm. Within an hour of setup, Angelina had exited her bus to a growing crowd and roaring applause. Without hesitation, she wielded the microphone and began working the bystanders and setting her hooks deep and early.

"Tell me what you think about convicted sex-offender Matthew Rising living right here, terrorizing your hometown." To another woman flanked by two ponytailed girls, she asked, "Are these your girls? Does his presence worry you?" The woman stuttered, palmed the tangled hair out of her face, and wrapped her arms around her girls. The wrinkle between her eyes suggested that if that mother wasn't worried before, she was now.

I'm not sure the KKK or Black Panthers were as adept at inciting a riot.

Ginger revealed in a practiced and seductive voice to her adoring crowd that she planned to broadcast live all afternoon and into the evening. This meant that her afternoon radio show would simply fade seamlessly into her nighttime television show. This announcement brought applause and catcalls from the growing audience, which in turn produced a well-rehearsed blush from Ginger. I flipped my hood up, pulled Wood's Costas down over my eyes, parked the bike, bought a soda from a vending machine, and sat on a bench, viewing the festivities.

Word spread, cars pulled in, folks mobbed the grounds surrounding the courthouse. Onlookers set up lawn chairs, and both a hot dog and shaved-ice vendor appeared out of nowhere. The city must have called in additional law enforcement, because sheriff's deputies from neighboring counties arrived en masse. The mayor showed and quickly took credit for everything. Ginger let him, then pounced on him for what she really wanted, which was the courthouse steps. The same steps they marched me down, handcuffed, some twelve years prior. Without the slightest thought to obtaining any type of required city permit, he quickly agreed and the Ginger Machine took over from there.

Within minutes, Ginger and her entourage had commandeered

the steps, transforming them into a primetime stage. Colorful flags, spotlights, even fans meant to blow her hair back were brought in and set in place. Seated at a glass table situated between the columns while the courthouse served as the backdrop, Ginger looked toned and fit. Short skirt, muscular legs. A makeup artist brushed her face while another woman fussed with her hair. Ginger had always dreamed of the spotlight. If I didn't experience such visceral disgust at the sight and thought of her, I'd be tempted to admire her—a self-made woman staring down on the world she'd created. The wind from the off-screen fans tugged at her perfect hair—auburn red had given way to jet black—and vacuum-sealed her blouse across her artistically crafted, perfectly enhanced plastic surgery chest, highlighting her personally trained and sweat-sculpted body. When the on-air light flashed from red to green, she proclaimed in a loud, articulate, triumphant voice, "This is Angelina Custodia, broadcasting live from the sex-offender epicenter of south Georgia." Her voice rose, as did the perception of her passion. "I am the sound of the silenced, the town crier, the mouthpiece of the muted and the muzzled, the declaration of the disillusioned, the voice of the victimized." Walking forward, the conquering hero, calm, resolute, finality in her tone, she pointed her finger at the camera. "Because you don't have to sit there and just take it!"

Man, she's good.

The several hundred crowding the steps of the courthouse agreed, and Ginger ate the applause like candy. At one point, she wiped away a tear and made some off-the-cuff comment to the audience about how she learned a long time ago that to do this job she "needs waterproof mascara" and that she would keep doing it "until they pry this microphone from my cold, dead fingers."

They loved that, too.

If she didn't make me want to vomit, it would have been comical.

Feeling a bit too exposed, I pulled my helmet back on and slid the visor down. I bought a shaved ice, straddled my bike, and continued to enjoy the festivities—illegally close. I felt like a voyeur.

Because I was in violation of my parole and she was not, I kick-started the bike and was easing off the clutch, hoping to pry my way through the crowd, when the show returned from commercial. Ginger, basking in her confidence, descended the steps and began asking members of the crowd:

"Given the deviant crimes for which he was convicted, how do you feel?"

"Does Matthew Rising's presence in this community give you pause?"

"Do you lock your doors at night?"

Wanting a better view of her, the crowd amassed in the street in front of me. Doing so funneled Ginger directly toward me, closing off my exit.

This was not good.

Scrambling, I hopped the curb, circled around the shaved ice trailer, and found that barricades had appeared out of thin air, closing off both the street and the sidewalk. I turned one-hundred-and-eighty degrees, eased down the curb, and ran directly into Ginger and her two cameramen. Our image appeared on the JumboTron at the base of the steps. She in all her glory and me in my dumb-looking but much concealing helmet. Concentrating on her surroundings and not the face inside the helmet, she asked, "Tell me, sir, are you afraid of Matthew Rising's presence in your community?"

I shook my head.

She chuckled and the cameramen inched closer. "You're not concerned about what he might do if given freedom in this town?"

Another shake.

Expressing her irritation that I'd not removed my helmet, incredulous that I was not in agreement with her riot-inciting speech, and wanting to prove for all the world to see that she would not back down from a man who stood nearly a foot taller, she—for the first time—attempted to peer through the plastic reflection on my visor, which was made all the worse by the two spotlights shining off the shoulders of her cameramen. Just inches from my face, she spouted, "Well, tell me, sir, what then do you want?"

I flipped up my visor, made eye contact, and said, "I want you to tell the truth."

As the color drained out of Ginger's speechless face, I eased off on the clutch and smiled as her producer clued into the fact that Ginger was completely tongue-tied and sent the show to commercial. Just before turning the corner, I glanced in my rearview and caught a glimpse of Ginger's stunned and ashen face. I'd caught her off guard. And she did not like it.

And I was pretty sure it'd never happen again.

CHAPTER TWENTY

For dinner, I sat on the porch and ate a can of tuna. Just before last light, I saw a small black shape, looked like a raccoon, walking timidly up the dirt road toward me. It would walk a few steps, sniff the air, then take a step, sniff, pause, and then repeat the process. It took it a long time to get close enough for me to make out that it was a small limping dog. As it neared the yard, it saw me on the porch and froze, nose in the air. I just kept eating my tuna. Driven by its stomach, it circled the mattress and stood some twenty feet from me. It was quite possibly the filthiest dog I'd ever seen, and I'm not sure which stunk worse, it or the mattress. When I stood, it jumped and ran back down the road into the safety of the woods. I grabbed my last can of tuna out of the pantry, pulled the top, dumped it onto a paper plate, and then walked out into the yard and set it on the grass where the dog could see me. Then I retreated to the porch. The dog circled upwind, his eyes up and keeping the plate between him and me. He reached the plate and quickly engulfed the tuna. Licking his lips, he looked at me as if to say, *That all you got?*

I laughed and spoke softly. "Sorry, pal. I'm cleaned out."

It was almost midnight, there was little moon, the pine needles made walking through the woods almost silent, and, even in the dark, I felt funny carrying the stuffed animal. If caught and arrested again, this would not help my case. When I reached the garden, I climbed the wall, let myself down, and walked back out onto the field Audrey had created. The fragrance greeted me. The scarecrow had been patched back together. More glue and duct tape and even some plastic wrap. Wood's gut had been reshaped and pruned. Everyone else seemed in their rightful place. I set the spider monkey on the shoulders of the scarecrow and turned to leave, but the nagging picture of Audrey crying stopped me. Beyond the garden lay the convent. I didn't know which cottage was hers, but if I peeped in enough windows and avoided any nighttime security they had, I could probably figure it out.

I didn't actually see the woman in the first cottage, but I saw her shadow and it was too large and round. The second was singing and not Audrey's voice. I thought the woman in the third cottage could have been Audrey, but when I drew close to the window her cat jumped up and looked at me. Audrey is not a cat person. Scratch number three. When I approached cottage number four, a series of motion lights lit up the side yards like a runway, sending me diving into a row of hedges. When the woman who lived there looked out to investigate, I realized she was too tall to be Audrey. Then something Dee said struck me. He said he'd been emptying trash cans and heard her crying. So I started looking for big trash cans needing drum liners.

Bingo.

The last cottage, maybe older and slightly smaller, sat apart from the other buildings. Lights inside showed someone inside walking room to room. I approached a window and, given that the curtain was halfway pulled, had a view of about half the room. Audrey walked out of one room and into the room into which I was looking. She passed across the room and out of my field of view. I could see the end of a bed and the bed shook once like maybe she'd sat briefly or set something on it. I squatted, crept to the other side of the window, and could see her sitting on the edge of the bed, reading the label on a pill bottle. Then she stood and returned back across the room. I squatted and followed her with my eyes.

She walked into the bathroom, where the mirror reflected the image of her turning on the shower and then walking back into the main room and standing in front of her closet.

Where she stripped naked.

Having not seen my wife in almost thirteen years, the sight shocked me. Not in a bad way. Rather the reverse. I've loved her from the moment we met in the training room, and I love her still. But she was no longer mine. The heart she'd once give me, she'd taken back. So while I sat there, spying on my wife, face flushed, a strange emotion crept over me.

Shame.

Like I was stealing something that wasn't mine. I turned and slid to my heels. The argument within myself was loud and incoherent and I'm not sure which side won, but as the voices raged, I crept back up, stretching my fingers up the brick and then pulling my eyes above the level of the sill in time to watch her walk back into the bathroom.

Wow, I love my wife.

While I tried to reinsert my jaw into its lower socket, she stepped into the shower and began washing her hair and shaving her legs. Feeling more and more like a Peeping Tom, I turned and sat on my heels until I heard the water cut off.

She toweled off, slid on an old pair of faded cotton pajamas, and climbed into bed. The pajamas looked familiar, but I shook my head. *Not possible.* Once in bed, she clicked on a small flat-screen TV and the video player below it. As the screen flashed and the blue screen changed to a rather grainy picture of an old football game, she clutched a pillow and tucked her knees and hands up under her chin.

At first the video didn't interest me, then I looked closer. It was me. It was us. High school. Senior year. At various times, she used the remote to fast-forward through plays, then slow-mo through others. She watched for an hour, then two. The games changed. High school switched to college, and Audrey stretched out on her side, watching my every move. The video included clips of interviews, sweaty pictures of me postgame talking about what we did right, where I needed to improve, etc. It showed my first Heisman win. My second. The night after we won our third national championship. Somewhere in here I realized I'd crept too close and fogged up the glass. I backed off and the steam dissipated.

When the video flashed again, I saw myself standing on the stage at the NFL draft. My name had just been called. Audrey was hugging me, crying. Guys were patting me on the back. Wood, the big teddy bear, was crying. Tears dripping off his nose. Another quick splice and the video switched to the ESPN news center. I was signing autographs with the audience, talking to a little boy, having my picture taken with him, and then my interview with Jim Kneels. Again, the video flashed and the screen rolled with clips of my arrest, my walking handcuffed out of the hotel room after twenty-four hours with Ginger, disgusted onlookers screaming obscenities. Clips of the story as it developed over the months preceding trial. People I'd never met debating over coffee on gleaming sets whether the fame suddenly went to my head or if I'd been like that all along and just finally got caught with my hand in the cookie jar. Then the trial. The witnesses. The claims. The grainy, shadowy video of someone that looked like me performing deviant acts. The jury deliberation. Finally, it concluded with the reading of the guilty verdict, and the judge's mandatory sentencing of me. The last scene showed me from behind, orange jumpsuit, my hands and feet shackled, walking through the double gates of concertina wire leading into Wiregrass Correctional. I was looking over my shoulder, my eyes searching the crowd.

I remember that moment—I was trying to find Audrey. Tell her I love her. But all I heard was the inaudible soul-emptying screams from the area of the parking lot where she'd collapsed.

It was nearly four a.m. when the video finished. She clicked off the TV, then the light, and the room went black.

I was about to turn and leave when I heard the first whimper. Then a muffled moan. Soon the dam broke and the wails came. To muffle her own cries, she buried her face in her pillow and emptied herself. This lasted a long time.

Finally, the light clicked on, and Audrey picked up the pill bottle she'd been holding when she first walked into the room. Her eyes were bloodshot and puffy. She twisted off the lid, poured one pill into her hand, sized it up, poured a second, and then quickly poured a third. Having swallowed all three, she clicked the TV back on and started the video over.

Ten minutes later, she passed out, and her limp body dropped the remote. A drunk sailor, she sprawled half on the bed and half off. Mouth open, one arm and leg dangling.

I sunk to my heels again, arguing with myself. Finally, damning the torpedoes, I skirted around the front of her cottage and tried the door, but it was locked. So I returned to my window and gave it a push. It budged.

I slid off my shoes, lifted myself up and through the window, and stood staring down on my unconscious wife. Needing to do something, I reached down, placed my arms beneath her legs and neck and lifted her onto her bed. The feel of her shaved legs, the smell of her skin, the muscles in her arms—I was not prepared for that. I lay her down, slid her legs beneath the sheets, wedged a small pillow between her legs, tucked the covers up around her arms, and then knelt next to her bed. I pushed her short hair behind her ears and only then noticed her pajamas.

Faded, tattered, worn thin, a hole here and there. They were mine. Had my initials on the collar. She'd bought them for me in New York, and I'd been wearing them the night after the draft when I woke at three a.m. for my workout. I had slid them off, pulled on my workout clothes, and stepped on the elevator. They were the last thing I touched before I left.

I sat there a long time. I traced her ear, the lines of her chin, the small of her neck. I wanted to kiss her, badly. Instead, I spoke the words I'd been wanting to tell her since I left the courtroom. "Audrey, I love you—with all of me."

I've done some tough things in my life, but one of the toughest was not crawling in that bed and wrapping my arms around my wife. The whisper kept me out, *She might be yours on paper, but her heart is not.*

I clicked off the TV and was reaching to turn out the light when the flash caught my eyes. I pulled aside the collar of her pajamas, and there, at the base of her neck, lay the dove.

Thinking back over the few interactions we'd had since I'd been out, I'd not noticed it, because each time she'd worn something like a sweatshirt or T-shirt that covered it. Tonight, I hadn't seen it when she was getting in and out of the shower because my eyes were elsewhere.

After all this time.

That's my Audrey. Still fighting. The presence of that dove around her neck meant that despite the storm that had tossed and raged around her, something in Audrey had clung to an anchor deep within.

I leaned in, pressed my lips to hers, and held there while her warmth melted me. I'd pressed my luck far enough, so I turned out the light and crept home as the sun was coming up over my shoulder.

CHAPTER TWENTY-ONE

When I reached the porch, that dog was sitting on the front step. His eyes and nose were trained on the trail that had taken me to school. When I appeared he stood and his tail wagged once. I knelt, held out my hand. He tucked his tail, lowered his head, and walked up close enough to let me scratch his ears.

He was nasty. Dirty. Scabbed. Covered in sores. Flies were swarming. He had either been beaten or hit by a car or both. Fleas were jumping all over him and his front left leg was infected and needed stitches. Lastly, thanks to what I saw squirming around inside the present he left me in the front yard—he also had worms.

"Pal, you fit in perfect around here."

As long as I rubbed his ears or scratched his tummy, he'd let me do pretty much anything I wanted. As I bathed him, and the dirt, grime, and mud washed off, it became apparent that he, whatever his name was or had been, was a Boston terrier with rather distinct tuxedo markings.

I was drying him off when Dee appeared for our workout. He said, "New friend?"

"Poor guy's had a rough go."

"He got a name?"

I shook my head. "Got any ideas?"

He pointed at the dog's chest. "Tux."

It fit. "A good name."

The only way I had to get him to the vet was the bike, so after our workout, I cranked it while Tux stood there looking at me as if I'd lost my mind. When I patted my lap, he walked in a circle, then stood waiting on me. I looked down, and he sat on his butt. I said, "Tux, how's this gonna work if you don't do what I tell you?" I patted my leg again. "Now, come on." He tilted his head sideways, stood, then gingerly climbed up on my leg keeping his back legs on the ground. I took that to mean that something hurt too badly to jump up there, so I lifted him gently. He planted his rear on my lap and rested his shaking forelegs on the gas tank. Wanting to make him feel safe, I wedged him between my arms so he could look out over the handlebars and then we eased out of the driveway. Once we got up to speed, he stood, seeming to like the wind in his face.

The vet was new to town, or at least new since I'd left, and I didn't know her. I hoped that meant she didn't know me and didn't follow football or the major news networks. I signed in and sat in a waiting room along with three other people who paid me little notice. That changed when the lady opened the door and said, "Matthew Rising?" When she did, all three heads popped up like they'd been shot out of canons. I whispered, "Excuse me," and carried Tux into the examination room.

The vet looked him over, stitched up his leg, gave him a shot of antibiotics into the infected area of his leg—which he didn't like—and then gave him two other shots to kill whatever might be squirming around inside him.

She asked, "Is he yours?"

"Found him yesterday. Today was the first time he let me pet him."

She scribbled a prescription and handed it to me. "Twice a day for a week." I folded it and put it in my pocket. She continued, "I think he's had a pretty rough go. He's malnourished. Very sick. Probably been beat or hit by a car. And I have to be honest and tell you that, even with all the drugs I just gave him, I'm not sure he'll make it. I also think he's in a good bit of pain, is suffering a lot. If that continues, you should consider…" She reached up and rubbed his ears. "Letting us put him to sleep."

Her tone of voice and the look on her face told me she was being kind, not uncaring. "How will I know?"

She shrugged. "If he starts sleeping more, doesn't move around much, appears to be getting stiff and doesn't let you touch him, you'll know he's in more pain than he can bear and he's started the slow, and in his case painful, process of dying."

For reasons I could not explain, that hurt me. I picked him up, cradling him. "Thanks."

She looked at me with an honest but caring look. "Sometimes we find them too late."

I held Tux in my arms. "Right now, I'm living on the singular hope that sometimes love heals things that seem impossible."

She smiled. "That it does. I'll hope with you. Let us know if we can help." She gently wrapped her fingers around his good leg and held it. "He's in good hands."

Obviously, she had no idea who I was, and I had no intention of correcting her. "Thanks."

I spent most of what little I had on designer dog food, some high-nutrition treats, a padded lamb's wool bed, and the prescription.

When I got him home, I fed him, gave him a treat, and showed him his bed, where he promptly curled up and went to sleep.

About that time, a horn started honking at what sounded like my gate. When it hadn't quit after ten minutes, I cranked the bike and idled down the road to where a man I didn't know stood leaning in to his Audi A8, pressing hard on the horn. Early twenties, he wore a baseball cap, khaki pants, oxford shirt, Rolex watch. I pulled up to the gate as he lifted his hand off the horn.

"Sir, can I help you?"

While the engine purred, he strolled around the car, carrying a bag. His shirt read ESPN. The smirk on his face made me pretty certain that I did not want whatever was in that bag. When he reached the fence that separated us, he tilted his cap back and seemed to chuckle. He did not look familiar.

He shook his head. "I can't believe it's you." Another half chuckle. "After all this time, I mean, it's really you."

I didn't respond.

Without warning, he tossed the bag over the fence. It climbed a few feet in the air and dropped onto the dirt at my feet. I never took my eyes off him. He nodded. "Go ahead. It won't hurt you." A final chuckle. "Least not nearly as much as me."

The brown bag had been stapled at the top. I knelt, hefted the bag, and then slowly pulled at the staples. I found a worn and hand-oiled NFL football inside.

I looked up but said nothing. He responded with, "You don't remember me, do you?"

Still I said nothing.

He adjusted the hat on his head. "Funny. I can't forget you." He paused, scratched his chin, then stepped up to the fence and hung his hands on the chain link. "It took me years to see this, but... you're the worst kind of human being."

I turned the ball in my hands. It read, *Mac, Blessings on your life and dreams. Matthew #8.*

The pieces fell together and I remembered. "You're that kid from the ESPN audience after the draft."

"And you're the pathetic lying fraud who betrayed us all."

I held the ball in my hands as he spat through the fence, turned, stepped into his car, and drove away.

I watched as his car disappeared. I turned the ball in my hands. At one time, it had seen a lot of use. When I looked up, red tail lights had been replaced by light-blue headlights. The expensive kind.

The windows were tinted too dark to see inside but when the Bentley pulled up to the gate, I could see a left hand. One large ring stood out. And there's only one type of ring that is that big and that gaudy.

A Super Bowl Champion ring.

The car stopped, and Roddy stepped out. Designer shades, designer watch, designer suit, designer shoes. He looked like a million dollars, and what he was wearing probably cost fifty thousand. He pulled off his glasses, walked to the fence, and smiled. A large diamond stud in his left ear. A single nod. "Rocket."

I shook my head. "I wondered when they'd send you."

He weighed his head side to side. "Don't shoot the messenger. I was looking for an excuse to get down here anyway."

I pulled open the gate, and he hugged me. After twelve years in the league, ten Pro Bowls, two Super Bowl MVPs, three World Champion rings, and a slew of endorsements to his name, he was fit and strong as ever. He said, "You got a few minutes?"

I opened the gate wider, and he drove that quarter-of-a-million-dollar car with a five-hundred-dollar detail onto my dusty road. I led him to the house, where we sat on the front porch and he stared at the disheveled mess around my cabin, and the charred remains of the mattress in the front yard. "Visitors?"

"Just some folks expressing their opinion."

He put his hand on my shoulder. "I saw the prison video." He shook his head. "It impressed a lot of people."

"I heard."

"They asked me to convince you to come out of retirement."

I squinted. "That's an interesting way to put it."

He laughed and opened the brown bag. Pulling out the ball, he read the signature. "What's the story with this?"

"It's complicated."

He stood, mounted a GoPro camera on his window, and tossed me the ball, backing up down the dirt road. "Come on. I know you're old and rusty, but I thought I'd do you a favor and make you feel like the man you once were."

The GoPro sat some thirty-plus yards from me. Maybe closer to forty. "That thing on?"

He smiled. "HD."

I tossed it back, weak, off course, and with too much arc. He raised an eyebrow and returned it to me. "Prison do that to you?"

I caught it and wobbled a duck back in his general direction. He flung it back at me, hard and tight spiraled. "You need me to remind you?"

I shook my head. "No. I can remember just fine."

He smiled and slid his glasses onto the end of his nose. "Then throw the ball."

I did as he asked. The ball left my hand, whistled through the air, and dissected the GoPro from its mount on the window. The camera went one direction, the mount the other. Roddy nodded in approval, retrieved the ball, and pitched it back. I caught it, set my feet, and shot a bullet at his head. He just had time to get his hands up before the pigskin split his part. He paused, smiled wider, and tossed it back. This continued a few minutes. After a dozen or so throws, he retrieved a pair of gloves from his car and mimicked shooting a syringe into his arm. "You sure they didn't feed you some juice in that prison?"

"Orange juice on Monday and Wednesday. Cranberry Tuesday

and Thursday. Fruit punch on Friday, Saturday, and Sunday. Room-temp water anytime you want it."

Having seen and felt enough, he trotted to me, handed me the ball, and then spread out wide to my left, the dirt road stretching out in front of us. He raised an eyebrow and waited.

I smiled. "You okay running in those shoes? I don't want you to pull a hammy and sue me when the team releases you."

"I can handle whatever you dish out."

"Red muscle thirty-two, sticky free china."

He chuckled and followed it with a slow nod. "Don't bite off more than you can chew."

"And don't get stuffed at the line."

He laughed louder and nodded. I snapped the ball and he took off. I loved watching Roddy run. Poetry in motion. And after a decade in the pros, he could fly. I watched him float, thirty, forty, fifty. When he hit fifty-five yards, I released the ball and he caught it in stride seventy-plus yards down the road. He trotted back, breathing slightly, and handed me the ball.

We returned to the porch, where I offered him a warm ginger ale that he accepted. We sat in the quiet a few minutes, neither talking nor feeling the need to. When he did speak, it was purposeful. He sipped from his soda can. "I know you've got a few things stacked against you, but they'd like you to consider trying out. Quietly. No press. Just you and me. Asked me to lean on you."

I stared down into my glass. "Roddy—" I shook my head.

He stood, pulled on his suit coat, and slid his glasses back over his eyes. The diamond glistened, matching his pearly white teeth. He straightened his coat, fixed his tie. When I reached out my hand, he accepted it and held it. He said, "I don't pretend to know what happened. If it's true—" He paused. Shook his head. "But I've played twelve years. Been with three teams and caught passes from maybe a dozen guys who stood behind center. None of them have what you—" He eyed the road. "Still got." He let go, walked to his car, collected the pieces of the GoPro, and then paused, holding onto the door. He wanted to say something else, but when it got to the tip of his tongue, he thought better of it and stepped into his car.

He shut the door, and the dust swirled behind him as he drove slowly out the drive. I whispered, "It means more than you know."

CHAPTER TWENTY-TWO

Tux slept for the better part of a week and into the second. Morning and evening, I worked with Dee, trying to straighten out his arm. Because Dee's desire to please his coach, win his approval, ran deep, so did the wound. Hence, progress on his arm was slow. I'm not knocking his heart; all players want to please their coach. Dee's case was different because he never knew his dad, and Coach Demon, like it or not, filled an empty place in Dee's heart. All coaches do. Problem was, he was filling it with violent tirades, poor coaching, and betrayal. And based on what I could gather, Dee would experience more betrayal before this season was over.

During the day, I laid low and kept clear of public places. And each night, I crept back across the half mile that separated us, hunkered below the window, and waited until I heard the remote control fall onto the floor. I lingered longer as Audrey lived out her nights in worn-out reruns and a self-induced coma. Sitting on the floor next to her bed, I'd slip my hand beneath hers, marveling at the calluses earned in her garden. I'd brush the hair behind her

217

ears, wanting desperately to trace the lines of her figure but feeling guilty at the thought. In that conflicted place I sat, bathing in the sight and smell and sound of my wife. And, yes, I worried a good bit about the unknown effects of the drugs on her life and how long she'd been taking them. Watching her shower proved she'd lost at least ten pounds since I'd been gone. Maybe more. And she never really had it to lose. In the dark, listening to her breathe, "life without parole" took on new meaning. Each night, the glue that held me to the floor grew stronger.

One Thursday night around ten p.m., I looked through Audrey's window to find her room empty. Scratching my head, I thought I heard laughter. A strange sound rising from the pious reverence of a convent when so many haven't spoken in years. What's more, the laughter was familiar. I hadn't heard it in a long time, but there was no mistake.

I climbed the wall and followed my ears, circling around to a large, well-lit building in the center. Well-lit wasn't a good place for me, so I shimmied off the wall and onto the roof of the building where the skylights had been opened.

I crawled on my belly, poking my eyes and nose over the edge of the skylight, staring down on the circus below. Audrey sat, legs crossed, on the carpet, looking through reading glasses at Dee, who was standing in front of her. Scattered around her were several multiple-choice tests where the bubbles had been filled in. A large table off to one side, a couch behind her, and a very large flat-screen TV hung on the wall. Reel-to-reel and VHS films filled one wall of shelves. The handwriting on the covers and spine was mine. *So that's where they went.* On the table behind them sat a messy stack of papers and one very thick book simply entitled, *SAT.*

The TV had been turned on, and frozen on the screen stood me. My senior year of high school, I'd been made the Joker of the Homecoming Court. In good humor, the school had revolted against me and said I'd already won enough awards, so I had been appointed court jester. It was a lot of fun. The night before homecoming, I'd performed a one-man skit, poking fun at myself. I'd slicked my hair over, wore a whistle on a cord around my neck, pocket protector, white tape around the nosepiece of my glasses, shorts hiked up, socks rolled up, and high-top sneakers. I was the epitome of a cliché nerd. My voice and stage presence was Patton. My body posture was Carol Burnett—meaning I stuck my butt a foot out over my heels at all times. And my voice was as close as I could get to the sheriff in *Cool Hand Luke* in his famous phrase, "What we have here is a failure to communicate." I had morphed myself into "Professor P.E.," and I was giving the gym class an exercise in how to throw the football. In my best Tim Conway impression, I was stumbling over myself, couldn't throw a spiral to save my life, rattling off about kinetic chain...it was marvelous fun. The school gave me a standing ovation. I think they enjoyed watching me let my hair down for once. The TV had been paused as I was demonstrating the catapult.

Below me, Dee stood center stage. Football in hand, a whistle around his neck, a pair of thick, black-rimmed glasses with a piece of white tape wrapped around the nosepiece, a pocket protector containing an assortment of pens had been taped to his chest, his shorts were hiked up to his armpits, and his socks were stretched to the tops of his knees. He had contorted his voice to sound older and, in all honesty, more constipated. His forehead was wrinkled and his hand motions looked oddly familiar. Lastly, his hips and butt had been shoved out. His entire body was one giant caricature. Of me. I listened and caught him in midsentence. "So, what we have here, young man, is a failure to commune-cate." He spun the football and rolled the whistle around his mouth. His accent was spot-on, and his imitation of the sheriff was better than mine. "This is a football, made of Grade A pigskin. It's not an egg. You didn't lay it. You throw it. Like this." More Carol Burnett. "See here—you are a giant catapult. Kinetic energy starts in your feet, travels up your shin bone into your thigh bone—"

Audrey was holding out one hand like a stop sign and laughing so hard she couldn't breathe.

He continued. "Into your belly bone. Which is in here." He made a circle around his stomach. "It swirls around in there before shimmying up your funny bone, your backbone, on into your neck bone and jawbone, spinning around your eye bone, and finally dribbling out your shoulder and finger bone. Now you want to hold the ball—" He mimicked a terrible grip and an awful-looking throw where the ball fell out of his hand and rolled around the floor. He kicked it every time he tried to pick it up. All the while, his voice had me pegged to a T.

In between breaths, Audrey managed, "Stop! I'm about to pee in my pants."

Dee ran both hands along the inside band of his shorts, lifted his feet like both heels were stuck in gum, and continued his impersonation.

He was fantastic.

With his left hand, Dee hit resume with the remote and we all three watched me, Professor P.E., hold class almost seventeen years ago.

In the video, I invited my sidekick, Miss Cleaning Lady, onto the stage to help demonstrate. Audrey walked up on stage, carrying a mop and wearing my jersey and a pink skirt in which the butt had been stuffed with an enormous pillow. She picked up a bag of about ten footballs and began throwing tight spirals out into the audience. The place went crazy. In the background, I attempted to critique an otherwise perfect throw, telling her, "No, honey, that's not, that's not the way you…" The audience was eating out of her hand. In homage to George C. Scott and his famous speech at the beginning of the movie *Patton*, I spun my whistle, marching left and right on the stage and spoke into the microphone as she continued throwing balls into the balcony. "Now, in tomorrow's game . . . we're not having any of this nonsense about holding our position. We're not holding anything. Let the Hun do that." I began thrusting my fist like a car engine. "We will be advancing our position continually . . ." The crowd loved it. Between her throws and my best attempt at Patton, we'd brought them to their feet.

With her bag empty, Miss Cleaning Lady slung it over her shoulder, curtsied for the audience, and kissed Professor P.E. on the cheek. "Thanks, Professor." Finally, she hooked her arm in mine and we bowed for the crowd.

Dee cut the video. Audrey sat up, wiped her eyes, and just sat there shaking her head, a smile on her face. She spoke both to Dee and herself. "That seems like another lifetime."

Dee began adjusting his nerd attire back to normal and commented, "You two made a pretty good team."

Several seconds passed before she responded. "Yes, we did."

They packed up, turned out the light, and the sound of their steps and Dee's continual mimicking of me faded away down the hall, leaving me on the roof staring up at the stars, wrapped in the sound of my wife's laughter.

And while part of me was jealous of their time together, the other part marveled at a man-sized kid named Dalton Rogers and the role he had played and continued to play in Audrey's life. Lying there, I realized that Dee had done and was doing what I could not.

He made my wife laugh.

And I loved him for it.

CHAPTER TWENTY-THREE

Mid-July. Dee arrived unannounced in my drive. I stepped off the porch and walked up to the van where he sat with the windows down and engine running. He was still wearing his apron with his name on the front and his pin, which read, THREE YEARS OF SERVICE. A sweat towel was draped over his shoulder, as the AC in the van was evidently not cooling too well.

"Thought you were working," I said.

"I am." He thumbed over his shoulder. The back of the van was packed floor to ceiling with canned and boxed goods and sodas and other nonperishables. "Every few weeks, we haul the expired stuff to the food bank in Valdosta. I'm headed there now." He spoke without looking at me. "I was just wondering if maybe... you wanted to maybe help me unload some of it—" He wiped his forehead. "Here."

It took me a second to realize that Dee was offering me food. "I can't—"

He raised a hand. "State law requires us to empty the shelves of expired food. If we do not give it away, I am required by that same law to deposit everything in the back of this van in a Dumpster."

"Dee, you should give that to folks who really need it."

He wiped his head again and kept staring out the windshield. "In the six weeks we've been working out, I've lost fat yet gained twelve pounds. All my pants are tight in the legs, big in the waist, and I feel like I'm wearing muscle tees. We're burning seven, maybe eight thousand calories a day, and you're working harder than me 'cause you're doing everything I'm doing faster, harder, and you're talking to me the entire time. I don't know what your weight was when we started, but—" This time he looked at me. "I know you've lost more than I've gained."

He was right. Groceries were scarce. I was withering away. Between working out with him and spending the nights with Audrey, I was burning the candle at both ends and putting back only a portion of the calories I was spending. I nodded. "You give me your word that this won't get you in trouble."

A nod. "I give you my word."

We carried five cases of food into my cabin. And he'd been smart about it, too. He didn't bring me Twinkies and cheese puffs. I unloaded cans of tuna and salmon and one entire case of nothing but steaks, maybe fifty in total, that had expired yesterday. He pointed, "Freeze them. They'll last." Another case included chicken and pork, pasta, rice. It was a king's buffet waiting to be cooked. My mouth was salivating with every box we unloaded. It also included soaps, shampoo, and a gallon each of dish and laundry detergent.

He checked his watch and started jogging to the van. "I better get. See you tonight?"

I tossed him a ball, which he caught in front of him, holding it there, his big hand wrapping around the laces. "How is it that you arrived at my house without that in your hand?"

He smiled and wiped his forehead. "So that's how it's gonna be, huh?"

"You know the rules. You better bring your A-game tonight. You'll need it."

He put his foot on the brake and dropped the stick in drive. "Old man—" He smiled, shook his head, and took his foot off the break.

"Dee?"

He turned to look at me.

"Thank you. Really."

After he'd gone, I walked inside and cooked two steaks in a pan on the stove. One and a half for me, and a half for Tux. Then I cooked two more. I ate for nearly an hour until I was too stuffed to stand up. Then I curled up on my blanket on the floor and slept with Tux tucked under my arm. It was the best sleep I'd had in a long, long time.

When I woke, it was dark. The clock read 9:47. I stumbled to the fridge and chugged from a water bottle. I washed my face in the sink and only then saw the note lying on the floor.

> Coach, I knocked and let myself in. Found you on the floor. Judging by the mess in the kitchen and the smell coming out of you, ;-), it looks like you got into the steak and potatoes so I let you sleep. You can take it out on me tomorrow morning. See you bright and early.
> P.S. This place is a mess. You should clean it up.

The note was resting beneath a bottle of Pine-Sol cleaner.

I was mad at myself for sleeping through our workout, but he was right. Maybe my body was trying to tell me something. For the first time in weeks, I felt rested. And not hungry.

*   *   *

I swung open the front door and there, hanging in front of me, was the biggest moon I'd ever seen. Call it a harvest moon, call it what you like, it was ginormous. The light outside was that beautiful glowing white. I didn't want to waste it, so I threw on some clothes and climbed up the Bucket. I cracked open a can of boiled peanuts and was digging my fingers around the bottom when a figure walked out on the football field below me.

He carried a bag of balls and began throwing into a net in the far end zone. Dee had improved. Anybody could see that. But while he had improved, there was something different tonight in his demeanor. His body language was muted. Heavy. Reserved. He was out there, going through the motions, but only about eighty percent. After a dozen or so throws, he gathered up the balls and then threw them again. Halfway through the third round, he stopped, walked in a circle, dropped the ball, then sat and stared out across the end zone and stands. I could see the weight on his shoulders from where I was sitting.

Moments later, I walked out onto the grass and quietly made my way to the fifty yard line. "You all right?"

My voice startled him. He jumped up but when he saw me, he nodded and then hid his face. His expression was oozing frustration and his shoulders were bubbling anger. He picked up a ball and flung it at the net.

"Dee?"

He wiped his nose on his shirt sleeve. "I was just trying to—" He pointed at the net.

I had a feeling I knew what this was about. Not all of it, but some. Every quarterback goes through a crisis of confidence at some point. Least, I'd never met one who hadn't. Myself included. I gently turned his chin, sizing up the look on his face without embarrassing him.

"Something bugging you?"

He nodded but didn't look at me. He wiped his eyes.

Dee was afraid of something. He was improving and he knew it. He also knew that the weeks to camp were winding down, and that with the possibility of success came the very real possibility of failure. He struggled to find the words. I knew where this was going. I'd been there. "Go ahead. Out loud. Voice it."

"What if I'm afraid?"

"Of?"

"Not being good enough."

"What's that called?"

He paused. Then whispered, "Failure."

"Go ahead. Louder. Spit it out."

He cleared his throat. "Failure."

"There. That wasn't so hard, was it?"

He shook his head.

"A valid emotion." I paused. "First things first—you want to play quarterback?"

He nodded.

"You sure? Nobody's making you. This is your chance to decide. You *can* walk away and be no less the man. We'll still be friends."

He looked at me and thought about it.

I shrugged. "Don't be fooled, failure is one of two possibilities. You could go to camp, forget everything I ever taught you, revert to your old ways, let that crazy coach of yours back in your head, and start throwing with that"—I mimicked his old throwing motion—"hitch."

He laughed. "Was it that bad?"

"Worse." I continued, "Let's be real honest. Failing, falling flat on your face, is possible. But—" I poked him in the shoulder. "So is succeeding beyond your wildest dreams." I laughed. "I want to let you in on a secret. You have more ability at your age than I did." He looked at me surprised. "That's right. Sitting here right now, you're better than I was at your age. Difference is this—when I was five or six, my dad brought me out here, to this very field, and played with me. In our minds, we filled the stands, put a voice over the loudspeakers, filled the air with whistles and yellow flags and coaches calling plays. We filled this place with laughter and dreams and the impossible. And we played that game until the sweat ran down our faces and mixed with the laughter. Out here, I fell in love with a game and learned how to play out of my dreams, and failure never really played into that. I wasn't trying to measure up. I was trying to become like someone else. Your problem is you've spent much of your life watching my film, and so you're comparing yourself to me. Don't do that. I've heard other coaches, some of mine included, talk about playing with a chip on your shoulder. Playing angry. *'It's a violent game, better fight violence with violence.'*" I nodded. "They're right about it being violent, but if they're honest, they play out of anger and hatred because they're afraid they won't measure up as a man. Won't be as good as so-and-so. They're trying desperately to answer the question, 'Do I have what it takes?' And I'm here to tell you that you've got it in spades." I spun the ball in my hands. "If I teach you anything, if I can have any influence on you at all, let it be this one thing." I waved my hand across the field. "This is a field where boys and men play. It's a game. Maybe the greatest game, but it's still a game. I guess to an alien, or somebody from another country, it looks like twenty-two large men chasing a piece of pigskin and stretching tight elastic pants in the process." He laughed and wiped his nose again. I patted the ground with my fist. "This should be fun. If it's not, if it turns into a chore or a burden, let's go do something else, 'cause it's too much work otherwise."

He laughed and muttered, "I heard that's right."

"Out here, I learned to love something and someone other than myself. You asked me to teach you the game of football this summer. Teach you how to be a better QB. But"—I shook my head—"other than your throwing motion, I don't think you really need me for that. But one thing I had that you don't is perspective. I love the game for the game itself. You love the game for what it might say about you."

He nodded. "Yes."

"Dee." He turned to face me. "You're good enough to play at most any school. That's not the question here, and you'll learn that soon enough. If you just want skills improvement, a lot of guys can do that. Some far better than I. But coaching your head and coaching your heart are two very different things." I spun a ball in the air. "If you want to succeed out here, you've got to risk failure." I waved my hands across the stands in the distance. "A lot of guys I played with equated losing with failure. And when we lost, they melted down. Chernobyl. But losing and failure are not one in the same." I paused. "Play this game long enough, and you will lose. Nobody's undefeated." I pointed up at the scoreboard. "When I was in junior high, Dad brought me out here after a Friday night game. The stands were empty. Field still painted. Scoreboard lit up. Sidelines littered with paper cups, mounds of melting ice, and spent athletic tape. He brought me out here beneath the lights. We ran around. Laughing. Throwing. Audibles. The same game we always played. But lately I'd been talking more about the scoreboard, of winners and losers, and what the board read at the end of the game. He'd been listening. So as I'm calling plays—standing right here on this very line—and my eyes are switching back and forth between him and that board of lights, he calls a time-out, walks over to the board, flips the power switch, and it goes black as night. Then he walks back to me and lifts my chin. I'm standing there wondering what in the world he's just done, thinking to myself, *What good is it if we can't see the score?* I can still see the smile spread across his face. He leaned in and whispered, 'Every time you step foot on this field or any other, you've got a fifty-fifty shot at losing or winning. So get over it. They're just numbers, and'—he pointed at the scoreboard then poked me gently in the chest—'and they are not the measure of your value.'"

Dee stared up at me. "I'd like to have met him."

"He'd have liked you. A lot. You're his kind of quarterback."

"What kind is that?"

"Explosive." I smiled. "With a good bit of style thrown in for good measure."

I stood up. "Come here."

He followed.

I walked him to the sideline and stepped across it. Outside the field of play. I pointed down. "You see that?"

"Yeah."

"What's it called?"

"Is this a trick question?"

I laughed. "No."

"Sideline."

"What's it do?"

"Creates a field of play."

I shook my head. "It's what separates us from all those folks behind us. This right here…" I stepped on the paint. "This is where we lay down all our fears. So many poor jokers are sitting around, remote in hand, afraid to buckle a chin strap, worried they might not measure up. About what might go wrong. Don't buy into the lie that says you don't count if you don't win. You count. You matter. Always have."

"That sounds like Mama Audrey."

"Yeah, well…she said it to me one time."

He wanted to ask me a question but hesitated. Something about it stopped him.

"Go ahead. Get it off your chest."

"I never knew either of my folks. All I know is that the woman who gave birth to me dropped me off and never looked back."

There it was. Right there. The wound we'd been dancing around all summer had bubbled up from its hiding place. The good news was that he trusted me enough to share it with me. To let me peek behind the curtain. The bad news was that it was soul-deep and had been plaguing him his whole life.

I put my arm around him. "For the record, I think she was wrong, but I don't know what she was facing. Don't know what she was up against. Or your dad. I just know they did. And selfishly, I'm glad they did."

"What? Why?"

"Because for twelve years, I've not been able to make my wife laugh. You have."

He nodded.

I locked my arm in his, standing shoulder to shoulder. "Cross this line with me. Be unlike all those cynical armchair wannabes behind you. Buckle up your chin strap and risk failure. What's the worst that can happen?" I inched my toes closer to the line.

He looked at me, surprised. "You've been afraid?"

"Sure. You've seen my videos. I wasn't playing pee-wee. Some of those guys are huge."

He laughed. "I thought you weren't afraid of anything."

I shook my head. "You need to quit watching *SportsCenter*."

He tucked the ball under his arm and broad-jumped way out across the line. From the other side, he turned, smiling.

I trotted across to the fifty and held the ball out under my imaginary center. *"Rocky top, blue seven Chevy wicked zulu. Hut-hut-hut."*

It was the most fun I'd had on a football field in a long time, and never once did he glance at the scoreboard.

After thirty minutes or so, we collapsed on the fifty, drenched, covered in grass and surrounded by sweaty footballs. He lay on the ground looking up at the moon directly overhead. It was daylight-bright outside.

He spoke to me without looking at me. He spoke quietly. "Thank you."

"Dee, play this game because you love it." I tapped his heart. "Play out of here." I placed my hand on his head. "Not here."

We stuffed all the balls back into his bag, and he began walking back to his dorm. He turned, "Rocket?"

It was the first time he'd ever called me that. Nicknames are a big deal among football players, and I'd been giving his a good bit of thought. I thought I'd found one that fit. "Clark?"

He looked confused. He shook his head. "What?"

"Clark. Clark Kent."

"Who's he?"

"Don't you ever watch the movies?"

"Yeah, movies in this decade."

"Boy, you need a keeper. You know, red cape, flies around the Earth."

He smiled. "Oh, yeah, that Clark."

He smiled. He liked the nickname. "Tomorrow is my birthday, and I was wondering if maybe you'd let me buy you some lunch. I can clock out at noon. I know a place where no one will know you. Or care."

"I'll be there."

I watched him disappear through the tunnel, marveling at the changes. The promise. And the effect all that had on my hope. Only then did I see the lone figure leaning against the far exit in the stands. She stood in the shadows. Arms crossed. Face hidden. Watching but disconnected.

I waved, but Audrey did not wave back. She turned, showing me her back, and disappeared.

CHAPTER TWENTY-FOUR

My clothes were starting to sour, and given my midday nap I wasn't too tired so I stuffed a pillowcase with dirty laundry and rode to town. The twenty-four-hour Laundromat was open. One florescent light flickered. I rode by slowly and, to my relief, it was empty.

I dumped all my clothes in one washer, loaded it with quarters, and sat while it began its cycle. The dryer read "seven minutes remaining," when a lady and two kids pulled up and walked in. I thought to myself, *What kind of mother brings her kids to the Laundromat at eleven p.m.?*

Evidently, the working kind.

She was obviously a waitress or something as she wore a shirt with her name on it and had a pocket full of what looked like tip money when she went to the machine to make change. I pulled up the hood of my sweatshirt, checked my pants leg, and sat staring at their reflection in the glass door of my dryer. She unloaded a little girl, maybe four, and a little boy of about nine. Maybe ten. The girl wore a dress, pigtails, flip-flops, painted toenails. The boy wore a number 12 jersey and carried a small rubber football. She spoke quickly to him, "Daniel, put that down long enough to help me unload!" He set the ball down and helped her unload and drag three laundry baskets of clothes out of the back of the car. The little girl sat on a chair coloring in a book while the boy sat down in front of the TV on the wall. He grabbed the remote, punched a button from memory, and ESPN flashed onto the screen. *SportsCenter* was just starting. He crossed his legs, tossed the ball, and sat glued to the picture. The mother loaded five machines and then attempted to buy detergent.

After she'd inserted her money and pulled the lever, and then pulled it again, she cussed, and then hit the machine. "No, please don't do that." The single-use box of detergent had fallen and lodged against the glass, preventing her from getting the one she'd bought and from buying any more. "Oh come on!" She banged the glass harder with her fist. "You're killing me." She then tilted the machine, trying to dislodge the box. No luck. Finally, she unloaded the machines, throwing the wad of clothes back into each of the baskets, picked up her daughter, told her son to "Come on," and began walking toward the door, dragging one basket behind her. Given the gallon I had sitting beneath my chair, I stood and offered it. "Ma'am, I'm not trying to be nosy, but I've got more than I can use—if you're needing detergent."

The look on her face told me she did not trust me, nor did she trust men like me, nor men in general, which probably explained why she was doing laundry at this time of night. But she needed clean clothes, and my detergent was her answer. She attempted a smile, set down her daughter, and palmed the hair out of her face. "You sure it's no trouble?"

"I'm sure."

She gathered her composure. "But only if you let me pay you for it. With money."

Sometimes, it's tough living in a world where we wound each other so deeply. Maybe I was growing more raw. Maybe things were getting to me. Maybe the reality of my life was starting to set in. Maybe my own anger was bubbling back up. I wanted to grab her, hug her, tell her life isn't supposed to be this way. That things will get better. That I was sorry for whatever had brought her here. And for whoever had done it.

I set the detergent on the table in front of her. "If you insist, but I'll never use it all. You're welcome to whatever you need."

She approached the table much like Tux the first time he'd walked into my yard. She nodded, said "Thank you," and began filling the machines. She then muffled something to her son and sent him over with five dollars.

He held out his hand. "Mister?"

I took the money from his hand. "Thank you."

He nodded and returned to *SportsCenter*, the man of the house.

After she got her kids settled and machines running, she walked over and pointed at a chair. "May I?"

I scooted over.

She sat and extended her hand. "Chelsey." I shook her hand. She attempted a smile. "Sorry for being short. Been a long day."

On the screen, the announcer said, "And in NFL news today—" Roddy's picture flashed onto the screen. "A certain Hall-of-Famer, the great Roderick Penzell, spent some time this week throwing with disgraced quarterback Matthew Rising." I turned away and tuned it out. "No worries." I glanced over my shoulder. "Got your hands full."

Oblivious to the TV or my picture that filled the screen, she let out a deep breath and something sweet spread across her composure. "Yeah. If my mom had taken me here this time of night, I'd have been sprawled on the floor, kicking, screaming, and letting her know what I thought about it."

I laughed. "Me too."

"They're good kids."

Behind me, Roddy spoke with reporters. The camera angle accentuated his diamond stud and chiseled jaw. "Yes, I spent time today throwing with the Rocket."

My machine finished, and I began quickly folding my clothes and stuffing them in the plastic bag. She probed. "You new around here?"

I considered lying. "Actually, I grew up here. Just...just moved back."

She nodded. "Where'd you go to school?"

The interviewer pressed Roddy, "Did he express any interest in playing in the NFL?"

I tried to fold loudly to drown out Roddy. "St. Bernard's."

"Oh." She smiled. "Rich kid."

Roddy responded, "He was pretty clear that he had no intention of trying to play professional football."

I waved across the interior of the Laundromat and my plastic laundry bag. "Yep. Silver spoon."

She laughed. It was a beautiful and easy laugh, and I imagined she'd had to use it a lot to survive this far in life. Having packed my bag, I dropped a T-shirt, and when I knelt to pick it up, I noticed she glanced at my ankle. Above me, the interviewer continued to question Roddy. It was also at this point that I noticed the young boy staring at me. "Roddy, how'd he throw?"

All three of us watched the screen. The only person in the room not trained on me was Cinderella, who was quietly engrossed in her coloring book. Roddy smiled that ten-million-dollar smile. "He threw well."

Reporters fired multiple questions at Roddy about my arm strength, release, speed, velocity, my perceived level of fitness. One reporter simply asked, "Does he still have it?"

Roddy paused. Thoughtful. Contemplative. Finally, he looked squarely into the camera. "Yes. Maybe more."

The interviewer chuckled, sounded doubtful, and pressed the microphone closer to Roddy's face. "Come on, Rod, we know you two are friends and you caught his last pass. You'd like to help him now that he's out, but tell the truth."

Roddy stepped forward, staring directly at the reporter. "If he did what he was convicted of doing, he is no friend of mine. He knows that, and I've told him so. But—" He turned back to the camera. "Regarding his ability, I've played over a decade as a professional football player. He was, and based on what I saw today, still is the best I've ever played with or against. Period."

Roddy flicked the microphone out of his face and walked off. The announcer regained his composure and said, "There you have it. Matthew Rising, former Heisman trophy winner, first round draft pick, and convicted felon, who just finished serving twelve years of a twenty-year sentence, recently paroled, spent time throwing today with All-Pro receiver Roderick..."

The woman turned to me, and her face turned white. Quickly, she turned to her daughter and held out her hand. "Sweetie, come here."

"But, Mama, I'm—"

She snapped her fingers. "Get over here right now."

"But—" The woman stood and scooped Cinderella off her feet, hanging her on one hip.

Time to go. I slung my bag over my shoulder and walked out. I buckled my helmet, started the bike, and was easing off on the clutch when the boy walked out. The football was tucked under his arm. He was holding a ball-point pen and a page torn from his sister's coloring book. "Mister?"

I turned off the bike. The mother stood at the door, ready to pounce, the daughter shielded behind her. The look on her face was not one of approval.

I took off the helmet. "Yes, son."

He extended the paper. "Did you really win the Heisman?"

I glanced at the mom, who was shaking her head. Then back at the boy. The mother took a step closer, then stopped. I looked down at the boy. "No, son. I didn't."

He pointed at the screen. "But—"

"We just look alike. That's all."

The mother exhaled and tilted her head back slightly. The boy said, "Oh. Okay."

He turned to go.

My voice stopped him. "But—" The mother's laser-beam focus returned to me. "That man was once a kid just like you. With a ball beneath his arm. He was probably about your—" I sized him up. "How old are you?"

"Ten."

"Well, I think you're maybe a bit bigger than he was. You keep growing and you could make one pretty good quarterback."

He smiled, tossed the ball, and said, "I know. That's what my mama says."

I looked at the mother, then back at the boy. "Well, you listen to her. She may be right."

When I got three blocks down the street, I had to stop. Couldn't see.

CHAPTER TWENTY-FIVE

I walked into my cabin and stood in the shower a long time, letting the hot water rain down my neck. I stepped out and was toweling off my hair when I heard, "Hello, Matthew." The hair stood up on the back of my neck. I pulled the towel off my head and found Ginger standing in the corner.

This was not unexpected.

She was wearing a long trench coat. High heels. Makeup. Life had been kind to her, as had her plastic surgeon, and to say she was beautiful and attractive would have been an understatement. "Hi." She sauntered around me while not necessarily toward me. She did this while unbuckling her trench coat.

I wrapped my towel around me and felt my fists tighten. She circled closer, tracing my shoulders with her index finger. When she got in front of me, she walked off a step or two, her back to me, then turned, facing me and slowly let the coat slide off her shoulders, hips, and calves.

I guess I don't need to paint you a picture.

Her voice dripped. "Miss me?"

I didn't want her in my cabin. Didn't want her within three states of me, but I did want to know one thing and I'd been wanting to know it a long time. I tried not to look where she was wanting me to look. Admittedly, I'd been in prison a long time. She continued circling. I'd seen sharks do the same thing on TV. She stood behind me when I spoke, "Why do you hate me?"

She smiled and traced the lines of my chin with her finger, mindful of how her hair, her body, barely brushed against mine. Her voice was sultry. Inviting. "It didn't start that way."

"What then?"

She moved back. "You had something I wanted."

"What?"

She stopped in front of me, looking up. Aware of how the light above showered her. Her hand rested on my dripping chest. "You." She patted my butt and started to circle again. "Your charisma. Others' allegiance." She stopped, her eyes locked on mine. "The power you wielded."

It didn't take a dummy to see she was playing me. She'd orchestrated this, and my history with Ginger told me we were just getting warmed up. I didn't trust her as far as I could throw her, so I kept an eye on her. But that was also problematic in that totally naked Ginger was, well, totally naked. She was also making me dizzy so I stepped off to the side, forcing her to swim in another direction. "Ginger, did it ever occur to you that maybe I was just a kid playing a game? And I happened to love a girl other than you."

She nodded matter-of-factly. "Yes."

"Then why not sink your teeth in someone else and leave me alone."

"Because I blamed you." Half a smile. "Still do."

"For what?"

She paused, weighing her words. "Things."

"Does the irony of your life ever bother you?"

"Irony?"

My internal radar sounded like a gong going off in my head. I had two competing emotions. One half wanted to turn and run. Fast. In the other direction. To get as far away from her as possible in the shortest amount of time. The other half wanted to break her in half, hurting her badly. There was also a third emotion, but I was trying desperately not to listen to it. I also had a pretty strong feeling that she knew all of this. She wasn't stupid. She knew that putting one finger on her would violate the conditions of my parole and land me back in prison. She'd scripted everything about this moment, and it was heavily weighted in her favor. "You've made a career, a life, off comforting women who've actually been raped when you don't know the first thing about it."

She tried to stuff her reaction but the look on her face told me I'd just dented her armor. I continued, "You're not really qualified to speak on it." She recovered quickly. I was in the process of slipping one leg into a pair of jeans when she seized on the opportunity, crossed the floor, stood me upright, and pressed herself against me. "Aren't you just the least bit interested?" She smiled and raised an eyebrow. "Twelve years is a long time."

I'd be lying if I didn't tell you I was tempted. I was. The touch of her skin, the softness, the invitation, the warmth of her body pressed to mine. There was a voice inside my head screaming at the top of his lungs, saying, "Dude . . . you deserve this. Trust me, you've earned it. Dive in." But as intoxicating as all that was, it suffered one major defect. One fault from which it could never recover.

Ginger's body could never do for me what Audrey's love had.

So while my lustful friend screamed at the top of his lungs, the memory of my precious and magnificent wife stood silently inside my heart. Beckoning. Prison didn't erase that. Couldn't.

Unaware that her spell had been broken, Ginger hung her arms around my neck and kissed me on the cheek. Moist, warm, lipstick lips stemming from a cold heart makes for tepid love. In all her conquering, Ginger failed to realize that Audrey and I had known one another. Shared our love. Our laughter. Our tears. Our best and worst. What Audrey and I had known was far more than just sex. I'm afraid that's all Ginger had ever known. Ginger had known the act of conquering, while emotively and physically, my wife had offered herself to me, given unselfishly, and pursued me—wanting nothing but my love in return. Despite her best attempts, Ginger with her A-game and her perfectly sculpted body, fueled by an insatiable desire for power, couldn't compete with that tender girl who'd given me her heart in high school. Ginger had been outclassed and was too dumb to know it.

I whispered, "Ginger, you don't hold a candle to my wife."

It was only then that I noticed someone standing at the front door. Someone looking in.

Instinctively, Ginger pressed tighter against me as we turned our heads in unison to find Audrey staring through the glass at the two of us. Disbelief and disgust blanketed Audrey.

Reality set in. Audrey and I were little more than game pieces, and Ginger was the giant hand moving us around the board.

Checkmate.

Ginger smiled—smugly, triumphantly—then separated just slightly, touching the tip of my nose with her finger and whispering, "Who holds the candle now?"

For the first time in a long time I felt rage. Rage because I knew no matter what I did, Ginger would never be satisfied. Never stop.

Ever.

And that meant Audrey would continue to suffer.

I pulled on my jeans only to look up and find that Audrey had disappeared from the window. When I put an unaffectionate hand on Ginger's shoulder in an attempt to lead her out of my cabin, the first of her two bodyguards walked through the door.

Goon number one was freakishly big. He was a tank. He stepped toward me and lifted his hand to wrap it around my neck, but I was in no mood for jousting so I sidestepped him and kicked at his knee. My heel kicked through his ACL, his knee snapped, he crumpled and hit the floor grunting.

Goon number two was more wiry, quicker. He flew through the air, took me off my feet, and hit me two or three times in the face before my left hook crushed his nose. His face exploded like a balloon, his eyes rolled back and he hit the floor, arms out, stiff, like a cockroach.

Amused, Ginger pulled on her coat and walked out, stopping just feet from Audrey, who stood paralyzed on the porch surrounded by the shattered pieces of what once made up her soul. Ginger took her time tying the belt of her coat and smoothing the smeared edge of her lipstick with her right index finger. She turned slightly, said, "Audrey," and walked to her Mercedes parked beneath the trees just beyond the cabin. Cranking the engine, she whistled for her dogs, punched the button that automatically folded the soft top into the trunk, and drove slowly out the drive.

I stood frozen beneath the shadow of suspicion. Audrey stood in the shadows of the porch, steadying herself with the railing.

I had just gotten "Audrey, I can—" out of my mouth when she bent at the waist, vomited, and then vomited again. I stepped toward her, but she held out a hand as the dry heaves wrenched her off her feet and sent her to her knees. This continued for several minutes as the veins rose on her neck and Audrey sought to catch her breath. I sat on the porch and hung my head in my hands, listening to Audrey vomit me out of her life. When she finally stood, she reached inside her collar, broke the chain around her neck, and dropped the dove on the porch. Wrapping her arms around her,

as if holding herself, she was walking off when I spoke. "Please...
let me."

She never turned.

An hour later, I stood staring through her window when Audrey
twisted off the cap to the sleeping pills. She didn't shower, and she
didn't change into her pajamas. She just sat on her bed and stared
at the pills a long time. On the bedside table sat a picture of Dee
and her following a game. He was sweaty, smiling, she was wearing
his jersey, her face was painted, her cheek pressed to his. She stared
at it a long time. After several minutes, she poured one, and then
a second, and finally a third into her hand. She tossed them into
her mouth, drank from a glass of water, and then sat there staring
at the bottle. Finally, she lay back and pulled her knees into her
chest. No remote. No TV. I didn't leave until her shoulders relaxed
beneath the sheets and her head fell limp. Only then did the pain
in my left hand register. When I looked down, I found the bone
broken, pressing up against the underside of the skin, and my hand
was swelling pretty good.

I soaked my hand in ice off and on throughout the night, which
brought the swelling down and helped pull out the tenderness.
It was pretty good and numb when I set it, but the second time
around was easier. Staring at my hand, the acrid taste of anger
returned.

In my mind, Gage's voice echoed, *Tell me...* I sunk my hand
elbow-deep into the ice, silencing the playback. I didn't want to
hear what he had to say.

CHAPTER TWENTY-SIX

I didn't have much with which to buy Dee a present, but I wanted to give him something that mattered. Something of value. He'd earned it and more. I rode down to the shade barn, pulled what I wanted off the wall, wrapped it in a towel, zipped it into an old duffel, and rode the bike to town. I parked down the street from the grocery and sat wearing my helmet until he walked out the front door, untying his apron. He waved at me, pointed at the van, and mouthed the words, "Follow me."

I should have been concerned about eating in a public place, but I found myself caring less and less about the restrictions placed upon my release. A good sign that I needed to take Wood's advice, pack up, and find a home in another state—several states away. But, to be honest, that didn't really appeal to me either.

Only one thing did.

Dee's camp started in a week, which meant my commitment to him was winding down. A part of me wanted to stick around and see him play—a strong part—but my presence here was causing Audrey, and me, a lot of pain.

I had a week to go.

Dee drove to the courthouse and parked in one of those angled spaces alongside. I glanced at the people mingling around. *You've got to be kidding me.*

He exited the van, trotted back to me, and pointed to the opposite end of the block and Mama's Po' Boys. It was a sidewalk sandwich shop where folks in a hurry bought sandwiches and either ate standing up, on benches in the park, or walking back to work. The smell was intoxicating.

He said, "You like po' boys?"

I handed him twenty dollars. "Absolutely."

He pointed to a set of benches set off to one side of the courthouse, shadowed beneath the oaks. A good spot. "Meet you over there."

I heeled down the kickstand and carried the duffel over to the bench. A few minutes later, Dee joined me. The sandwiches were fantastic. I ate mine in about five bites, as did he, so he ordered two more and we ate those as the mayonnaise dripped down our chins. We made a glorious mess.

He eyed my black-and-blue and swollen hand. "Want to talk about it?"

"You don't miss much, do you?"

"I think it was you who told me that quarterbacks need to see what others miss. It's what makes us good at our jobs."

"That I did." I glanced at it. "Just because they unlock the cell and open the gates doesn't make you free."

He nodded and didn't ask any more questions. We sat in the quiet a few minutes. I asked him. "Birthday today, huh?"

He smiled. "Seventeen."

I handed him the duffel. "I own very few things of value. I thought maybe you'd like to have that. It's... special to me."

"Can I open it?"

"Yep."

He smiled. "You wrap this yourself?"

A chuckle.

He unzipped the bag, held the present, and unwrapped the towel. He looked at me in disbelief, in astonishment. "I can't accept this."

"You deserve it. And after the summer I've put you through, you've more than earned it. I want you to know that you're *that* good. And I wouldn't tell you that if you weren't."

He held the first of my two Heisman trophies in his hand. "But—"

"Dee, I want to tell you something." A tractor trailer passed on the road next to us, and a couple eating ice cream walked by on the sidewalk. I looked away until they passed. "I want you to know that I didn't expect this...you...this summer. It's been... it's been one of the greatest joys of my life. I mean that. Being with you has reminded me of the game I once loved and why I loved it. I want to thank you for that." I paused. "Technically, I'm old enough to be your dad, but I feel more like an older brother or uncle or... anyway, what I'm saying is, I'm proud of you."

"But?"

I didn't like saying good-bye, and I could tell he didn't like the thought of me saying it. "I'll be leaving when you go to camp."

He nodded and looked away. We sat beneath the slight rattle of the oak leaves. He broke the silence. "I was kind of hoping you might stay and watch my games. Help me—" A forced laugh. "Navigate my coach."

"I'll check on you."

He didn't respond. He zipped up the duffel. "Thank you for this. It means a lot."

We stood, eye to eye. He was heavy. Only then did I realize I hadn't given him much of a present. Certainly not the present he wanted. He asked, "Can you tell me why you're leaving?"

"It's complicated."

He stood tall and straight. Eye to eye with me. Hurt and anger covered his face. He spoke through tight lips. "I've done everything you've asked me this summer and never once uttered a complaint. So why don't you try?"

"My being here is painful to Audrey. And to me."

He lifted the duffel over his shoulder, took a step, then turned back. The first tear had already slid down his cheek. "You ever stop to think that maybe your leaving is painful to me?" He shook his head, set the duffel on the bench, and began walking to his van. Halfway there, he turned. "I been left all my life."

I watched him climb into his van and then returned to my bike. But not before dumping the duffel in the nearest trash can.

CHAPTER TWENTY-SEVEN

It was dark when I returned home. Wood was standing on my front porch, accompanied by two sheriff's deputies along with a woman wearing a suit and another man in plain clothes wearing a badge and a holstered pistol. Wood shook his head as I walked up the porch steps. "Rocket, I had nothing to do with this, and as your attorney I'm instructing you to keep your mouth shut." As he said that, I noticed two other people were unloading the contents of my pantry and freezer into coolers in the back of one of the deputy's cars.

The woman approached me and said, "Mr. Rising?"

I didn't respond.

She was nearly a foot shorter than me. She continued. "Does the name Dalton Rogers ring a bell?"

I studied her as a crew of people gathered around her. I noticed Wood glancing at my hand. "I'm sorry. And you are?"

"Deborah Cunning. District Attorney." She proffered to the

man wearing plain clothes to her right. "And this is Zane Adams, Assistant District Attorney."

I took Wood's advice and kept my mouth shut.

She handed me a piece of paper. "This is a search warrant for your premises. Mr. Mason informed us that he was missing some groceries. A lot of groceries. Now I can't prove that you took them, but I'm pretty sure I can prove that Dalton Rogers did. And I'm curious how it is that you came to possess them. Given that their retail value exceeds a thousand dollars, that is grand theft. And while I'm at it, just what is the nature of your relationship with Mr. Rogers?" She slid on her glasses, propped her hand on her hip, and waited.

I spoke slowly. "Am I under arrest?"

She smiled and patted me on the shoulder. "I'll be in touch." When she reached the bottom step, she stopped but didn't turn to look at me. "Wood, please inform your client that he's not allowed to leave this county."

Wood didn't respond.

She turned and slid her glasses down on her nose. "Dunwoody, I want verbal confirmation in front of witnesses that I have served you notice and that you are to inform your client. Do you understand?"

He frowned. "Debbie, I heard you the first time. So, with all due respect, go pull your panties out of a wad."

The deputy behind Debbie smirked and then quickly erased it off his face. They loaded up and created a dust storm driving out. When the dust cleared, Tux crawled out from beneath the cabin and stood next to me, sniffing the air.

I scratched my head. "That's one blitz I did not see coming."

Wood shook his head. "Me neither." He turned to me. "Where'd you get all that food? I mean, if you were hungry—"

I waved him off. "Dee was taking it to the food bank. Showed up with a van full. Offered it. I was 'bout to gnaw my own arm off. He said it was all expired, couldn't be sold, so I loaded up."

Wood looked at me. "Something's fishy here."

"Tell me about it."

He glanced at my hand and raised his eyebrows.

I shook my head. "You wouldn't believe me if I told you."

"Try me."

When I finished telling him the story, he spat. "That woman has bigger gonads than ten men put together." He pulled his car keys from his pocket and said, "I better get to the office. No telling what Debbie is cooking up. I'll be in touch."

I picked up Tux, and the two of us lay in my hammock on the porch. I had lots of questions and few, if any, answers. Seconds later, Ray appeared at the edge of the yard. Hands in his pockets. I don't know how long he'd been standing there, so I asked. "How long you been there?"

"Long enough."

He walked across the yard, climbed the porch, sat next to me, and stared out across the yard. Content to sit in the quiet, he did. Finally, I asked, "You heard?"

He nodded. "Word spreads pretty quick 'round here when it comes to you."

"I don't suppose you walked all the way over here in the dark to tell me that."

"No." He shook his head. "I did not." A pause. He put his hand on my shoulder. "You know I been at that school a long time?"

His tone of voice caught my attention. "Yeah."

"And that means I have keys to every door."

I nodded.

He pulled a toothpick from his shirt pocket and began picking at his teeth. "And when the Sisters need a lock changed, they bring me in 'cause they trust an old man with arthritic hands."

"Okay."

"The records room is hidden in one of the back offices. It's got three locks on it. I got keys to all of them. Yesterday, I got to thinking about Dalton Rogers and what might be in his file. Just wondering if anything in there could help him. A starting place. So I rummage through the file and there's no file. As in, there was one, but it's gone. His name is on the file, but most of the contents are missing. Then I got a call yesterday afternoon from Miss Audrey 'cause she had this weird feeling like somebody had been in her place. Rummaging around. Said she'd thought it many times." He looked at me. "I didn't have the courage to tell her it was you."

"You know about that?"

"Matthew, I'm old, not dumb."

"You tell her?"

"'Course not." He kept picking at his teeth. "But then I went over to change her lock. She was out in her garden. I walked over to her bedroom window looking out across the incredible world she's created and I just stood there marveling at what she's done and there she is out there toiling in that sun. Just working away and then I turned to go and when I did, I noticed a file folder sticking out from underneath the edge of the bed." He scratched his head and turned toward me. "So, given what I know about her and given what I know about Dalton and given what I know about how she's poured her life into him and given that I knew that file was missing, I let my curiosity get the best of me, and I slid it out. Sure enough, it was his file."

If I was mildly interested when he first started talking, he had my full attention now.

He stood, pulled his handkerchief from his back pocket, and wiped both eyes. He then pulled a single key from his shirt pocket and set it on the steps next to me. Without another word, he turned and disappeared in the woods.

*   *   *

It was after dinner when I crept up to Audrey's window. The last couple of weeks, she'd been skipping dinner and going to bed earlier. Sleeping twelve to fourteen hours a day had become her medication. A single light in the bathroom cast a dim light across the room. Audrey lay in bed, mouth open, body limp. Her self-induced coma. I used Ray's key, let myself in, and tiptoed to the edge of the bed. She never moved. I slid my hand beneath the mattress and the box spring and found the folder where Ray had left it. The name read DALTON ROGERS. I carried it to the bathroom and opened it. Midway through, I found the birth certificate. There, in black and white, the words jumped off the page.

The blindside was more than I'd expected.

I sat on the edge of the tub and closed my eyes. I could not believe it. Refused to. My mind raced. *How?* Then I read the date, backed into the calendar, and the light clicked on. I closed my eyes and sat rubbing my temples. *How long had she known?*

I set the folder on her table, the birth certificate lying on top. I locked the door behind me and started walking. I wanted her to know that I knew.

CHAPTER TWENTY-EIGHT

I walked back to the cabin in the darkness. Halfway there, I stared down the road and saw a man running toward me. The motion was Dee's. He approached, breathing heavy, and he'd been crying. Still was. He had lost all control of his emotions. He screamed in anger. "They cut me."

"Wait. What? Who cut you?"

"Coach."

"Why?"

"Some guys with badges showed up, told him they've got me on video stealing food, and now they've got the food as evidence. Told my coach they intend to charge me with grand theft unless I tell them what really happened."

He walked in circles around me as the pieces fell into place. *Clever,* I thought to myself. *Very clever.* "And they want you to tell them I stole it."

He continued, "That's just for starters. They want me to tell them the *nature* of our relationship. Like, how well I know you.

How much time we've spent together. Have you ever put your hands on me. They said they had an unconfirmed rumor that we'd been working out. Every day." He threw down his hands. "Who told them that?"

"What else?"

He wouldn't look at me.

"Dee. What else?"

"They said you'd be back in jail by tomorrow night. Prison by the middle of next week."

I let out a deep breath. I had always thought that I might lose this chess game. I just didn't think it'd happen this soon. I said, "Dee, go home. There's something I need to do."

He wasn't really looking at me or waiting for an answer. He was crying out in pain. "What on earth can you possibly do?"

"Dee?"

He stomped in a circle around me.

I put my hands on his shoulders. "Dee?"

He finally stopped and looked at me. He was cracking from the inside out. "I want you to do one more thing for me."

He began crying. "Man——" The reality of our summer and my life was hitting him full force. "You're going back to prison!"

His shoulders shook when I wrapped my arms around him and hugged him. I stood there, just hugging him. The sobs shook his shoulders. I whispered, "I've always been going back to prison."

He wrapped his arms around me and squeezed. A bear hug. Afraid to let go. "Why! Why'd you do this?"

"I need you to do me one more favor."

Exasperated, he spoke. "What?"

"Get some rest. I've got a few things to do and I'll be in touch."

"You want me to sleep? What are you talking about?"

"Dee, I need you to do the one thing that no one wants to do—I need you to trust me." He looked at me. Searching for hope. "Can you do that? Will you, please?"

He wiped his face on his shirt sleeve and nodded.

I patted him on the shoulder. "I'll be in touch. And don't make any plans for tomorrow evening."

"I've got to work. Still have my job at school."

"Call in sick. And answer your phone if it rings, even if you don't know the number. It's probably me."

He wanted to ask me a mountain of questions. "Not now. It'll make sense tomorrow."

He nodded, turned, and disappeared through the woods.

When I returned to my cabin, there was a manila envelope sitting on my front steps. A lone DVD lay inside it. No note. It didn't need one. I slid the disc into the player and watched a well-edited video of every workout I'd had with Dee. Morning. Evening. Whenever I put a hand on him, the video played through it once, then sliced back in a slow-motion version. Particular attention had been paid to any time I patted him on the butt. Words scrolled up from the bottom of the screen. "This is an edited version of over seventy hours of video. Both the edited and the unedited versions have been sent to the Court."

The message was clear.

When I walked in, a similar-looking manila envelope and DVD lay on Wood's desk. Wood was digging through a stack of law books, and his face was painted in worry. "Matty—" He began stuttering. "I think she's got you by the—"

I cut him off. "Can I use your phone?"

He slid it across the table without looking at me.

"What's Roddy's cell number?"

He glanced up, irritated. "What?"

I spoke slowly to make sure he understood me. I had a feeling his head was spinning. "What is Roderick's cell number?"

He dug through a book on his desk, and I dialed the number. I put him on speakerphone, and Roddy answered after the first ring. His voice betrayed his smile. "I wondered when you might be calling me."

"I need a favor."

"Been waiting for you to ask me that."

While I told him what I wanted, Wood looked at me like I'd gone loco. And by the time I'd finished the call, he was speechless and shaking his head. "You've lost your mind."

I sat on his desk and crossed my hands. "You still want to be my agent?"

He shook his head. "No. Absolutely not."

"Good, then I need you to do a few things." When I finished telling him, he sat at his desk and sunk his head in his hands. "Rocket, I can't do that for you. To you."

"Wood, look at me."

He didn't look up.

"Dunwoody?"

He looked up.

"I don't have time to argue with you."

"I'm not arguing. I'm telling you, emphatically, no."

I leaned in closer. My face a foot from his. "Are you my center?"

He looked away. "Don't do that."

My voice rose. "Are you my center?"

No answer.

"Wood, I have one play. The play clock is ticking. Do you want to sit this one out?"

A long pause. He stood and held eye contact. He blinked and pushed a single tear out of his eye, which trailed down his cheek and spilled onto his shirt. I'd seen blood do the same thing. His voice cracked when he spoke. "I'm your center."

I walked to the door. "Then call the huddle."

CHAPTER TWENTY-NINE

Before every game, I, along with my coaches and players, would watch film and then piece together a strategy of what we thought would work against the opponent. It's what we hoped would happen. We called it a game plan. Sometimes it worked. Sometimes it didn't. When it didn't, it was up to me to read where the defense was beating us and call an audible. That was my job. And it was something I was good at—at one time.

The problem with a game plan is that you never knew if it would work until you were in the game.

Wood would do his part. Roddy his. Now the wait began. *Would they show?* I had no idea. Needing to clear my head, I shoved my hands in my pockets and struck out on a walk. The night had turned cool, or at least cooler, and it felt good. It smelled like football. Kicking up dust in front of me, I remembered something my dad had told me a long time ago: *You can only control what you can control. Don't worry about what you can't. Won't change anything.*

A while later I found myself staring at the shade barn. The moon was high and bright. Casting our shadows below us. Below me, Tux growled. The hair standing up on his back. In the distance, I saw someone with a flashlight walking across the field en route to the barn.

I cradled Tux, quieted him, and we followed at a distance. She opened a side door and strode in. We crept in through an end door and opposite her, out of sight and sound. Her flashlight landed on one of several boxes stacked on a wall. She lifted the lid off the box, leaned over it, rifled through its contents, and finally pulled something out. She held it up in front of her, put the lid back on the box, and returned out the same door she'd come in. Before she left, she straightened a picture on a wall, glanced quickly around with her flashlight, and disappeared out the same door she'd come in.

In Audrey's absence, I pushed open the door and stood staring up at all that I'd once accomplished while Tux sniffed the dirt and peed on all the support timbers. I took my time, sifting through boxes and staring at the displays on the walls. The memories flooded. Old cleats, jerseys, shoulder pads, helmets, game balls, awards, framed listings of achievements and records, newspaper articles, magazine covers. Each memory was tied to a sweet place in me, but when I walked up close and drank from the spigot, the aftertaste was bitter. As a disconnected observer, I examined my life, and when it struck me, I didn't fight it. The sum of my life accounted for nothing. A forgotten dustbin in south Georgia. And without Audrey, I'd done nothing. I stood among the rubble and ruins of a world that had long since crumbled around me.

I opened the front and rear barn doors and then cranked open the vents along the lower walls, creating a vigorous draft. Standing in the middle felt like an elevator shaft lying on its side. I poured the kerosene around the base of the timber and lit the match. I'd always loved that smell. The kerosene caught and began licking up the side of the wood. Within seconds, it'd climbed to the roof and was crawling along the underside to the far end.

I turned from the fire, picked up Tux, and began walking away. Flames climbed out of the barn, showered me in heat, and cast a bronze shadow on the road before me. A quarter mile away, I turned and watched as the flames lit up the night sky, showering the air in sparks, heat, and the residue of memory. In less than five minutes, the insatiable appetite of the fire had consumed the barn, which had crumbled and filled the air around me in flittering ash. Out of fuel, the fire receded into a pile of heat and cinders. By morning, there'd be little left.

Just a black stain on the face of the earth.

But it had been a beautiful fire. I only wish Wood had been here to see it.

CHAPTER THIRTY

I slept fitfully and woke before daylight. As if someone shook me. Memories and images were flashing through my head like a projector. I showered, dressed, and slipped out the front door. Minutes later, I scaled the wall and then lowered myself into the garden. I wanted to walk through one last time. Imprint it into my mind—so I could come back here. I walked slowly, studying every detail, every bush, leaf, rose petal, smell. I marveled at what Audrey had done. Out of nothing but weeds and dirt, she had created and nurtured a living, breathing cathedral. I was proud of her.

And I wished I could tell her that.

The sun broke the skyline, parted the clouds, and began burning the mist off the ground. I sat on a bench and rested my head against the wall behind me. I closed my eyes and sat there breathing, imprinting the smell in my brain. Just feet away, I heard, "What do you remember?"

Audrey's voice surprised me. When I opened my eyes, she stood to my left. Barefooted. Jeans. Hands dirty. Looked like she'd been up a while.

"About us?"

She shook her head. "About life."

"Hope and promise."

She chuckled. A hurt laugh. "Really."

"The hope of what might be and the promise of sharing it with you."

She must have been tired because she dropped her guard relatively quickly. She nodded thoughtfully. "In the recesses of my mind—" She waved her hand across her garden. "Before all this."

I tried to get her talking. "How you doing? You okay?"

Evidently, she wasn't that tired. She flipped her switch, raised her guard, turned cold, and ignored me. "Dee says you're finally doing it. That you made the call."

"You mean today?"

"Dee appeared last night, giddy. We sat and talked a long time. Said he can't wait to watch this. Said it should shut the critics up forever."

I laughed. "I don't know if anything shuts them up, but it might quiet them a while."

She nodded. "Experience talking."

Obviously, she hadn't figured it out yet. Neither had he. "Wood and Roddy are taking care of all the details. Should be quite a show."

"Roddy." She shook her head. "Only one of him." She turned to me. "Where will you end up?"

The garden caught my attention. "Don't know. I asked Wood to handle the first round or two of calls. After that we'll talk. But wherever, it doesn't really matter."

She sat on the bench opposite me, gently tracing her toes in the jet-black dirt. "He loves wearing that earpiece."

I chuckled. "Yep."

If my soul had been starving for water and the last twelve years had been a desert, these last few minutes had been an oasis and I was standing in a waterfall.

I drank deeply.

We sat in the quiet. The sun slowly lighting the world. Hummingbirds shot like F-16s in the air around us. Doves perched on the walls about us, cooing, calling to one another.

She spoke. Not so much to me as into the air around us. "I love it here."

My window was closing, and I felt it. I said, "Audrey, can I say something to you?"

She looked up at me, and in her eyes I did not see anger or rage. I saw a broken and lonely girl. She waited.

"I just want to tell you that I'm sorry and I love you."

She blinked. "Is that your confession?"

"I confess that I love you more today than the day we married. And I confess that I'm really sorry for what happened to us. To you. To our life together."

She blinked again and nodded but said nothing. She was either too tired to fight or maybe she needed one tender moment amid the ten thousand that threatened to kill her. I stood and stared out across her garden, out across the one moment in our lives when all the world was right. The thought came to the tip of my tongue. I held it there, wondering if I should let it out. Finally, I did. I said, "You know, this wasn't the play that I called."

She looked up, confused. "What?"

I waved my hand out across the garden. "This . . . it wasn't what I called in the huddle."

"It wasn't?"

"No." I shoved my hands in my pockets and started toward the ladder. Doing so brought me within two feet of her.

Her voice was soft. "But you audibled at the line." She nodded. "It's on video. You changed the play at the line."

I smiled. "You saw me act like I was changing the play at the line. The audible you hear isn't the play that Wood and Roddy run." I shook my head. "I wanted them to think I'd changed it based on their coverage. That they'd boxed me in. It's what the other side was expecting. But it was all smoke and mirrors. And it's how Roddy got open. Only Wood and Roddy knew the call."

She looked stumped. "But how'd they know?"

I turned. "The morning after we lost the national championship? You woke me up, changed my workout schedule, scheduled Roddy and Wood. I called it that morning."

She considered the ramifications of this. "You mean, they knew the last play of the following season, the morning after you lost?"

I shoved my hands in my pants and started walking.

Her voice followed me. "Matthew?"

I stopped.

"You called the last play of the season before the season even started?"

I stopped. "Yes."

"Why?"

"Because sometimes the other side is better. Stronger. Faster. I knew then that they would be. That they could beat us. So I gave the three of us an assignment. We worked on it all summer and through the season. Wood's job was to give me four seconds. Period. Roddy knew exactly where in the end zone he needed to be and how many steps it took to get there and how much time and how high he had to jump. And I knew the vertical leaps of the three DBs that might be covering him. I even had footage of them playing intramural basketball. I knew how high they could jump. So I knew exactly, within an inch or two, where that ball needed to be, and Roddy did, too. Calling that play a year earlier is the only reason it worked a year later." I paused. "Great QBs are great, not because they have the strongest arms or fastest feet, but because they can anticipate and read defenses. It's the one skill you can't coach."

She looked out across her garden. Confused. Slowly the pieces fit together and when they did, the sum of them pulled down slightly on her lower jaw. She sat in silence, astonishment setting in, and as I turned, I saw a glimmer of something in her eyes that looked like hope.

Her words fell softly on my shoulders. "Matty?"

The word soothed me. I let it rattle around inside me. It echoed, resonated, and settled softly near my heart. "Yes?"

Her tone was motherly. Caring. Slightly defensive. "Can Dee read defenses?"

"At his age, better than I. But he's young. And he hasn't seen this one coming. This one will catch him off guard."

She covered her mouth with her hands to hide her smile, but she couldn't hide the tears.

I walked off as the clock tower sounded.

CHAPTER THIRTY-ONE

Ray shook me awake an hour later. I rubbed the sleep out of my eyes and met him on the porch, where he offered me a cup of coffee. I knew what he was doing. We both did. He was saying good-bye. We propped our legs on the railing, blew the steam off our mugs, and sipped in silence for several minutes. Finally, I said, "I'll miss the Bucket."

A nod. "I'll miss seeing you on it."

I glanced at him. "Will you help Audrey with—"

He held up a hand and stopped me. "Who you think drove him to the orthodontist? Taught him to drive? Got him his first pair of cleats? His job at the grocery? Don't plan to stop now."

"Thanks."

He continued, "In truth, he be taking care of her now." Tux curled up at Ray's feet, letting out a deep sigh. Ray finished his coffee, stood, dusted off his pants, and, stopping behind me, put his hand on my shoulder. "I'll come see you." He wiped his eyes with a handkerchief. "Soon as you get settled."

I patted his hand, and he disappeared through the trees.

Tux and I spent the day alone—and out of sight—on top of the Bucket. If they came to the cabin, I'd at least see them coming. I napped, ate a little, drank lots of water, and stretched late in the afternoon. I climbed down around five p.m. when Wood appeared. He rolled his window down and gave me a thumbs up. "All set."

We were quiet a minute, neither really knowing what to say. Wood knew where this was going, and he knew there were no easy answers. Finally, he spoke. "You sure about this?"

"No. But…" I shrugged.

He attempted a joke. "It's nice to know you're human."

"Oh, I'm human all right."

"You can still call it off."

"You know better than that."

"I'll be with you on the other side of this."

"You'd do well to get on with your life. Put all this behind you."

"I'll get on with my life, but I'm not putting you behind me." He paused. "Matter of fact, I, uh…I been meaning to ask you something." His tone had changed. Something tender. Caught me off guard. "Laura and I were wondering if you minded if we named our son Matthew."

"She's expecting?" I had no idea.

He nodded, smiling.

"How long have you known?"

"Had the ultrasound this week. He's definitely a boy."

I laughed. "Wow. Really?"

He chuckled. "Laura's been telling me we need to get cable, but I just never listened to her."

"Evidently not."

"So?"

"Yes. Yes, absolutely."

"While you're in such an agreeable mood—" Wood wasn't finished. He had something else on his mind. "How would you feel about being his godfather?"

"That might be tough from prison."

"Doesn't matter where you are."

"Laura really said that?"

He looked up at me. "When I told her about today, about what you're planning, she broke down. Told me if I didn't talk to you about all this that she was coming down here herself."

I chuckled. "You married well, Dunwoody."

He smiled, chest swelling. "That I did."

"I'd really like that. Yes. Thank you."

We were quiet a few minutes. Finally, he spoke. "You know, if you want, I could get out of this car, give you the keys, and you could just start driving. And I'd be willing to bet that when they found out you did that, everything would settle and disappear. You could start over someplace other than here."

I considered this. "The thought did cross my mind."

He waited. "But?"

"You remember that Orange Bowl?"

He closed his eyes. "My head still hurts. What were those two brothers' names?"

"Chip and Dave—"

He cut me off. "Russell."

"Yep."

He pressed his hand to his head as if the memory still hurt. "Those guys were tough. One would stand you up and hold you a second while the other just cut you in half."

"And you remember how they shut us down for fifty-eight minutes."

"I do."

"What finally worked?"

Wood chuckled. "Sneak up the middle."

271

"Didn't work the first time, did it?"

"Nor the second or third."

"Then came—"

He laughed from his belly and cut me off again. "Fourth and forever."

We both paused as the memory replayed itself across our minds.

I said, "You remember standing in that huddle? Before that last play?"

Wood kept laughing. "Man, Roddy was so pissed."

I stopped him. "Wood, this is fourth and forever."

He stared out through the windshield. His lips were tight when he spoke. "I miss that."

"There's someone I miss more. And she needs to know it." The clock was ticking. I tapped on the side of the door. "Better get going."

"Yeah. I want to get there in time to make sure everything's in order and to tell Damon where he can shove his clipboard."

"I'd like to see that."

"Want a ride?"

"I'll walk."

Wood stared out his windshield and his voice softened. "Last time through the tunnel."

I nodded. "See you in a few."

At a quarter to six, I peered through the trees at the stadium. The sidelines were packed with people. Television crews had brought cranes onto the track to get a close-up and elevated view of the field. The knot in my stomach tightened. *Could I pull this off?*

Roddy had made good on his promise to get the word out via Twitter, and it must have worked because the lower section of the stands was packed. Must have been a thousand people. Wood stood on the sideline, deflecting a vocal barrage from Coach Damon, who was effectively muted by the crowd of reporters, scouts, and coaches swarming the field. True to form, Wood had changed into a suit and what looked like his secret-service earpiece, which I thought was a nice touch.

Dee quietly appeared next to me. If his father had been black, his father's influence on his skin color had drained out of him. Completely. He looked at me. "What'd you say?"

I let out a deep breath. "I said I'd like a chance to reenter the NFL. Formally."

"It worked." His excitement grew. "You're really trying out?"

"Something like that."

He shook his head, mesmerized by the crowd. Awe pulled down on his jaw while his smile spread his lips. "Must be twenty-five to thirty teams over there. And twice as many cameras." He snapped his fingers. "I just met a photographer from *SI*. Coach, *Sports Illustrated* is here. The lens on his camera must have been"—he extended his arms widely as if he were telling a fish story—"three feet long."

Mesmerized, he was staring at the field. I was staring at him. "Dee?"

He turned, curious. Oblivious. "Yeah?"

"I need you to do me a favor."

His eyes returned to the field. One toe started tapping the ground. "Anything. Name it."

I placed a ball in his hands. "Try out with me."

The toe stopped tapping and the last of the color drained out. "What!"

"One last workout."

"But—" This is about the time he understood what was going on and began shaking his head. "No."

"Dee. Look at me."

He wouldn't.

"Dee?"

273

Still nothing.

"Men are coming to my cabin today. They may be there now—" Slowly, he lifted his face. "They're going to arrest me. Send me back to prison."

He shoved me hard in the chest. "Why'd you do this? Why didn't you walk away when you could?"

"Dee, she's just using you."

"Who? Why?"

"That's not important. If not you, she'd be using someone else. She tends to come at what I love. No matter who it is. Always has."

He turned. Faced me. Eyes asking the question his heart had long since wanted to voice.

"Do this for me, please. Walk out there and play a game with me." I tapped his heart. "Just play a game with me."

He dropped the ball and began shaking his head. Finally, his shoulders shook. The sobs came soon after. His voice broke. "But prison—"

I straightened him up, lifting his chin. "Steel bars can't kill me. But these bars on my heart?" I searched the stands for Audrey. "I need a little help with those."

The cameras caught our movement when we walked out of the trees on the far side, sending people scurrying off the sideline. We met them in the end zone. Everybody in the bleachers stood and began chanting, "Rocket! Rocket! Rocket!"

Wood managed the crowd around us and made space for Roddy to pass through with a few of his friends. They were younger guys, and I only knew them by reputation. Roddy introduced them. "Guys, Rocket. Matthew..." He gestured to his buddies. "Posse."

I shook their hands. "Thanks for coming. Guys, this is Dee, but I call him Clark Kent. If it's all right with you, I've asked him to help me out."

Roddy handed me a pair of cleats. "As you requested. You need me to remind you how to put them on?"

I laughed. "Probably."

He held up a second pair and pointed to Dee.

I responded, "Yep."

He handed the cleats to Dee, who held them like an egg. Dee looked at me. "Can I accept these?"

I laughed.

I turned to the crowd of reporters. There must have been fifty video cameras pointed at me. "I'd like thank everybody for coming out on such short notice. I realize that's rather high maintenance of me, and—" Most everybody laughed. "That's not my intention. After a short layoff..." More laughter. "I am officially expressing my intent to reenter the National Football League." Several reporters began shouting questions, but Wood raised his hands and silenced them. I continued, "I know all of you have questions, and we'll get to each one. But I've invited you here this afternoon to assess my ability. To let you see me in person and determine for yourselves if you think there's a spot for me in the league. I know many of you have doubts about a video made of me in prison. If I were you, I'd have doubts, too, so you're in good company. I have a bit of a history with rather fantastic and unbelievable videos." Most got the joke and the uncomfortable laughter spread. I paused. "I'll address that on the field." I turned to Dee. "I've asked a good friend of mine to join me today." All the cameras moved to Dee. What color had slowly returned to his face immediately fled. "This is Dalton Rogers." I smiled. "You might keep an eye on him, as you'll be hearing more about him." I turned back to Wood. "You got the bird?"

He held his earpiece with one hand while speaking into the other. Whoever was listening on the other end quickly responded. Wood smirked. "Ready."

"Mount up. We're headed south. You can catch up." I turned back to the reporters. "If I were you, one of my first questions about me would deal with my level of fitness. Of strength. Can I play through the fourth quarter and into the fifth?" I paused to let that settle in. "For the record, this is the same workout I've done since I was here in high school. For those of you who have vehicles, you're going to need them. For those of you who don't, don't worry. Have a seat. Get comfortable. The show will start momentarily." I turned to Roddy, his guys, and Dee. "You ready?"

Roddy laughed. "Old man, I'm ready for whatever you think you're man enough to dish out." He pointed at my and Dee's tattered black boots. The video cameras followed. "You sure you want to run in those?"

I placed a ball in Dee's hands. "Show them how it's done."

We ran through the woods, climbed up on the tracks, and started south. I watched Dee out of the corner of my eye. He'd turned the corner. He was running like a deer. When the helicopter appeared overhead and filed in behind us, with Wood staring down and a harness-mounted cameraman recording our every move via live-feed, Roddy thumbed over his shoulder and said, "What is that?"

I patted him on the back. "That's Wood. Broadcasting what we're doing on a giant screen on the field we just left. You always did like an audience." Roddy cussed under his breath and quickened his step.

After a mile, Dee stretched his legs, covering two railroad ties at a time, then three. He followed the drill to the letter. At five miles, we turned around. One of Roddy's fellow receivers had dropped off, the other was sucking wind and lagging behind. Roddy was talking in my ear. "You're trying to kill me, aren't you?"

"Nope." I pointed at Dee. "Just trying to show them what he's made of."

He hollered beneath the noise of the helicopter. "My contract doesn't say anything about running on any railroad track, and if it weren't for that camera above my head, and the fact that Roderick Nation is watching this live, I'd give you the finger and tell you where you could put this railroad track."

I always loved playing with Roddy. The trash-talking was priceless.

At ten miles, we were clicking off close to five-minute miles. We ran down off the tracks, up the dirt road, past the cabin, and hit the base of the Bucket at full stride. We were all suffering, but we were also flying.

Behind me, I heard Roddy laughing. Halfway up, I tapped Dee on the shoulder. "Go on." He found his last gear—the one we'd spent all summer creating—and Roddy struggled to catch him. When we got to the top, Roddy put his hands on his knees and looked at Dee, "Boy! Who is you? What college you play for? You SEC? PAC 10? Big 12?"

I laughed and started trotting down. "Come on, you're about to find out."

On the field, we laced up our cleats and started throwing the ball around. Pretty soon, we led into drills. Then patterns. Routes. Multiple reads. We spent a lot of time at twelve- to fifteen- to twenty-yard routes. Hitting outside shoulders, timing patterns. These were the bread and butter. The money routes. A lot of folks put a lot of emphasis on long balls, but it's the short, quick routes that win. Death by a thousand cuts.

I stayed close to Dee, stayed in his ear, and talked him through. "Remember the junkyard. The throws are just the same." I pointed at Roddy and his posse, helping Dee make the connection. "Michelin, B.F. Goodrich. MINI Cooper. Pirelli. Goodyear. Remember the catapult. And follow through." He nodded, settled in, did everything I did, and began firing bullets.

Somewhere in here, he threw a pass to one of the other receivers and it tore the receiver's glove at the seam. "Oohs" and "aahs" erupted out of the receiver core. Pretty soon, they started calling him Superman and Kryptonite. The banter proved to be a windfall, as the other receivers were soon lining up to run routes for him. Dee was in the middle of his count, audibling to his receivers, when he stopped, turned to me, winked, and then finished his count.

That's when I knew.

I stood back behind him, letting him have the center of the field. A few minutes later, Damon broke his clipboard over his knee and walked out of the stadium through the tunnel.

After about twenty minutes of underneath routes, Dee called an audible at the line and hit one of Roddy's guys on a forty-two-yard post with very little air beneath it that brought the scouts to their feet. And when he hit Roddy in stride on a fifty-five-yard fly, everybody in the stadium hit their feet and ESPN began broadcasting live from the field. Roddy brought the ball back to me and whispered, "You done playing, prison boy?"

I looked out across the field and heard the echo of my father. His smile. Our laughter. I saw Wood's sweat-stained face in the huddle. The scoreboard. I remembered the smell of cut grass, wet paint, and the singular sound of a girl who held my heart in one hand and a penny-filled milk jug in the other—screaming at the top of her lungs.

Despite my pain and the conclusion that was swiftly coming, I remembered the wonder and majesty and beauty of this game. I remembered my love.

And when I lifted a heel, setting Roddy in motion, and began my count, *"Blue forty-two, blue forty-two. Hot check razor. Hot check razor,"* the bars melted.

Roddy ran behind me, taunting me. "You sure you can throw it that far? Don't want you embarrassing yourself in front of all these people."

Roddy reached the left hash. "Hut-hut-hut."

I snapped the ball to myself, and Roddy looked as if he'd been shot out of a gun. While everyone in the stands and on the sideline saw just me and Roddy on the field, I read the linebacker's outside swim of the corner, telling me that he was closing off the inside and Roddy was going long into the corner of the end zone. I dropped five steps, read my weak side receiver who'd been stuffed at the line, faked to a back in the flats to draw the safeties, and then turned, ducked under the defensive tackle who'd beat my left-side tackle, rolled right evading the outside linebacker, set my feet, pulled down on my left arm, and launched a rocket into the corner of the end zone, where Roddy wasn't yet but would be in about two and a half seconds. The ball spiraled, turned nose down, and Roddy caught it seventy yards downfield, in stride, over his left shoulder in the corner of the end zone.

That one got them talking and silenced the critics.

Turning, I spotted Audrey for the first time. She was sitting in "her seat," cheering, wearing Dee's jersey. I waved once. She placed her hand over her heart and mouthed the words, "Thank you."

I pulled down slightly on my collar and showed her the dove around my neck.

I threw for almost an hour and ESPN2 covered the entire workout live.

At eight p.m., Wood blew the horn and Dee and I gathered in the middle of the field where we began fielding questions. The first reporter shoved a microphone in Dee's face and said, "Dalton, what college do you attend?"

"Um—" I smiled as Audrey slipped through the crowd where Dee could see her and she could hear him. "I'm a senior here at St. Bernard."

The response was effusive.

One of the reporters asked, "How old are you?"

Dee looked at me and I nodded. He said, "I'm seventeen."

That brought the volume up until one young reporter in the front put two and two together. I watched his face as the pieces fell in line. He eyed my ankle, then Dee, then me. When he asked the question, I heard the words leave his mouth in slow motion. "But Matthew, isn't that a violation of your parole?"

You could hear a pin drop.

I spoke loud enough so everyone could hear me. "Yes, it is."

While silence settled over the crowd and no one knew what to say, a black Crown Vic drove out onto the track. I was thankful she hadn't gotten here sooner, but maybe she had and was just waiting for those three words. I turned to Dee as she elbowed her way through the crowd. "I don't think you'll have any trouble playing this year." I smiled. "Or next."

The reality of what we'd just done, of what he'd done, of what I'd done, began to set in. He nodded, and Audrey slipped her arm inside his. I was glad he had her. And she, him.

Debbie stomped onto the field and spoke with great volume so everyone knew she had the floor. Which she did. "Matthew Rising, you have the right to remain silent. Anything you say or do—" Her agents spun me around, handcuffed me, and were leading me to the car when Audrey stepped between us. She stared up at me. Her whisper was broken. "You have something that belongs to me."

I bowed my head and she lifted the dove off my neck, holding it in her hand. The chain draped over her shaking hand and dangled between us. Dee noticed she was shaking and put his arm around her.

What bars remained, shattered.

I pressed my forehead to hers and said words twelve years in the making. "And you have something of mine." I kissed her cheek. "Always have."

CHAPTER THIRTY-TWO

The reality of my return to prison occurred about the same time the electronic lock of my cell door clicked solidly into place. I sat on my cot and stared at my surroundings. Not much had changed. My life in sixty-four-square feet. They'd removed my anklet when I arrived, which was a strange sensation. Free but not.

Wood said that an anonymous tip had alerted authorities to my relationship with Dee. Evidence of this was the unedited video coverage of our workouts. The same I'd seen in the DVD taped to my door. Wood explained the case against me was open and closed. His experience with me and videos was not good, so he suggested I plead guilty. I told him that I was and that I intended to. He said that, by statute, the judge would rule that I serve out the remainder of my first sentence and add to that another ten years for every infraction of my parole. Given the video, we both knew what that meant.

The morning after our workout, the athletic director, along with many of the boosters at St. Bernard's, had a rather short meeting with Damon. Dee was named the starting quarterback. Debbie had dropped any and all charges against Dee regarding the food he gave me. Now that it was proven the food had been expired, his boss even offered him his job back. In the month after my return to prison, the first three games of the season came and went. Dee played well beyond our expectations. Last Friday night Dee threw six touchdown passes and ran for three more. *Street & Smith's* had him ranked in their top twenty, and he was climbing weekly. Cut from the tether of rejection that anchored him to his past, he'd blossomed, proving Audrey right.

Every soul has an anchor.

I had not let Dee come see me because I felt that seeing me in here would be too tough on him. Okay, too tough on me. I didn't know how I would live out the rest of my days in this steel box. I hadn't come to grips with that. I just knew that I'd been let out for a reason. That reason was to find Audrey and love what and who she loved: Dee. And I'd done that. And something in me found great pleasure in having done so. I cannot explain that. All I know was that when they shut that prison door behind me, I was lonely and there was a piercing pain in my heart, but I wasn't angry.

Maybe the only comfort I had was knowing that Audrey would be okay. That day at the field, I saw relief in her. And release. Wood has been sitting next to her at all of Dee's games, shaking a penny-filled milk jug right alongside her. He told me that she looked better, not so gaunt. No black circles under her eyes. Even gained a few pounds. And that every time he saw her, she was wearing the dove—not hiding it. I was glad about that. Really. He said she'd been working some in the garden. She'd shown him the recreation of the play, even showed him his likeness on the field. He'd laughed. He said she was making some changes. Even planted a young oak tree next to the wall.

I don't know what happened that last day on that field. I would not say that Audrey grew to trust me, nor would I say that she had forgiven me for what she believed I'd done. But she learned to live with it. She saw what I did for Dee and while that did not erase the past, it made the memory of it not so painful. The torment was gone.

———

Gage appeared at seven p.m. with a transistor radio and folding chair. He sat on one side of the bars, and I lay on my bunk on the other. We rested the radio between us. Several of the guys around me leaned against their walls and listened. Fourth game of the season and it was homecoming. St. Bernard scored early and often and, from the sound of things, Dee was in control of everything around him. In the second quarter, the announcer said that he just learned there were over forty college scouts in the stands. I smiled. Word had spread. It'd worked.

At halftime the seniors paraded across midfield. Dee had asked Audrey to walk with him. I'd like to have seen that. As each senior began the walk with their folks, or whomever they'd chosen to walk them out, the announcer spoke about the achievements of each one. When Dee and Audrey started at the goal line, the announcer attempted to speak but was drowned out by applause and stomping on the metal bleachers. I could see Dee escorting Audrey out along midfield, his helmet under one arm and Audrey locked in the other. And in my mind's eye I could see Audrey's smile—her pride in and for him.

The announcer said, "Ladies and gentlemen, Dalton Rogers is a graduating senior with a 4.27 GPA. For the last three years, he has stocked shelves and bagged groceries at a local grocery store. Until a few weeks ago he was unsure if he'd be able to go to college..." We could hear laughter from the folks in the stands. "But with all the events of the last few weeks, he now has over fifty Division I offers to choose from. Dalton is, as of today, *Street & Smith's* number one high school pick in the nation." At this point, the applause drowned out the announcer. When he was able to continue, he said, "But Dalton says while he is grateful for that, he is more grateful to the two people who made it happen, Audrey and Matthew Rising." There was no applause this time. Just silence. "Dalton says that he was orphaned as a child and left at St. Bernard's. He has no memory of his biological parents, and St. Bernard's is the only home he's ever known." In the background, we heard a high-toned whistle and somebody screaming, "Dalton, we love you!" The announcer again, "Mama Audrey, as he calls her, helped raise him. She's the closest thing to a mother he's ever known. She taught him how to read, tie his shoes, and throw a football. He says the two of them, thanks to her extensive video collection, have watched over a thousand hours of video analyzing the quarterback play of Matthew Rising." The announcer paused and said, "As an aside, I'm told you can ask Dalton about any game in the Rocket's career and he can tell you what plays were run, where, and the score of each game. He says that while he has watched countless hours of video, and heard the stories and rumors and legends of Matthew Rising, it was only this past summer that he got to know him when Matthew was paroled from prison. He credits Audrey with teaching him the mechanics of football, and in a large sense, making him the quarterback he is today. Without her, he'd not be here, but he says it was not until he met 'the Rocket' that he fell in love with the game on a deeper level and learned how to play it out of his heart and not his head. He says he realizes folks may not understand that, but Matthew taught him how to play out of what he loved, and not what he hated or what he feared. He says if it weren't for Mama and the Rocket, he'd not be here tonight, and, with their permission, he'd like to dedicate this season to them."

There was silence in the announcer's box. In the background, a single clap started. The radio announcer picked up on the source.

"Folks, that single clap you hear is Dunwoody Jackson, Matthew Rising's former center and agent. Those two have been friends a long time." Wood's clap was followed by a second. Joined by a third. Then hundreds. Then thousands. Soon it was raucous. The announcer said, "For you folks at home, I've never seen this before. Dalton Rogers has stepped away from Audrey Rising, in an attempt to give her the spotlight, so to speak, and when he did so, both sides of this stadium have taken to their feet and given her a long and loud ovation. The cameras have moved in and she is surrounded on the fifty by news media and other personnel. That's a pretty good smile right there."

The second announcer chimed in. "And although it's just a guess, I'd say those are tears of joy and not sorrow."

The first announcer picked it back up. "I don't know what Mrs. Rising is feeling at this moment, but the look on her face tells me it's pretty good. For those of you who don't know, Dee changed his number this year to number 8 in honor of his friend and coach, Matthew Rising. Oh look—she's just walked over to Dee and hugged him." A pause. "Audrey Rising has taken off the coat she was wearing to reveal that she is also wearing a number 8 jersey." A pause. At this point, the first announcer began questioning the second. "Ken, I can't tell for sure, but is that an older jersey that Mrs. Rising is wearing? Looks like it's got some wear and tear on it."

"Yep, George. It's been a while since we've seen a jersey in here like that one. It's, I'd say, at least a decade old." Another pause. "Folks, we've just received confirmation up in the press box that Audrey Rising is wearing a number 8 jersey that is more than a decade old, which could make it Matthew Rising's jersey. And she's just turned around where we can see the back and there are two names on the back of the jersey. The first is 'Rising' and the other just below it is 'Rogers.' Wow. That's quite a statement. No matter what you think about the events of the past, this is a strong moment for that lady and that young man. She's is going on record, telling everyone she believes Dalton Rogers is of the same caliber as Matthew Rising. And that's saying a lot. During his career, she was a vocal, animated, and passionate advocate for her then husband. Even earning the name 'Spider Monkey.' For those of you who don't know, Audrey Rising is, or was, I'm not quite sure, the wife of Matthew Rising. Following his trial, she disappeared and it's only been in the last few weeks that she has resurfaced in the public eye."

The second announcer interrupted the first. "Yeah, George, it would appear that she has spent the last decade or so of her life selflessly raising Dalton Rogers."

George continued, "Evidently, she's done quite a job. That lady right there has my deep respect and admiration. She did then and she does now. To know what she's been through, and yet here she is, this is really something special." The announcer paused while they listened to the cheer coming out of the bleachers. They let us listen while the stadium roared. One side yelled, "Dalton," while the other side answered with "Audrey." The announcer continued, "I've covered a lot of games, and I've never seen anything like this one. This is one for the books. Folks, we'll be right back."

I smiled in delight. Not because of my part in it, but because I was proud of Audrey. Especially when she, Ray, and I were the only three that knew the truth of the birth certificate. There might be a fourth, but I couldn't be certain of that.

Gage propped his feet up on my cell bars, peeled the wrapper off a Snickers bar, handed me half, smiled, and didn't say a word. No one did.

CHAPTER THIRTY-THREE

Sunday morning rolled around, and Gage tapped on my cell door. He was not carrying a football. He said, "You got visitors."

I sat up. "Wood?"

"And your wife."

His tone of voice told me this was not a social visit. I stood up. "They okay?"

He shook his head. "Doesn't look like it."

I extended my hands and he cuffed me, led me out of my cell, out of our building, down a razor-wired fence, and into the cement-and-steel building with few windows that we affectionately called Oz. Inside, somebody behind some wall or curtain controlled all the levers to our lives.

I walked into a large room with several stainless steel tables and stools all bolted to the floor. The tables were bare, no windows, nothing that could come loose and be used as a weapon in the event that someone in the room got into a disagreement. Gage pointed at a table and I sat. He slid the chain of my cuffs into an eyelet in the center of the table and locked it. This kept my hands visible and on top of the table at all times. Around us, multiple cameras recorded our every move and sound. They'd been used more than once to aid in the truth of a case, and evidence discovered here could be used either for or against any of us.

Gage turned to me. "I am required to tell you that you are not allowed to receive anything from anyone and you will be strip-searched when you leave here regardless."

I stared around Gage at the door, waiting for Audrey. "Got it."

Gage leaned in. "Given what you've gone through, it has been suggested by the eyes behind those cameras that we put you on suicide watch." He glanced up in the direction of the cameras. "That said, you'd do well to control your reaction to whatever walks through that door."

"Thanks."

Gage left me alone with the cold, echoing silence of the stainless room. In a few minutes He pushed open the door and appeared with Wood in tow, followed by Audrey. My heart jumped into my throat.

Dee was not with them.

Locked to the table, I could only partially stand, making my greeting rather pathetic. Gage nodded at me and backed into a corner. Present but not.

Wood walked over and hugged me. He was teary. Audrey stood at a distance. Her eyes were puffy and she'd been crying. A lot. She was wearing jeans and a sweatshirt, and her hands were tucked up inside the sleeves. She looked cold. The dove hung outside the sweatshirt and glistened under the reflection of the fluorescent bulbs above. I spoke softly to her. "Wood said you been taking care of Tux." She nodded. I tried to get over the uncomfortable part of this. "He likes tuna with a little mayonnaise and a few cut-up pickles. Loves pickles."

Wood spoke for her. "He's turned into a pretty good watchdog.

Anybody peeks in her window and he goes ballistic. 'Bout bit my head off when I picked her up."

Audrey wasted no time. "Have you talked to Dee?"

"No."

"Do you know where he is?"

"What?"

Wood spoke for the both of them. "He's gone."

"What do you mean, he's gone?"

"This was lying on her breakfast table this morning." Wood slid a folder across the table. It was Dalton Roger's folder that Audrey kept under her bed. Across the front, written in Dee's handwriting, it read:

You should have told me. You both should.

Wood looked at Audrey and waited. A moment passed before she spoke. "After the game last night, I fell asleep with the light on. After he went out with his friends, Dee must have come by to check on me. Sometime after midnight." She rubbed her hands together. "He's been doing that since..." She waved her hand across the prison then continued. "All I can guess is that he turned out the light and somehow saw the folder because—" She proffered the folder, suggesting I open it.

I opened it. His birth certificate was missing. I looked up, first at him, then her. "That's not good."

The cold, hard environment of my world matched that reflected by Audrey. She was doing everything she could to keep it together.

I'd never felt so helpless in my entire life.

We sat in silence. None of us knew what to say. Audrey broke the silence. When they words came out, they were soft—as if the speaking of them hurt her. "He bought a train ticket early yesterday morning with my Visa."

"Where?"

She paused but wouldn't look at me. "New York."

I felt like someone had kicked me in the gut.

She continued, "He won't answer his cell phone." Audrey looked away as the tears rolled down her cheeks.

My hands were tied. Literally. I offered what I could. "I can petition the prison to allow me to call her, but that'll take a few days at the soonest. And…there's no guarantee that they'll grant my request." I shrugged. "He's not technically family, so it's not classified as an emergency." I looked at Wood. "Wood, you mind—?"

He cut me off. "Wouldn't take my call."

That left it to Audrey. Wood knew what I was thinking and answered for her. "Wouldn't take hers either."

I searched in vain for comfort—to say or do anything that would ease Audrey's pain. Helplessness bled into despair. We sat in the quiet a few minutes. Behind them, Gage quietly cleared his throat and held up five fingers, as in, five minutes remaining.

As the clock wound down, the door opened. It surprised all of us, Gage included. The warden appeared; his face expressionless. He pushed open the door, held it, and motioned someone to follow him.

Dee walked in. Followed by Ginger.

I felt my fists tighten and, out of the corner of my eye, I witnessed a visceral bodily reaction from Audrey. I slid my hand a few inches across the table, rattling my chains in the process, and gently slid my hand beneath Audrey's. To my surprise, she let me.

Dee scanned the room and then immediately walked over to Audrey and hugged her. "It's okay, Mama. I'm sorry."

If ever a voice spoke everything a heart needed to hear in a single word, it was that one, *Mama.* He kissed her cheek and held her, letting the hug reinforce what his mouth had spoken. He then hugged me. "How you holding up?"

"Better now."

Ginger stood at a distance, a shadow cutting her face in half. Dee held the chair for Audrey and motioned for her to sit. She did. Dee sat next to her. This left Ginger standing and alone.

Ginger was wearing jeans and a sweatshirt. She looked tired. She wore no makeup, had no bodyguards and no entourage. Gage appeared next to the table, and the warden looked at me and then Audrey. He then spoke to Gage. "All the time they need."

Ginger approached the table in much the same way Tux had first approached me. Yet to make eye contact with anyone, her eyes were bloodshot and scouring the floor. The warden spoke to Ginger. "Just signal when you want out."

Ginger looked up at me, and then Audrey. She pointed at the only available stool at the round table. "May I?"

Wood had bowed up and the veins in his left arm had popped up like rose vines beneath his skin. She sat, folded her hands, and finally spoke. Her voice was broken.

As was she.

The woman who sat before us was not the woman I'd witnessed on the stage of the courthouse. She started, "When I was a girl, long before any of us ever met, my dad—" She bit her lip. "He did things." She shook her head and paused. A long pause. "After... he told me no one would ever want me. I believed him. How could they? So I became the girl that all of you met in high school." She attempted a smile. "Ginger." She rolled one thumb over the other. As she spoke, Audrey had slid her other hand on top of mine, now holding both of mine with both of hers. Her hands were trembling. Ginger continued, "I told myself that everything would be better if I could convince someone of value to love me." A shrug. "Someone of the highest value. I made my way through the boys, thinking each one would erase... but they didn't." She looked up at me as a tear trickled down. "Then I met you. And you... you were kind to me. And to make matters worse, you didn't want anything from me. That made me only want you... want to be yours... more." She sunk her head in her hands, trying to catch her breath. Doing so exposed her fingers. Her nails had been bit to the quick.

She returned to me. "The night I came to your room in high school with the ring—" She laughed. "There I stood, offering you what I thought you'd never refuse, and you did. I left there thinking I wasn't good enough for you." Her eyes bounced to Audrey. "You'd given your heart to another." Another pause. "I left your room and went to a party, where I got introduced to a drug I'd never used. I woke up with bruise marks on my neck—" She paused. "And pregnant." A longer pause. "To this day, I do not know the identity of the father."

She let this sink in, then returned her gaze to me. "I blamed you. And that's when I decided that if I couldn't have you, I'd destroy you. You had the world at your fingertips. More power than one person should ever command. I had nothing. My life was ruined. What did it matter? So I became what I've become." She hung her head in her hands and spoke with her mouth to the table. "Nine months later—" She shook her head, changed direction, and looked back up at me. "I was content to let you rot in prison, sending you postcards yearly on the date of your arrest, until you were paroled and . . ." She laughed out loud. Incredulous, she said, "You—" Her voice broke. "You did the one thing I couldn't or wouldn't do and had never done." She turned to Dee and reached out her hand to touch his, but thought better of it.

Dee sat calmly. Taking it in. He was quarterbacking this play, and whatever was about to happen, he'd already set it in motion.

Eyes staring at the ground, she pointed at Dee. "Then yesterday, my s—" She stuttered and then stopped herself and chose another word. "Dalton came to see me yesterday. I thought I could remain unaffected by him." A shrug. "Detached." She shook her head, then fidgeted in her chair. "To my surprise, he didn't ask me why or spew hatred. He didn't ask me for anything. He simply told me that I'd already cheated him of his mother." Ginger's voice choked to a whisper and she lifted her head to look at me. "He then asked me not to cheat him of the only dad he's ever known."

She stood, reached into her pocket, and pulled out a DVD, which she laid on the table. She palmed away the tears. Her resolve was returning. Wood's jaw rested on the table and his head was spinning to put the pieces together. Ginger let out a deep breath. Finally, she motioned to the DVD and looked at all of us. "My attorneys advised me against it." She rubbed her temple and ran her hand across her eyes, then looked at Gage, who signaled into the camera above him and immediately the lock clicked and door swung open.

Ginger sunk her hands in her pockets and took a step to leave. She paused, then turned to Audrey and spoke with a tenderness I'd never heard come out of her mouth. Torment streaked her face. She held her eyes closed a long second and the words hung on the tip of her tongue a long time. When she opened her eyes, the color matched the dull, steel table that chained me to the earth. The only thing more painful than watching her speak the words was hearing them. She was looking at Audrey when she spoke. "He told the truth." She swallowed. "Every word. Always has."

The events that followed were foggy, and the chronology remains muddled. I don't remember Ginger leaving, don't remember Wood jumping up and hugging Dee and then dancing around the room, and don't remember the warden telling Gage it was okay to let them celebrate. I do remember my wife vaulting the table that separated us, grabbing my chains, pulling with both arms and pushing with both legs and screaming at the top of her lungs. "Somebody cut these chains off my husband! Let him free! Cut these chains right now! Somebody break these chains!"

I remember standing in the peaceful eye of a swirling storm that had erupted around me and smiling at her. "Audrey."

She wasn't listening.

"Honey."

She paused, and the third time I spoke, my voice shook her loose from the hell she'd been living in. I smiled. "Audrey?" Her eyes found mine. "They're okay. I'm free."

I remember her tackling me, wrapping her arms and legs and body around me and burying her face in my neck and sobbing from a place in her soul that had been buried since the trial. With words from her mouth, Ginger had cut Audrey's chains, and I remember the sound of pain leaving her body. I remember her taking my face in both her hands and pressing her lips to mine and holding it. And I remember us crying. And laughing. I remember hearing my wife laugh.

I do remember that.

Exposed beneath eight cameras, chained to the table that was bolted to the concrete floor inside four sets of double electronic doors, four-foot-thick walls, three electric fences topped with concertina wire, and two guard towers where armed snipers stood with rifles, I'd been cut free.

And there on the playing field that had become my life, my wife had crossed the sideline and was fighting for me.

Again.

CHAPTER THIRTY-FOUR

Following the pandemonium, the warden uncuffed me as Audrey commanded and led us to a room where we, along with several other prison officials, including Gage, watched the video. With no script, no makeup, and little introduction, Ginger launched into her story. She told it with a straight face, vivid detail, and a keen memory for dates.

Ginger admitted to lying in high school about the bruise marks on her neck, confirming that I had nothing to do with it. She told about the date-rape drug used on her both on the night that she threw the ring at me and the night Wood and I rescued her at the railroad warehouse and how she would use it later on me. She told how she woke up from that nightmare a seventeen-year-old mom and that she wouldn't recognize his father if she bumped into him. And how she wrongly blamed me for all of it. She relayed the events surrounding the railroad warehouse where Wood and I saved her. How I broke my hand that night and then played the following night. And then she relayed, in vivid detail, the events that took place in the hours following the draft. How I'd awakened at three a.m. for my workout. She knew I'd been working out the week prior in the fitness center in the basement. She laced the first few paper cups with the drug and the water cooler itself, and when I began drinking the water in the cooler, she was afraid she'd given me too much. She said she'd purposefully chosen her route to the elevator and her room by the number of cameras that would record our movement and that when she walked in and put her arm around me, that I was incoherent and too heavy and she thought she'd never get me to her room. She then described how she led me, as shown by the security cameras, both in the fitness center, hallways, and elevator, out of the fitness center, down the hall, up the elevator, and into her hotel room, where two teenage prostitutes lay passed out beneath the same drug. She told how she'd hired a male prostitute to fill in for me—who, fortunately for Ginger, died of a drug overdose a year later. She paid him to star in a grainy and dark video in which he engaged the underage girls in various acts—recorded prior to my entrance. She explained the doses she'd given them, guaranteeing that they wouldn't be able to remember anything. When all four of us—Ginger, me, and the two girls—woke in the same bed the following day as the police broke through the door thanks to an anonymous tip, the girls naturally believed it'd been me. They had no reason not to. She also relayed how, following the trial, she had created a fake company that served to free girls from the sex trade. The company was a cover to privately return them to Malaysia. She gave them enough cash to live several years and had not heard from them since. Following the safe return of their only clients—ever—the company closed its doors. Finally, Ginger explained how she and the fill-in staged her final act—her own "rape." How she paid him $10,000 to "make sure it looked authentic." The swollen eye, busted lip, lacerations, bruises. At her invitation, he had literally knocked her unconscious. Ginger had bought the drugs, drugged the girls, paid the guy, taken the beating. She had planned it all for the better part of two years.

Open and shut. No wonder the jury bought it.

Ginger ended the video by speaking to Audrey directly. In simple terms, she said, "Matthew told the truth. From the beginning. Every word. When he stated under oath that he had no memory of any of this, he wasn't lying. The drug I used is classified as an amnesiac. It's designed to make you forget. Once I got him to the room, he was comatose, quite nearly dead, and incapable of any of this." She then detailed the amounts and doses and on what schedule it was given to me—holding up her notepad taken from the bedside table, which showed her handwriting in pencil.

To nip any speculation in the bud as to why she chose now to speak up, she spoke with clarity. "I was content to hang my misery around Matthew Rising's broad and beautiful shoulders and let him live out his days in prison." Here Ginger cracked and cried a long time. The video continued. When she collected herself, she said, "But then, despite all the reasons you had to hate me and the world around you, you took an abandoned kid under your wing, nursed him back to health, and taught him…how to love." She shook her head once. "And as if that wasn't bad enough, you both knew—all the while—that Dalton Rogers was, and is, my son." She trailed off and tried again. "I can't—" Emotion choked whatever was to follow.

At the video's end, she stared at the camera. "I would ask for forgiveness, specifically from you, Audrey and Matthew, for mercy, but I don't deserve either. And I know it." She shook her head, stared off-camera, and the video faded to black.

I sat there with my mouth open. If Ginger had been in prison for most of her life, then her confession was her attempt to fling wide the door. Now she'd have to deal with the court of public opinion.

Sitting in that room, surrounded by a lot of whispering people we did not know, Audrey looked at me, shaking her head. Her hands covering her mouth. The reality of the past twelve years cracking down the middle. Her entire body trembled, rocked violently. I've only heard the sound that exited her one other time in our married life. Then, it had entered her. Now, it was leaving. Exiting. I wrapped my arms around her and listened as Audrey emptied her soul. Moments later, she pressed my face between her hands and managed a painful whisper. "Forgive me?"

I shook my head. "There is nothing to forgive."

The story spread, consumed the media outlets. Much of prime-time coverage was given to Ginger's continuing confession. To her credit, she went on the air that day on her own program, took no callers, broke for no commercials, and confessed to the world. A day later, she accepted an invitation to an hour-long nighttime news program out of New York.

Given the evidence and the public outcry, the District Attorney, along with assistance from the Governor and Warden, fast-tracked my release whereby Audrey and I went into hiding. With what little we had in savings, we rented a car and drove the coast of Georgia, hopping from cheap hotel to cheap hotel. It wasn't glamorous, wasn't Hawaii, but we didn't care. We walked on the beach, shared as much of the last twelve years as we could remember, told the good and the bad. She wanted to know about life in prison, about my fight with the man, if I was afraid. When we were alone, she traced the lines of my scars with her fingers and kissed each one. Finally, she would kiss my chest, above my heart. I wanted to know how she ended up at St. Bernard's, about the garden, how she'd met Dalton, about the video in her bedroom, and how long she'd been taking sleeping pills. We held hands more often than not, seldom were beyond an arms' reach, and spent hours each day, her skin pressed to mine, wrapped around each other like the vines in her garden. To protect ourselves, we didn't watch TV, listen to the radio, or read the newspaper. A total media blackout.

The following Friday night, we drove back into town and watched Dee's game from the top of the Bucket. Wrapped in a blanket, safe from the crowd, we saw Dee become the quarterback, and man, he was meant to be. We watched in amazement as he broke free from the chains of his past and found his stride.

At halftime, the announcer stated that he'd heard from a reliable source, Wood no doubt, a special guest was in attendance at the game tonight.

He said, "Ladies and gentlemen, you may not be able to see him, but I'm told he's within the sound of my voice. So let's welcome the most decorated high school player in the history of high school football, two-time Heisman trophy winner, three-time national championship winner, and the number one pick in the NFL draft, Matthew 'the Rocket' Rising, back to the field he helped build."

The crowd hit their feet and began stomping the stands. "Rocket! Rocket! Rocket!"

We sat safe and alone atop the Bucket. It was a fun moment.

The announcer returned, and we watched as Ray ran out onto the field, carrying something about the size of a bath towel. He spoke into the microphone. "Rocket, I know you can hear me. I been waiting a long time to say this." He turned toward us, and even from this far we could see his smile spread from ear to ear. "We'd like to re-retire your jersey."

The crowd liked that, too.

Audrey was sitting between my legs. My arms wrapped around her. I whispered, "Probably be a good idea. The thing didn't smell too well then. Can't imagine what it smells like after a decade."

The game continued, and the announcer's words echoed in my ears. I heard his words describing me, but they seemed hollow.

As if they somehow didn't fit. Clothes that were the wrong size. Yes, that Matthew Rising had walked into prison, but I'm not sure that Matthew Rising walked out. What I'd learned since my release was that an entire population had risen up around what I might have done had I played. They'd conjectured and theorized ad nauseam. They'd spent the time between my incarceration to my release thinking about me playing, dreaming about me playing, and regretting that I hadn't played. They'd even included my persona in video games. From bars to living rooms, park benches, and board rooms, all had been filled with this conversation.

When I walked out a free man, I walked into the middle of a conversation that had been running a long time. A conversation about me that had not included me—in which I'd played no part. Had no say. The barrage of questions via the media was constant, and it caught me and us off guard. In prison, I felt forgotten and, in order to survive the hell in which I was living, I'd thrown daily with Gage. Laid down my dreams. Sweated out my anger. The football-loving public had not done so. A few diehards were still packing in the beer and wearing my jerseys. Selling them on the Internet. As if it mattered. We quickly learned that they just couldn't understand how I'd so easily given it up. They saw me throwing in the prison video, they saw my tryout with Dee, and they thought for sure my goal was to pick up where I'd left off.

This left me scratching my head, so we kept our distance from any and all crowds.

When the stands had emptied and Dee had finished with interviews and responding to questions about our whereabouts, Wood, Dee, and Ray met us on the fifty. A tender and quiet homecoming. Wood didn't need to ask us how we were doing. Our faces said it. Dee had showered and was wearing his letterman jacket. The same one he wore for this week's cover of *SI*. He handed Audrey the game ball. "For you."

She stood holding the ball, turning it in her hands. After

a moment, she kissed him. "I've always been a sucker for quarterbacks."

Wood interrupted the long silence and held up his phone. He said, "I know you two want to take some time. You got it. All you want. I'm just registering it on your radar that my phone is ringing off the hook." It vibrated as he was speaking. He turned the face plate toward us. "See what I mean?"

I'd thought long and hard about this. If the last few days had shown me anything, they'd proven that Audrey was still pretty raw. Her emotions were all over the board, and we needed time. I wanted to rent a house in Alaska, fifty miles from anyone, and spend time remembering us.

I said, "I know you all would like to see me—" I smiled. "Try out for real. Join a team. But we…need to take a year, or two or three or ten, and just remember each other. Be married. Laugh. Forget…all this." I wrapped my arm around Audrey. "A few years back, I laid that dream down. I have no idea what I'll do, but… Audrey is my focus. My whole world." I turned to Wood. "Can you just tell them that for me?"

He nodded.

We stood there, our little huddle. Audrey's eyes scanned the stands, the field, the world around us. She looked at me, licked her thumb, and then wiped something off my cheek. Wood laughed. "Not much changes."

She shrugged. "Well, I can't have a crusty hanging off his face."

Dee shook his head. "Nice, Coach. Really. Way to represent."

Audrey squared to me and chose her words. A wrinkle formed between her eyes. She stood tall. Not below me, not above, but eye level. Alongside. "Matthew, do you love me?"

The others inched forward, wanting to hear my response. I wasn't sure where this was going and wasn't sure I wanted to have this conversation in front of all of them. I eyed them and then nodded at her.

I studied her, realizing how, in just a week, she'd transformed from the frail woman in her cottage chewing on sleeping pills to the woman standing before me. I'd take either, but I much preferred this one. She stepped closer, the intensity spreading across her face, and poked me in the chest. "Matty... do you love me?"

The first time didn't bother me so much, but the second time was starting to ding me a bit. I couldn't figure out what she was getting at. I whispered beneath my breath, "Honey—"

Her head tilted to one side. Her voice was soft. The words spilled from her heart and cracked when they exited her mouth. "Do you love me?"

"Audrey, I—"

What happened next I did not see coming. In hindsight, Wood and Dee did because they were filming it with their phones. She set the ball in my hand, kissed me, and stepped back. "Show me."

Dee posted the video on YouTube, Wood began answering his phone, and life quickly returned to crazy.

CHAPTER THIRTY-FIVE

One week later

The lady dusted my collar. She was new. Not the same intern. "Moldone's Off 5th?"

Audrey sat next to me smirking. The lady was commenting on my pinstriped suit. "Yes," I said. "I asked Moldone if he had any prison orange, but he was fresh out."

She chuckled. One of the things I'd learned in a short period of time was that, given everything that had happened, people didn't know how to react around me. Most everyone had thought, with good reason, for longer than the last decade, that I was/am a deviant pervert who should have been buried beneath the prison. That mind-set takes more than a few seconds to change. Given that, I tried to make folks comfortable, and talking about where I'd come from in stark contrast to where I was had become a fun and ice-breaking way to help others with the transition.

She laughed, raised an eyebrow, and looked at Audrey. "Not sure about orange, but this color makes your eyes dance."

She gave me my marching orders about the audience, when

they'd be coming in, about the extra security guards who'd been brought in to make sure no one got out of hand, and that Jim would be walking through "that door" in twenty-three minutes.

I pointed at the audience who'd just walked in and were flashing cameras. "You mind if I mingle?"

"Help yourself."

I stood, unplugged my cord—which struck me—and then walked over to the railing where folks sat in hushed silence. I put my hands together and couldn't contain my smile. "The last time we did this, things didn't end too well. I'd like to remedy that." I scanned the crowd, but there were so many spotlights shining down that I couldn't make out faces. I turned to the producer's box, pointed, and mouthed the word, "Lights." The lighting instantly changed and lit the audience. "Ah, much better." I turned to a guy up front and extended my hand. "Hi, I'm Matthew Rising."

He hopped up, shook my hand, and patted me on the shoulder. He had two chins, more like jowls, and they bounced as he smiled and began speaking ninety miles an hour. The rest of the night went much like that. I found people genuinely happy, happy for me, for us. And just as many people wanted to talk with Audrey. Take our picture. Not just mine. After ten or fifteen minutes, they could have turned off the lights in the studio because my wife was glowing.

Having taken several pictures, I stopped and spoke above the crowd. "This is going to sound a bit crazy, but prison does crazy better than any place I've ever been --" Laughter, I'd learned, was a pressure valve to a room, and it was true here. They laughed. And in that laughter I heard a silent whisper of collective thanks— *Thanks for not holding it against us that we thought such horrible things about you all this time.* It was true. This is life. Welcome to Earth. I continued. "Last time I was here, there was a kid, Mac was, or is, his name. He's not—"

Before I finished speaking, I heard a door shut behind me. A guy wearing an ESPN hat walked out of the producer's box. The light was shining in my face, so he walked around front where I could see him. He held his hat in one hand and extended the other. "Matthew."

I shook his hand. "Hey, Mac, it's good to see you again."

He nodded, tried to speak but couldn't, and motioned to the producer's box. Then he pointed to the large screen beyond the stage. A video flashed. The last time I was here. The video playing above me was of my meeting Mac. Our conversation. Me signing the ball. Taking a picture with him. When it finished, he said, "You're the reason I'm working here. I'm one of the assistant producers on the show tonight. And I cannot tell you what a privilege and honor it is to have you back."

Sometimes handshakes just don't cut it, so I hugged him. In a strange way, I was proud of him. He turned to an assistant, who tossed him an NFL ball, and he held it out to me. "You mind?"

"Love to."

I signed several balls for the audience, took what felt like a hundred or so pictures, and the iconic Jim Kneels walked in. We were scurrying to get back to the stage when he held up a stop-sign hand and said, "I'll come to you." A laugh. "You've earned it."

The audience laughed along. For thirty minutes, Jim and I signed balls, took pictures, and talked with the audience. It was magical.

Finally, he gestured to the stage. "Shall we?"

The assistant plugged me back in and we sat, Audrey slipping her hand in mine. The red light flashed to green, Jim looked at his notes but thought better of it and set them down. Deliberately. He turned to me. "Where were we?"

A great opening. The ice shattered. The audience stood to their feet, and it was several minutes before Jim could quiet them. He turned to Mac in the production booth and spoke with a smile. "We might need more than an hour."

Finally, I spoke. My emotions had been all over the place, and I'd learned that it didn't take much to poke them through the surface. "We were talking about dreams, and what happens when they all come true."

The audience hit their feet again.

Audrey sat on one side. Dee on the other.

Jim smiled, still leading the dance. "A little gray in your face since I saw you last."

"Prison does that to you."

Jim countered. "Let's play a word game. Tell me the first words that come to mind when I say words like...prison."

"Loneliness untold."

"Football."

"Joy unspeakable."

"Audrey."

"Promise kept."

He paused, letting my answer hang in the air, shifting gears.

"Word is that you're leaving this room en route to a building a few blocks down the street where a few folks are waiting on you."

"We are."

"And those contracts are worth a lot."

I smiled. "That's what I'm told."

"Do you realize that you are, as of this moment, one of the most highly sought after endorsers of products ever?"

"No, I didn't, but remind me when we leave here and I'll speak to my agent about his abject failure at mentioning that fact."

The camera panned to Wood who stood with hands folded. One of the assistants held a microphone to his mouth so the audience could hear him. Wood said, "I didn't want his head to get swollen."

Jim responded, "And if it does?"

Wood pointed to Audrey, who reached in the purse next to her chair, pulled out a knitting needle, and showed it to the audience.

Jim smiled. "Will all of this change you?"

"I sure hope so. I would like to build a house with a soft mattress, air conditioning, a fridge in every room so I can eat whenever I want, and a shower that I don't have to share with a bunch of sweaty, hairy men."

More laughter.

"First purchase?"

"We're talking to an agent now about buying an apartment in Athens."

"Georgia?"

I nodded.

Jim smirked. "Care to tell me why?"

While Dee had chosen where he'd like to play the next four years, none of us had spoken of it. Walking onto the set, Dee asked me if I thought it'd be okay to let the cat out of the bag tonight, or if by doing so did I think he was attempting to steal my thunder?

Told you I love that kid. Albeit, a big kid.

I thought it was a great idea, and I told him so.

So when Jim asked, I turned to Dee. Dee smiled and spoke with the charisma for which he was becoming known. "So they have a place to stay when they come to watch me play."

More raucous applause from the audience.

Jim didn't miss the opportunity. "Is that official?"

Dee responded, "Yes, sir, that's official."

Jim crossed his legs. Signaling a turn in the conversation. "Where do we go from here?"

I pointed toward the EXIT sign. "Same place we were going last time you asked me that."

Jim nodded. "Touché." A measured pause. "Last week, the league structured a combine, just for you. A first in the league. Word is that scored as high as any quarterback ever. How do you respond to that?"

"They need to check their equipment and bring me some analgesic." The audience laughed. I leaned back, crossed one leg over the other. "I'm currently the oldest rookie in the history of the NFL. So, for starters, I'd like to make the team. Coach Ray tells me they've already written 'Geritol' above my locker and stocked it appropriately." More laughter. "My dad gave me a gift when I was younger—he taught me to love this game we call football. And I do. For reasons I can't express well, I do. A bunch of guys are thrown into a field and given the right to run with reckless abandon between two painted lines. I love it. I love everything about it."

Jim motioned to an assistant, who carried an easel onto the stage. Three magazines sat lined up on the ledge of the easel. Jim stood, allowed the cameras to follow him, and motioned to the first, which quickly flashed onto the large screen above us. Jim continued, "*SI* has covered your career from the beginning." He picked up the first, flipped through, then held it up for the camera to move in close. "This one hit the shelves some sixteen years ago." The camera focused on the title, THE GOD OF FRIDAY NIGHT. He weighed his head side to side then nodded in approval. "First time a high schooler ever graced the cover."

Audrey squeezed my hand as we stared up at a much younger me. Jim tapped the cover with his finger. "You look a bit younger."

I nodded. "That was BP."

Jim raised both eyebrows. "BP?"

"Before Prison."

Everybody laughed.

He picked up the second—released the week I was drafted—sucked through his teeth, and again the camera focused in. I'd always liked that picture. The angle had been taken over my shoulder, looking out across the field with the goalposts in the background. I liked it because it focused on the game. On what could be. He read the title out loud: CAN THE GOD OF FRIDAY NIGHT REIGN ON SUNDAY? He set it back on the easel and glanced over his shoulder at the audience. "Didn't really get to answer that one, did we?"

Audrey spoke up loud enough to be heard by the audience. "Not yet."

Several in the audience whistled. Some clapped. Jim raised a finger and said, "Well played."

Finally, he picked up the third, which was obscured by a black cover. He held it up in front of him. "This hits the stands tomorrow. I've asked if we could unveil it here. *SI* has graciously agreed." The camera zoomed in. Dee sat up straight. Mac in the control room played a drum roll over the sound system. When Jim lowered the black sheet, I was staring at the audience. I wanted to see their faces.

Their individual and collective expression told me what I wanted to know. As did the immediate standing ovation.

SI had contacted us last week and asked to shoot some new photos for this week's cover. I'd agreed, but with a stipulation. At first, they'd balked, and pretty soon I was having conversations pretty high up the food chain but when I explained, they agreed to come take a look. Once they arrived, we showed them around and they got rather excited.

It would be another first.

We'd not seen the picture until now. We had spent the morning at the prison, shooting pictures of me in my cell, throwing with Gage, throwing through the electronic window, etc. These were all filler pics for the story. Not the cover. The cover they'd shot late in the afternoon with the sun going down. The light was magical.

During the shooting, the totality of what we were experiencing hit us, and both Audrey and I had become overwhelmed. We shed tears often. None more so than in these last few pictures. The emotional dam that she'd built up over the last twelve years had started to crack and crumble. More and more pieces broke loose as the days passed, and that photo shoot took out a big chunk. The result meant that our eyes were teary. We looked like we'd been crying because we had. A vein had popped out on Audrey's temple. As a result, the camera captured a vivid, raw, and honest emotion.

It was my favorite picture. Ever.

The picture on the cover showed Audrey in her garden. She was wearing my high school jersey, standing next to her scarecrow. Stick over her shoulder. The dove hung at the base of her neck. A football at her feet. Dirt on her knuckles. The photographer had stood on the wall and angled the camera down, taking in most of the garden, the oaks and clock tower in the background. The title read:

DO YOU BELIEVE IN REDEMPTION?

Below that, in small letters, the subtitle read:

The Life and Times of Audrey Rising

The nearly fifteen-page article was our story—Audrey, Dee, and me—as seen through Audrey's eyes. What she saw, felt, and experienced over the last eighteen years from our meeting on the training table to our last meeting in prison to discovering Dee to planting her garden. Three publishers in New York heard of the article and have already made offers to buy her story. She's told them she's talking it over with her agent and that she'll be in touch. Wood thinks it's worth more than their offer so he's taking his time, which is fine with her. They'll come around. She told us that she'd tell it for free. Wood and I agreed it'd be our secret.

Jim flipped through the article, then spoke to the audience. "Folks, it's the first time *SI* has ever devoted such space to the wife of a player." He looked at Audrey. "And the first time a wife has ever landed on the cover."

Audrey held back the tears as long as she could, but when Dee hugged her, another chunk broke off.

For so long, Audrey had stood in my cheering section, rooting for me, screaming my name, leveling linebackers and getting escorted out of the stadium, that I relished a role reversal. I loved cheering for my wife.

Jim returned to his seat while the audience quieted, and Audrey dabbed her eyes with a tissue. He crossed his legs and looked at me. "Well…" Seconds passed. The dance wasn't quite over. Ever the professional, his voice rose. His finger rested on the title while his eyes looked at me. "Do you?"

A long pause. "A few weeks after I was sent to prison, my wife retreated to a convent, where she bumped into a little boy who stole what remained of her shattered heart." I patted Dee once on the knee. "He filled the hole that my absence left. So, like any good mama, she dug into his file and discovered the truth of who he was: he's the son of the woman who destroyed our life. Audrey knew this about four weeks after I'd gone to prison, so I'd say the wound was pretty raw. At that point, she faced a decision." I gestured to Dee. "Does she cast him off? Shove him aside? Make him pay for what she believed that his biological mother and I did to her?" I shook my head. "Audrey held his hand, wiped his nose, cradled him in the dark, taught him how to throw, showed him—of all people—videos of me, and shared her love with him." I turned to Dee. "Look at his eyes. Whose are they?" The camera focused close on Dee's face. Ginger's picture appeared next to him on the screen. The resemblance was obvious. I continued, "I think Audrey knew that the moment she first saw him. It's why she checked his file. She had to know." I shifted in my chair. Audrey looked down.

Jim interrupted me. He spoke softly to Audrey. "Is this true?"

Audrey glanced at Dee, patted him on the leg, and attempted a smile, nodding slightly. A long silence settled over us and the audience.

I continued. "Several miles down the road"—I shifted in my seat—"two hundred and forty four, to be exact…I was staring up through bars and drowning in my own hatred. Rotting from the inside out." I held up my hands. "I wanted to kill Ginger, and if they'd have let me out…" I nodded.

I pointed to Gage in the audience. "Then one day he reached down in my cell and asked me a real simple question. He said, 'Tell me what you love.'" The camera panned to Gage. A long pause. "I remember struggling to remember, to get the words out. I said, 'I love my wife.'"

I remember him nodding, unlocking my cell, and telling me, "We can build on that."

I glanced across the audience. At smiles. In the booth at Mac. At Wood. Dee. And finally at Audrey.

The world had come full circle.

I spoke slowly. "The bars of my cell were toothpicks compared to those inside me."

Silence.

I turned to Jim. "My wife fell in love with a little boy that she had every right to despise, and I walked out of prison having laid my anger down. No bars on my heart. I didn't do that to me and I didn't do that to her. Only one thing does that." I paused. "You asked me a question the first time I sat here, and the answer I gave was true then. It's true now. My favorite moment in any game occurs in the huddle, when the faces behind those face masks are all staring back at me. Silently, intently, asking me what I'm prepared to do. Amid their pain and sweat and often the reality of getting their tails kicked, they want to know if they can believe in me. If I'm worth their hope. Strip away all the exterior polish, the gloss, the commentary, and all the conversations, and that's the wonder and majesty and magnificence that is this game we call football. The ones I love need to hear something from me, and what they need to hear is not where things went wrong, not where something could have happened that didn't, but what I know to be true." I shrugged. "Jim, I know I love my wife, I love Dee"—I pointed at Gage and Ray—"I love those men sitting there." I pointed at Wood. "I love that big teddy bear there." A pause.

Jim interrupted me. "And Ginger? Do you hate Ginger?"

I spoke softly. Simply. No need to elaborate. "No."

"What emotion do you feel?"

"Pity."

He raised both eyebrows, asked again. "Not hatred?"

"Hatred is a commodity I couldn't afford in prison. Too expensive then. Too expensive now."

"How so?"

"I couldn't live every day with that stuff bubbling up inside me." I pointed at Gage. "Gage taught me that. He found me in a bad place. Picked me up. Showed me I had a choice. I couldn't change my circumstances, but I had a lot to say about who I was in the midst of them. And who I became. Gage helped me, showed me, how to lay it down."

"The DA has not decided, but the word is that you two are not pressing charges against Ginger." He looked at Audrey. "Is this true?"

"It is." Audrey chose her words. "Don't get me wrong, I'm dealing with what happened. I have to fight back being angry. At what was taken. Stolen. From us. And much was stolen."

The audience stood to their feet and cut her off with applause. Jim joined them. Me too.

When we sat, Audrey continued. "So, no, I'm not putting her on the Christmas card list, but when I look inside..." She pulled my hand to her. "When I look at what we need—at what I need—we don't need Ginger in prison. It accomplishes nothing for us. I can't speak to what the DA will do or not do, but my question for you, Jim, is 'to what purpose?'"

He looked at me and thumbed over his shoulder at Audrey. "Wow, she's good."

I smiled. "She's just getting warmed up."

He laughed. "You agree?"

"I do."

"Most of the United States wants Angelina Custodia's head on a platter."

I nodded. "And there was a time when I'd have put it there for you."

"When I called and spoke to Angelina Custodia just a few hours ago, she was, let me say, emotional. I'd say even broken, by the fact that you have said publicly you have no intention of sending her to jail for the rest of her natural-born life."

I shook my head. "Ginger's been living in prison a long time. Steel bars won't change that."

"So you really have no problem letting her off the hook so she can fade off into the sunset with her billion dollars and the dynasty that she built on your back?"

"It didn't buy her happiness then. Won't now."

"You're not jealous? Envious?"

I held Audrey's hand. "I have everything I need and everything I've ever wanted." I held up a finger. "And remember, if my life had gone the way we had initially scripted it, I'd have never met"—I put my hand on Dee's shoulder—"Dee. And," I nodded to Audrey, "as tough as it is to say, I wouldn't trade him for twelve years that followed my script."

Jim looked surprised. "You mean that?"

"I do."

The audience stood and stayed there a long time.

My emotions had risen into my chest, and the words were slow in coming. Holding Audrey's arm with one hand, Dee placed his other hand on my arm and spoke for the three of us. Kindness framed in confidence. "Their love did what her hatred could not. And never will."

Jim waited for my answer, but my throat had choked off my voice so I just pointed to Dee, nodded, and shrugged. Doing so shook loose a tear that trickled down the right side of my face. Audrey brushed it with her thumb. I grabbed a tissue from behind me, wiped my nose, and tried to poke fun at myself. "I need to get off this stage before I turn into a soaking-wet mess." The laughter helped me find my voice. I figured we needed to end this so I tried to speak with a tinge of finality—and hoped Jim would let me get away with it. He did. "My coaches tell me that I'll make my starting debut three weeks from Sunday against last year's league-leading defense."

Not quite finished with me, Jim chuckled. "That's called 'baptism by fire.'"

"Feels like it, too." Not wanting to break my rhythm, Jim proffered, making room for me to close. "The thing is this...my life is complete. I am content if I never play another down." I looked from Mac to Wood to Gage and Ray, from Audrey and Dee to Jim. Finally, my eyes came to rest on the three magazines propped on the easel. Our life in black and white. "There is a God of Friday night, but I am not Him." I let out a deep breath and sat back.

Jim paused, shook his head once, and turned toward the audience. "Folks, Audrey and Matthew Rising."

While the audience stood again and filled that room with raucous applause, Audrey pulled my cheek to her lips, kissed me, and whispered in my ear. When she spoke, one hand touched my face, the other traced the lines of the dove. "That's the thing about hope."

Audrey, Dee, Ray, Wood, and I rode the elevator down to the basement parking lot where Wood's hired limo waited. The driver opened the door, they filed in, and I stood staring at Wood. He whispered something into his secret-service earpiece and I said, "Nice touch. We could've walked."

Wood eyed the car then wiped his eyes with the back of his suit sleeve. "Shut up and get in the car. I'm hungry and all this talking and crying like a bunch of women hasn't helped any."

Following the party, Audrey and I returned to our room where we lay awake, talking, staring at the lights of the city and at one another. It was a lot to take in. And I'd be lying if I told you the emotion didn't catch up with me and I didn't shed more than one tear. I did. I cried like a baby. We both did. We laughed, too.

Seems like I'd just fallen asleep when my alarm went off at three a.m. I hit snooze and lay there. Waking up. Thinking about everything before me. The enormity of it all. Audrey hooked her bare right leg around both of mine and then wrapped her right arm over my chest, tucking her right hand under my left arm. She wiggled her left hand beneath my right arm, clutching my bicep. The dove around her neck rested on my chest. The spider monkey was perched. A crowbar could not have pried her off me. When she spoke, her voice betrayed her smile. "Don't even think about it."

I laughed. "Honey, I—"

She cut me off. "You think that guy in prison was tough? Try and step one foot out of this bed."

"I told Dee I'd meet him—"

"And I told Dee to sleep in."

"But the guys I'm competing against are—"

"I don't care if you're lined up against Zeus, sitting atop a winged Pegasus, and he's throwing lightning bolts."

"You're really not letting me out of this bed, are you?"

She slowly readjusted and tightened her grip. "Think of it more like an audible at the line."

I turned off the alarm and closed my eyes. A good call.

ON *A LIFE INTERCEPTED*

Tallahassee, Florida, 1989.

When I stepped out of the car, I remember the sun being hot and shining directly in my eyes. Over my shoulder reverberated the *thump-thump* of distant rap music but it had yet to circle around. That would happen in about three minutes. Lastly, I remember the sensation of carrying around a lot of muscle I no longer needed—and really couldn't use.

I had driven with my roommate, David, to the Tallahassee Mall to pick up a few things for school. We were sophomores. He had been in Tallahassee a year, was soon to pledge Sigma Alpha Epsilon, and had zeroed in on a career in finance or law. Dave had his collective stuff together. I'd moved to Tallahassee a few days prior, having just transferred from Georgia Tech, and was, for the first time in my memory, not playing organized football. My collective stuff was scattered from Atlanta south to Jacksonville and west to Tallahassee. And though I did my best to mask it, I was not in a good place, and something in me was ticking.

We would discover this shortly.

*   *   *

Exactly one year prior, I'd walked on at Georgia Tech and, wonder of wonders, made the football team. Childhood dream come true. Unlike some of the other rookies, I came into camp in shape and placed third in the twelve-minute run behind another rookie who would later spend twelve years in the pros and win two Super Bowls. Throughout the course of training camp and then the season, I'd paid my dues. I'd gotten faster, could jump higher, see the field better, respond quicker to the speed of the game, and all of my clothes were tight—except in the waist. In practice I had made a few interceptions, had been named rookie of the week twice, and—as evidenced by the scars on the front of my helmet, face mask, and shoulder pads—was not afraid to hit pretty much anybody. Late in the season during practice, I lined up against our first string offense. In back-to-back plays, I toppled a senior fullback and sacked our starting quarterback, prompting a senior veteran to pull the tape off my helmet—a rite of passage for rookies indicating that everyone on the team now knew my name and no longer needed the tape to remind them.

Following the season, I hunkered down in the weight room and when the winter strength competition came around, I tested out as the fifth strongest of all the skilled players. My single day cumulative total for squat, clean, and bench equaled a half a ton. It feels better to say half a ton, than a thousand pounds. Either way, it was a lot of weight. My body weight was up to 193 pounds and my body fat was down around five percent.

In my mind, I'd made it. Hard work had paid off and I'd done what few thought possible. My dream was coming true and living out the rest seemed a likely possibility. One of my coaches had actually uttered the word, "scholarship." As in, if I kept working hard, I could earn one.

Sometimes I wish the story ended there.

Spring rolled around, I pulled on my shoulder pads and laced up my cleats with a bit of confidence. I can distinctly remember running around the field with some idea of what I was actually doing. Gone was the naive rookie. A seasoned soon-to-be-sophomore now stood in his place.

Then came sideline drills. It's a tackle drill that focuses on angle of pursuit. Our free safety had the ball, mimicking a running back. He was a freak of nature: 6'4" and two hundred thirty plus pounds; ran a 4.5 in the forty; and during the winter strength training I saw him squat five hundred fifty pounds with little trouble. The following year he would become a key figure on the team that won the National Championship. So, as I'd done a thousand times in my life, I picked my angle, pursued, and tackled him.

I felt the pop before I hit the ground.

I remember lying on the grass, staring up through my facemask, thinking to myself, "That hurts. A lot." I knew the difference between hurt and injury and this was not hurt. I pulled myself up, hobbled back to the huddle, finished practice by letting others take my reps, and finally limped my way into the locker room. The pain in my lower back was taking my breath away, and something in the alignment of my hips seemed off center. Sitting in my locker, sweat mixed with tears, I pulled off my shoulder pads and had a pretty good idea that I'd never put them on again. The following day the doc stared at the X-rays. Even I could see the crack.

For almost fifteen years, football had been my identity. Pop Warner, junior high, junior varsity, varsity, team captain, Georgia Tech…You get the point. I'd been building toward something. Yet, when I was walking across that Tallahassee Mall parking lot, I knew my dream had crumbled, and as I sifted through the ruins of what was once me, the only thing I'd built was an angry crater. My emotional posture was akin to a man standing in the mirror scratching his head asking one question, over and over: *Without football, just exactly who am I?*

The *thump-thump* grew closer as we walked to the door of the mall. When the Ford Bronco passed, several loud bodies bounced around, rocking the Bronco slightly side to side. Then one arm extended out of the car and flung something at my head. The Barry Manilow cassette grazed my temple and landed on the asphalt next to me.

That's right: Barry Manilow. I found that rather disrespectful.

I'd just spent the last year *not* letting bigger, faster guys shove me around and treat me like I wasn't worth the dirt between their cleats. My pride whispered from the rubble inside me and said, "Nope. No sir. Not here. Not now." So, I raised my right hand and told them they were number one in my heart.

Pause here a second. You see that picture of me? The one with my hand in the air? It's not my best moment, and I was about to figure that out. I deserved what happened next. Dave did not.

Before my hand had come down, the brake lights flashed, tires spun in reverse, both doors opened and five guys jumped out pumped up on each others' adrenaline. They filled the air with waving arms and F-bombs. I remember thinking, *This might hurt* and then all Hades broke loose. I fought my way to the door of the mall thinking Dave was ahead of me but when I got there, he was not. Not inside. Not at the door. Not next to me. That's when the sound behind me caught my ear. It was the *thud-thud-thud* of ten feet kicking somebody. I turned and found Dave on the ground, wrapped up in a fetal ball, trying to guard his face.

Dave and I had been friends since the crib. Literally. Over the course of our younger lives, we played football, watched football, collected football cards, talked, eat, slept, and dreamed football. And come high school, while he had gravitated toward basketball, he didn't miss many of my games and when it came to